About the Author

MARGARET DUMAS is a technical writer and computer software executive. She lives in the San Francisco Bay Area, where she is at work on her latest novel and is still in search of the perfectly balanced life.

the Balance Thing

Also by Margaret Dumas

How to Succeed in Murder

Speak Now

the Balance Thing

Margaret Dumas

HARPER

NEW YORK . LONDON . TORONTO . SYDNEY

HARPER

This book is a work of fiction. The characters, incidents, and dialogue are products of the author's imagination and are not to be construed as real. Any resemblance to actual events or persons, living or dead, is entirely coincidental.

HarperCollins books may be purchased for educational, business, or sales promotional use. For information please write: Special Markets Department, HarperCollins Publishers, 10 East 53rd Street, New York, NY 10022.

FIRST EDITION

Designed by Nicola Ferguson

Library of Congress Cataloging-in-Publication Data
Dumas, Margaret.
The balance thing / Margaret Dumas.—1st Harper pbk.
p. cm.
ISBN-10: 0-06-112772-8
ISBN-13: 978-0-06-112772-4
1. Single women—Fiction. 2. Friendship—Fiction. 3. Dating (Social customs)—Fiction. 4. San Francisco (California)—Fiction. I. Title.

PS3604.U48B35 2006
813'.54—dc22 2006041185

06 07 08 09 10 ❖/RRD 10 9 8 7 6 5 4 3 2 1

the Balance Thing

One

When you're looking for parking in North Beach you have plenty of time to examine where you've gone wrong in your life. It sort of forces you to go slowly and consider all your options. I was finding it increasingly annoying because—like finding a place to park—introspection is not an activity I generally build into my schedule.

I don't waste mental cycles kicking myself for not cashing in my stock options before the bubble burst. I don't examine my face in the rearview mirror and wonder if at thirty-three I'm starting to look like my mother. And I don't generally obsess about my boyfriend—possibly because I don't generally have a boyfriend.

However. The question that persisted as I slowed to evaluate a hand-holding, sunlit couple—who, it turned out, were not getting into a car and opening up a parking space—was the same question that had been announcing itself with increasing frequency and mounting urgency over the past few weeks: *Greg?*

Lately it seemed he was everywhere. It wasn't so much that he'd developed a habit of showing up unexpectedly; it was more as if he'd come over five weeks ago and never left. His *Office Space* video was on top of my television. His Head & Shoulders was in my shower. He didn't even have to be there to be there.

Even now he was in my passenger seat, nattering on about—I tuned in briefly, heard the words "Internet baseball fantasy league," and tuned out again. He was sucking all the air out of the car.

I admit I had only myself to blame. If I'd noticed that what had, for me, been an I'm-bored-so-I-might-as-well-have-coffee-with-someone situation had, for Greg, been an if-I-just-hang-in-there-she's-got-to-fall-for-me-eventually scenario, this could all have been avoided.

But I hadn't. I'd let all the warning signs slip by and had never seen it until that night he'd come over to help me rearrange my furniture. Then *bam*—just as soon as he'd positioned the throw rug and the sofa at exactly the thirty-eight-degree angles I'd specified, he'd pounced.

I know I should have pushed him away. Or at least verified that this was just going to be sex between friends, no more meaningful than a game of racquetball, and not the beginning of something (*shudder*) beautiful.

But I hadn't. Because despite my better instincts . . . well, one gets swept up in these things. And although I knew it was imperative to set some firm parameters immediately after straightening my clothes, he'd made his post-sex declaration first—complete with puppy-dog eyes—"What are we doing next weekend?"

We.

One goddamn moment of weakness and by the following weekend his Peanut Butter Cap'n Crunch was in my kitchen.

I changed lanes to avoid getting caught behind a bus and was instead caught behind someone trying to make a left turn. "Whoops." I could feel Greg's loopy grin without looking over at him. "You're spanked. That's why I always stay in the right-hand lane."

I forced a smile. He wasn't really a bad guy. Most people seemed to classify him as a sort of likable flake. And professionally he had a reputation as a good-bordering-on-inspired programmer. At least he'd managed to hang on to his high-tech career better than I had. So there was no logical reason why I shouldn't be perfectly happy to spend half my life looking for a parking space just so we could buy the damn cannoli for the stupid party his idiot friend was throwing that night.

Maybe it was my attitude.

"Hon, can we find an ATM before we park?" he asked. I braced for the inevitable. "I think there's a Smells Fargo around the next corner."

Smells Fargo. Not Wells Fargo, the real name of the bank. Smells Fargo. Every time, every time, *every time*.

I wondered if he even realized he was doing it anymore.

I know we all have these little unconscious things. And the point is, they're little things. You have to look beyond them. You have to remember all the little unconscious things he does that *don't* make you want to hurl the car into oncoming traffic.

"There it is," he sang out. "Smells Fargo!"

I watched my knuckles turn white on the steering wheel. It was time for Greg to go.

. . .

"AW, SWEETIE." This was accompanied by a crinkled-brow frowny face from my friend Max. "He broke up with you?"

"Hell no," I said, "I broke up with him. When are the girls supposed to be here?" I looked across the crowded restaurant toward the door, hoping to catch Connie and Vida as they came in. From the look of things, they'd have to force their way through a gang of suburban moms in the throes of a Union Square–induced shopper's high.

I glanced over to find Max biting his lip. Actually biting his lip to keep from saying what I knew he was dying to. I sighed. "Say it."

"You're insane."

When it comes to offering opinions, Max never needs to be asked twice.

"He was driving me insane," I said. "But only in the right-hand lane."

"He was nuts about you," Max said. "And he was cute, and let's not forget he was nuts about you."

"He was nuts all right."

Max gave me an accusatory look. He was six-foot-four with jet black hair, deep gray eyes, and a body that was as near perfection as his five weekly appointments with a personal trainer could get it. Luckily, he was also just Max, and he didn't intimidate me for a minute.

"Okay," I allowed, "he wasn't nuts. He was perfectly sane. Annoying, but sane." I shrugged. "He'll make some dandruff-prone, pun-loving, cereal eater a lovely boyfriend someday. Can we change the subject now?"

Max took my hand in both of his, and I couldn't help noticing how much softer his skin felt than mine. "Becks, I'm you're oldest friend in this town, and we've seen each other through the good men and the bad, so believe me when I tell you, and I say this with love"—he took a moment to give me a totally sincere look—"you're going to die alone."

"Very funny." I withdrew my hand and patted him patronizingly on the arm. "I hope you've got better material in your show."

Max Trop, which of course was not the name his parents had given him, led two very different lives. By day he was a dermatologist with a thriving practice near enough to Union Square that his clients could schedule their Botox injections or microdermabrasion appointments conveniently between a little shopping spree at Saks and lunch at the Neiman Marcus Rotunda. By night—at least for the past few months—he was one of four first-time producers attempting to mount a musical-theater-topical-cabaret-snappy-patter-and-sing-along show that would put the classic San Francisco favorite *Beach Blanket Babylon* on notice that a new showbiz kid was in town.

Max's eyes narrowed. "Nice try. You think if you mention the show, you'll distract me. How self-centered do you think I am?"

I held my hands about a foot apart. "This much?"

"More. But I'll spare you because the girls are here, and neither of us will get to talk about anything but the bridal event of the century for the rest of the day."

Connie and Vida were excusing-me and pardoning-me their way through the crowd, trying to squeeze what looked like a half dozen large shopping bags each between the tables.

"Should we help them?" I asked, although between

Vida's lithe athletic grace and Connie's former-debutant manners, they weren't having much of a problem.

"I was thinking we could pretend not to know them." Despite this sentiment, Max stood and scooted chairs around to make more room.

Connie reached the table first, flung the packages around her, and collapsed into a chair, somehow managing to avoid compromising her flawless posture. "So here's the latest," she said. "Vee thinks I shouldn't sleep with Ian until after the wedding."

"I didn't say that." Vida deposited herself into the chair next to me and reached for my glass of water. "I just said I read an article about it." She took several large gulps. "I was dying for that." She looked around the table at us. "You know, reclaiming the mystery before the wedding night."

"Mystery is overrated," Max said. "But if you're looking to inject a little spice, I know this great shop on—"

"Anyway," Connie said firmly, "it's a stupid idea. Ian and I have been living together for two years. It's a little late now to play hard to get." She scooped her long, perfectly highlighted hair away from her face, then dropped it straight down her back. "We both know exactly what we're getting and we're both completely content."

"How romantic," Max murmured.

I gave him a warning look, but apparently Connie hadn't heard him. Maybe she was too busy being content. And why not? She was thirty-four years old and had everything the magazines told her she should. Great career as an events planner—she basically got to throw fabulous parties using other people's money. Great guy—or at least great for her, if a little bland for my taste—who ran his own company and worshiped the ground she walked on. Her just-slightly-too-intellectual-to-be-a-supermodel looks completed the package. She had that toned sleek look that racehorses and girls who grow up with a good deal of money seem to share. It had taken a tremendous effort of will not to hate her when we'd met.

"What's going on with you two?" Vida asked. She had finished my water and was eyeing Max's when the waiter came with reinforcements. "You looked like something serious was going down when we came in. Thanks!" The last word was addressed to the waiter and accompanied by one of Vida's you-can-take-the-girl-out-of-Southern-California-but-you-can't-take-the-sunshine-out-of-the-girl smiles. But she frowned when she turned to me. "Did you get laid off again?"

Oddly enough, I wasn't insulted by the question. Since the high-tech crash I'd been laid off—*ugh,* it's too depressing to say how often.

I had done well in the boom years, though. I'd planned carefully and worked hard and had graduated from the ranks of computer-show booth bunnies to become an associate product marketing manager right on schedule. And I'd just been promoted to the lofty position of marketing manager for a sizable software company when said company lost 87 percent of its market value in one week.

They "restructured" and suddenly I was out on my ass, which had definitely not been the next planned step on my career trajectory. My only consolation was that I'd managed to pay off most of my credit cards and make a down payment on a loft before everything fell apart.

Since then I'd developed an amazing knack for signing

on with companies that were on the verge of their last corporate gasps. One memorable time I'd actually shown up on my first day to find that the company had declared bankruptcy that morning. More than one person had suggested I was the Typhoid Mary of high tech.

"Becks, you didn't get laid off!" Connie looked momentarily panicked. I didn't think for an instant this was due to any genuine concern about my professional well-being. She just didn't want me to plead financial hardship and back out of being a bridesmaid at the international festival of excess that was to be her wedding.

In all other aspects of her life, Connie was a perfectly reasonable adult. But when it came time to plan the wedding, her insanely wealthy parents had convinced her that the concept of "too much" would not apply. It hadn't taken much convincing.

The extravaganza would include a flight to London and a week at some *chi chi* hotel, followed by transportation (possibly via magic pumpkin coach) to a country manor house where, over the course of another week, the wedding of the century would take place. Leading up to the main event would be more cocktail parties, formal dinners, and tea thingies than I could keep track of without a part-time assistant.

I'd need killer outfits for every gathering, not to mention a bridesmaid dress that looked like something out of a Merchant Ivory film. So Connie was very concerned about my cash flow.

"If you'd been keeping score, you'd know I don't have a real job to get laid off from these days," I told them. Then I shrugged. "But don't worry. I've still got Vladima."

Silly, really, but there it was. Despite a business degree

from Stanford and several years of experience working in serious, grown-up marketing departments, I was currently earning a living as the voice of a kick-ass vampire/vixen in the Internet-based animation phenomenon known as *Vladima Cross—Defender of the Night.*

It was a complete fluke. Ages ago I'd briefly been the Product Marketing Associate for a computer animation tool, and I'd had the rather clever idea that we should make little animated movies showing how to use the software. Using animation to teach animation. Brilliant, right? Except that the actress who was supposed to come in and record the voice of the cartoon instructor never showed up. And since it had all been my bright idea, I'd had to fill in for her.

Eventually the animation company tanked, but not before a poorly socialized artist/programmer named Josh Fielding had gotten so used to hearing my voice that he'd wanted nobody else to record the extremely campy dialogue of his cartoon vampire heroine.

It wasn't something I'd want in the alumni newsletter, but, hey, it paid the bills. And it had to because lately I couldn't score a second interview for a marketing job. The vampire business, on the other hand, was booming. We were just getting ready to go live with *Vladima XVI—Daemons of the Night.*

"Sure she has a job," Max said smoothly. "Three guesses what she doesn't have."

"Oh." Connie looked relieved. "Is that all? She just broke up with Greg?" Connie turned to Vida. "How long did he last?"

Vida looked up from the menu and squinted. "She wasn't seeing him on Valentine's Day. I remember because we went to that 'bring a used boyfriend' party at Jennifer's place. Oh, I think that's where she met Greg." She did a quick calculation. "So if it's April now, and that was mid-February, he probably made it six, maybe seven weeks."

"Not bad." Connie nodded absently while looking over the list of lunch specials. "What do you think pushed her over the edge? The growly thing when he ate?"

"Probably the whole deal about not killing spiders because they're our friends," Vida guessed.

"No," Connie reconsidered, "my money's on the way he said 'for all intensive purposes.'"

"You're both wrong," Max informed them. "It was Smells Fargo."

"Are you three sure you don't need me for this discussion?" I asked them. "Really, it's okay, because I'm right here."

They all looked at me for about two beats, then resumed the conversation, leaving me out of it. Which was fine. I needed the practice. I was going to die alone.

Two

Despite the firmly held belief among my friends that the only problem I had was the lack of a man I could stand for more than two months straight, I had bigger concerns. The most pressing of which was the increasingly large gap in my résumé. My real-world résumé. The one that didn't mention my connection with the computer-generated undead. My biggest problem now was that I hadn't worked—aside from voicing Vladima—since my most recent layoff. Almost five months ago.

And it hadn't been for lack of trying. Convinced that a lot of the game was knowing who to know, I had developed a phased, systematic approach to networking. I'd gone through every contact on my BlackBerry and created a spreadsheet with specific categories for everyone. Where I'd met them. What we had in common. Where they were now. What they could do for me.

And then I'd started making calls. And I'd kept making calls. Because my initial results had been dismal. Apparently not one of the dozens and dozens of people I'd cultivated over the years was now in a position to help me.

Either that or I was doing something wrong.

Looking over my call stats, I tried to objectively assess where my approach might be weak. As I thought about it, I realized that what I'd been doing, when you broke it down to basics, was telemarketing. I was the product, and the people on my networking list were the leads. And what did every telemarketer have that I didn't have? A script.

I grabbed the laptop and began.

LIST OF ESSENTIAL CONVERSATIONAL POINTS

- GREETING: Keep it light and informal. Confidently assume they remember you and greet them as they would great one another. Try: "Hey, how the hell are you?"
- PRELIMINARIES: Let them know you've followed their careers and demonstrate your delight at their successes. Inquire as to their happiness in their present positions.
- PRIVACY: Do not let them draw you out about your recent period of unemployment. (Never use the word unemployment.) Be cheerful and vague. Change the topic.
- EMPLOYMENT STATUS: Wait for them to bring it up. Surely you will be asked where you're working. That is the moment to casually mention that the right offer (and there have been many) hasn't come along. Present yourself as very, very desirable and very, very choosy.
- THE CLOSE: Do not be obvious. The initial contact is simply to plant the knowledge of your availability. If they instantly suggest a position with their

> group, that's a bonus. But *under no circumstances* must you ask about one. Let them hang up feeling refreshed by your conversation and reminded of your stellar attributes, not hounded by your blatant need.

After a certain amount of time spent adjusting the font and margins, I faced the fact that eventually—no matter how perfect the talking points were—I would still have to pick up the phone. I took a deep breath, visualized a successful conversation, and dialed.

"MITCH? HEY YOU! It's Becks Mansfield! From Tarantula!"

One of the creepier aspects of the Internet business was the tendency to name companies after spiders. It's the whole Web thing. I should have realized the company was doomed just by the name. Tarantulas don't really do webs. They're nesters. And the World Wide Nest didn't quite have the right ring to it.

But this wasn't about the past. This was about networking. According to my spreadsheet, Mitch Hastings had landed a director gig at PlanetCom. He had three stars in the "Useful" column.

"Becks? Hey, how the hell are you?"

Excellent. And proof that I shouldn't have chickened out of using the "how the hell are you" greeting.

"I'm good, great. How are you? Congratulations on the new job!" No gushing, just an easy familiarity.

"Yeah, it's pretty cool here. Where are you these days?"

The fateful question. Remember, be cheerful and vague.

"Oh, you know, I've been taking a break. I really wanted to do some traveling, you know?"

"Yeah, sure. Sounds great."

Was there a touch of wariness creeping into his voice? I upped the nonchalance a level, broke my own rule, and skipped straight to the Employment Status point. "Besides, none of the offers I've been getting really do it for me, you know? I mean, I'm just not excited enough to want to commit."

"Sure. It's better to wait for the right thing."

Okay, he was relaxing again. I could backtrack to the Preliminaries.

"So, how do you like it there at PlanetCom?"

"Yeah, it's great, but Becks—hey, I've got someplace to be. But it was great talking to you. Let's grab a beer sometime, okay?"

"Great!" Keeping it bright. "See you soon."

I hung up cursing, robbed of my close. The whole point had been to refresh his memory about how fabulous I'd been to work with, and let him know that I'd be open to entertaining the right offer. Then, the next time he heard there was trouble in his marketing department—and when wasn't there?—he'd think, "Bingo! I'll just call Becks and talk her into coming here and sorting everything out. Good old Becks." And he'd smile fondly and I'd have a job.

Instead, he was probably sitting in his director's office right now, thinking, "Good old Becks. I wonder when she lost it. Maybe she has a drinking problem."

I ALLOTTED MYSELF twelve minutes for that line of thought, walking laps around the ground floor of my loft. It was a big space, with twenty-foot ceilings and a glass wall at one end looking out on a courtyard I shared with my neighbors. On the opposite end of the room a spiral staircase led up to the sleeping deck.

I looked around the place as I made my circuits. I wanted to put a huge mirror over the fireplace. I wanted to install bookshelves all the way up the wall by the stairs. I wanted to paint the bathroom purple. But mainly, I wanted to be so busy I wouldn't have time to think about redecorating. I wanted a job.

"LEON!" I SOUNDED surprised and delighted, even though I was the one who had placed the call. "How the hell are you? It's Becks!"

I'd worked with Leon Stevens for a while at WiredGlobe. I had even, in a fluke of organizational restructuring, been his boss for about three weeks. Just long enough for me to have been handed the dirty work of laying off the entire department before I'd been let go myself.

"Becks! How the hell are you?"

It really was the magic greeting. "I'm good. I'm great. What's new with you?"

"Oh, you know." He sighed, and I could picture him scratching behind his ear in that kitten-with-a-flea way he had. "I'm totally busy, totally stressed out. Same as always." He laughed. "I'm sure you are too."

"Me? Oh, no!" I tried to sound surprised, despite the fact that we were following the script to the letter. "I'm totally chilled. I've taken a real break."

"Really? A break? You?" He sounded skeptical.

"Yeah, well, I really wanted to just take care of my life for a while, you know?"

"Since when have you had a life?"

I laughed, as if it was a shared joke. He went on before I had a chance to come up with a clever reply.

"Hey, Becks, great talking to you, but I'm late for something. See you soon, okay?"

"Sure, great, Leon."

He took the time to cackle "A life!" before the line went dead.

It came back to me that I'd always hated Leon. I paced some more. Of course I had a life. Wasn't I currently walking laps in my loft? A loft is a life. Wasn't I going to be a bridesmaid for Connie? Being in a wedding is a life. Didn't I have a—well, no I didn't have a boyfriend anymore, but having a boyfriend isn't having a life.

Having a job is having a life.

I cursed and referred to my spreadsheet.

The sad truth of the matter was that I'd already gone through most of my A-list resources. I was now clearly in the realm of these gosh-I-haven't-seen-you-in-ages-how-*are*-you sort of guys, and with most of them I couldn't really remember many personal details. Like whether they had wives, or children, or pet iguanas.

I stared at the phone with loathing. Part of me knew I didn't have to get another marketing job right away. Believe it or not, showing up in a recording booth every so often and saying things like "Impale this, you filthy worm!" was lucrative enough that I didn't have to worry about making the mortgage.

But it wasn't about the money. It was about having a *career*. At this rate I'd never make director by thirty-five, and that meant I could kiss being a VP by thirty-eight goodbye. And as for being made CEO by forty . . . doubtful.

Aside from all that, the simple truth was that I missed my old life. I missed the press tours where I never quite knew what city I was in. I missed waking up with a jolt of adrenaline as I realized how packed my day's schedule was. I missed being too busy to think of anything other than my next deadline. I missed the old me.

I picked up the phone and dialed.

"HEY, STU! IT'S BECKS! How the hell are you?"

The third time was not the charm.

"Becks who?"

"Becks Mansfield"—keeping it light—"from CyberVision?" Damn! Why had I put a question mark at the end of that?

There was an uncomfortable pause.

"Becks Mansfield?" Disbelief.

"Stu, you remember—"

"Becks Mansfield from CyberVision?"

"Yes!" Now it was clicking for him. "How the hell are you?" Brightly.

Another pause.

"How did you get my number?" Not the response I'd expected.

"Oh, gosh . . ." *I Googled you, you idiot.* "I heard you were—"

"Why in the hell would you ever call me?"

Okay, we were way off script here. "Stu—"

"I can't believe your nerve."

It may take me a while to catch on, but I was definitely cluing in to the fact that Stu was not pleased to hear from me. *"Um . . ."*

"You don't even remember, do you?"

"Well . . ." Remember what?

"The post-launch review meeting?" he prompted angrily. "The one where you pointed out thirteen different ways I'd fucked up the—"

"The X32 launch!" I finished for him, everything falling into place. "Right! Of course! That was a complete disaster. What ever happened to—" Oh. I had a feeling I knew what happened.

"They fired me!"

I winced. Why hadn't I remembered that? "Well, Stu, I hardly think you can blame me for that." Could he?

"You bet your ass I can!"

"But, Stu, I was only offering constructive criticism. I mean, the point of those review meetings was to learn from our mistakes, right? And let's face it . . ." No, better not go down that road. "But look, you've landed on your feet, right? And, really, you can't fault me just for being direct."

Apparently he could. "Direct? You were a complete bitch!"

Okay, that stung. I had no idea how to come back from that.

"Good-bye, Becks."

Click.

I stared at the receiver. I took a breath. I knew that, statistically, there were bound to be people in my professional past who remembered me less than fondly. And I knew that, statistically, women in the workplace are called bitches in direct proportion to how high they climb on the corporate ladder. Also, statistically, women who can deal with that fact generally do better than those who can't.

I knew in my heart I was one of those women. I could deal.

I hung up the phone and closed the laptop. Because I also knew I could deal a lot better after a massive amount of ice cream.

Three

I think you're crazy for wanting another stupid marketing job anyway." Connie's opinion was not blunted by the silk-organza-with-hand-sewn-pearl-accents bridal veil engulfing her face.

"That one's too stiff," I told her. "I thought you wanted long and drapey. And I don't see what's so crazy about trying to get my career back on track."

"Are we still on the job thing?" Vida entered the elaborately feminine dressing room with her arms full of something sheer and silky. "Seriously, Becks, why don't you just enjoy the time off?"

"It isn't time off unless it's time off from something. And I don't have anything, so it's just time. Wasted time." I looked at the new veil, which Vida offered with the resigned fortitude of a handmaiden who realizes she isn't destined to please the queen. "That's nice."

Connie wrinkled her nose. "Too plain. I want simple and elegant but not plain."

The handmaiden rebelled. "Well, you're going to have to explain the difference to me because the last thing I brought in was 'too fussy.'"

Vida was definitely not in her element at Bridal Elegance. As usual, she was wearing sunscreen instead of makeup, and her straight blond hair was in a ponytail. She wore cargo pants and a long-sleeved polo with a software logo on it—her office clothes. She'd come straight from her job as a coder at one of the big tech companies on the peninsula.

Vida went surfing before work every morning she could, and I knew if I got close enough to her, I'd probably still be able to catch a whiff of riptide on her skin. She was sure and graceful on a surfboard, but surrounded by bridal flounces she looked about as comfortable as Rambo in a tea shop.

I heard Connie's voice from somewhere inside a cathedral-length cloud of sheer white silk. "I hate this."

Tempers were getting frayed. Luckily, the saleswoman had years of experience to call upon. She poked her head inside the creamy satin drape and asked the magic question. "Does anyone here need champagne?"

AN HOUR LATER, a much more mellow bridal party had identified the perfect veil (perfect was the theme for Connie's wedding) and moved on to another room and the tricky subject of bridesmaid shoes for Vida and me.

"They need to be high enough so you look good, but low enough so you can dance all night," Connie said with authority. "Just because the dresses are full-length doesn't mean that nobody will see your feet."

I must have made some sort of harumphing noise because both Vida and Connie looked at me.

"What?" Connie asked. "What's wrong with the shoes?"

"It's not the shoes," I said, although at an average price of three hundred and twenty dollars there was plenty wrong with them. "It's just that, unless you find me an eligible Englishman, I don't really need to worry about dancing."

My friends exchanged glances.

"What?" I demanded.

"You can't date an Englishman," Connie told me.

"What do you mean I can't date an Englishman? Is that part of NAFTA or something? They can have our wheat, but we can't have their men?"

Vida gave me a serious look. "NAFTA has nothing to do with England," she said. "It stands for North American—"

"I know what it stands for," I snapped. "I just mean, what rule says I'm prohibited from dating an Englishman?"

Connie sank onto one of the shoe department's fringed ottomans and considered a black Stuart Weitzman pump with a little crystal bow on the front strap. "Well, Becks, you know how you are."

"How am I?"

Vida handed me a Marc Jacobs ankle strap stiletto and a straight answer. "You're a steamroller. You crush every man in your path."

"I do not!" I turned to Connie with the expectation she'd defend me.

Instead she nodded briskly. "You do, Becks. You walk all over them."

"I do not!" I said again.

Vida removed the shoe from my hand and replaced it with a refill on the champagne. "Think about it," she said. "When was the last time someone broke up with you? You're totally the one who dumps them."

"And over the silliest things," Connie continued, her

attention on a kitten-heel mule with a little fur pom-pom. "I mean, we always know when it's coming because you start making fun of them behind their backs."

"Oh, that's so true," Vida sat beside me eagerly. "You totally do that. And then, about a week later, everything they do irritates you—"

"And then poof," Connie finished, "they're gone."

"I'm not like that!" I protested. "It isn't me! It's them!"

Connie gave me a highly significant look while Vida nodded in satisfaction.

"What?" I demanded.

"Nothing. You're right. It's them." Connie agreed. "But here's a question— Who's the one picking them out?"

"What?"

"You totally dismissed Sean," Vida said.

"Sean who?" My head was beginning to spin. I'd set out that morning perfectly prepared to drink too much at lunch and spend too much on wedding stuff. Having my recent disastrous dating history dissected and thrown in my face had not been on the agenda.

Vida compressed her lips briefly before answering. "He's the guy from the mayor's office that I introduced you to at Connie's engagement party."

I searched my memory. "Oh, Sean. I thought he was gay."

My friends exchanged pitying looks.

"He isn't gay," Vida explained to me, speaking as though I was a rather slow five-year-old. "He's perfect for you. He's got a great job, a great house—"

"And a sailboat," Connie supplied.

"And he has a degree from the London School of Economics," Vida continued, ticking off the meritorious qualities of this guy I could barely remember. "And season tickets to the opera and—"

"And a boyfriend he keeps in a little place on Potrero Hill," I concluded.

"He's not gay!" They both insisted loudly. The saleswoman poked her head around the corner with a curious expression on her face. She probably thought we were discussing the groom. She opened her mouth as if to speak, then smiled brightly and backed out of the doorway.

"Maybe it's time we were going," I suggested.

"He's not gay." Vida refused to be distracted. "I know someone he used to date, and she said he was unbelievable in bed. Apparently he did this thing—"

"The point is"—Connie cut her off before Vida could provide any details of Sean's advanced sexual technique—"that you, Becks, when presented with this perfectly good specimen of the single male of the species, didn't even take a second look."

"Right," Vida agreed. "Sean didn't jump up and say 'I'm interested' so you didn't even notice him. Instead, you went out and got involved with Greg." She scrunched her nose in distaste as she said his name. "Who was an okay guy but totally wrong for you."

"But he did all the work. He called you. He pursued you. He fell right into your lap," Connie said.

"Until you kicked him back out again," Vida concluded. "Right on schedule."

I behaved in an un–Bridal Elegance manner by chugging the rest of the bubbly. It gave me time to recover.

"Wait a minute." I turned to Vida. "If this guy Sean is so perfect, why don't you go out with him?"

"Becks, it's not like there's one man who's perfect for everyone. He's so not perfect for me. But he was completely perfect for you." She sighed and looked at herself critically in the mirror. "Besides, he's one of the huge number of men who don't seem to realize I'm a woman."

"You're not." Connie's matter-of-fact statement came from somewhere behind a rack of white silk stilettos. "You're one of the guys." She reappeared holding a Manolo Blahnik with a completely unreasonable heel. "But we're not talking about you. I'm the bride and therefore the rightful center of attention."

Vida and I performed synchronized eye rolls.

"Hang on," I said, "you can't just blast me like this and then change the subject. Do you guys really think my radar's that off?"

Connie gave a martyred sigh and sat down. "Fine, but I don't have the time for you to fight me on this," she said. "Your only problem is that you're date lazy."

Oh God. Had she been cruising the self-help aisle at Barnes & Noble again? "What does that mean?"

"Date lazy," she explained. "It means you don't put any effort or thought into who you date."

"I do too!" I protested. "I have a whole list of rules." I began counting them off. "Don't date a guy who wears more jewelry than me, don't date a guy who uses *party* as a verb, don't date a Taurus because they're emotionally unavailable—"

"Becks, that's not what she's talking about," Vida cut off my recitation, which could have gone on much longer. "What she means is you don't ever go out with a guy you totally want to go out with."

"Of course I do."

Connie snorted. "You're never the one who chooses. You date the guys who approach you, instead of making the effort of finding someone you really want."

"Exactly." Vida nodded. "You're date lazy."

"I am not," I said firmly. "I just have better things to do than troll bars looking for some mythical Prince Charming."

"We're not talking about bars, and we're not talking about Prince Charming. We're just talking about opening your eyes a little bit and looking around at the men you meet. Geez, it's like some guy has to conk you over the head and say 'please go out with me' before you even think of him as a prospect. And then what do you do? You consult your stupid list of rules, and if he gets a passing grade, you go out with him. Do you stop to ask yourself if you're even interested in him? No! And so of course you end up turning into a total bitch and dumping him six weeks later because you shouldn't have been going out with him in the first place!" Vida sank onto a nearby couch looking exhausted.

"Gosh, Vee, tell me what you really think."

"We just want you to be happy, Becks," Connie said. "Like me." She gave the Manolo a critical eye, then dropped it with a look of distaste.

I almost said something about how I didn't know if it was realistic to rely on some guy to make me happy, but I didn't want to get yelled at anymore. Besides, Bridal Elegance was hardly the venue for that conversation.

"You just need to think about it a little bit," Vida suggested. "For God's sake, you have a point-by-point plan for every other aspect of your life, why don't you come up with a man plan?"

"A man plan." I nodded. "Right. And then I'll make a wish on the evening star, and before you know it, he'll ride right up to me on a white stallion."

"Fine," Connie sniffed. "Don't listen to your best friends. I don't know why we're even having this conversation when my entire wedding is in jeopardy over your stupid shoes!"

WE'D GONE from the bridal shop to a restaurant, and from there to a bar, and by the time we called it quits the shoe crisis had passed, and I was willing to admit to a certain inattention to my love life. I still didn't think it was my biggest problem, but after the fourth margarita I'd stopped arguing.

When I got home, the light was blinking on my answering machine. "Could that be Prince Charming himself?" I mumbled as I reached for the button.

But it wasn't.

It was better. It was Mitch Hastings.

It was a job.

Four

Three days later I presented myself to the receptionist at PlanetCom prepared to knock them dead—despite the fact that I knew absolutely nothing about the job I was interviewing for. Mitch had been pretty vague about the details. He'd just said there was a project in a horrible mess and he'd thought of me. I told myself that was because he knew I was brilliant at solving problems and not because the phrase "horrible mess" called me to mind.

The first person I spoke with seemed as clueless about the position as I was. But she was just a recruiter sent from human resources. She was only there to get me to sign a few nondisclosure forms and verify that I was indeed Rebecca Mansfield, Marketing Genius, before taking me to the real interviewers.

She led me down a series of hallways, making lefts and rights and more lefts and leaving me with no hope that I'd ever be able to find my way back without an escort. Of course, I'd have an escort. The big pink tag I'd been instructed to wear around my neck clearly stated that I was not to be set loose in the building alone.

Actually, as I watched the candy-colored stripes on the

HR rep's pantsuit streaming down the hall ahead of me, I reflected that the security seemed a little over the top. There were cameras in every corridor, and everyone I saw moving purposefully from closed door to closed door wore a color-coded picture ID badge. Stripy suit had to keep pulling her (bright orange) badge out and swiping it in readers as we went farther into the labyrinth of commerce that was PlanetCom.

I knew the company's major focus was on wireless communication, which was presumably a pretty competitive marketplace, but I'd never seen this level of corporate paranoia. I started to get a little excited. Maybe what they were doing was so earth-shatteringly, groundbreakingly revolutionary that corporate spies were just dying to get their hands on it. Maybe, after all this time, I was on to a winner.

I started peeking at the little placards outside the rooms we passed. The personality quirks of high-tech companies often show up in the naming scheme for their conference rooms. I worked for one place that held meetings in Yosemite, Yellowstone, and Joshua Tree. The implication was that they were into some sort of "green" technology, but no. They produced a hideously boring (which is not how I marketed it) customer contact tracking system.

If I was trying to learn anything about PlanetCom from their room names, I was out of luck, unless I could infer anything from A207E or S99F. I couldn't for the life of me figure out the meanings behind the codes, which was possibly the point.

At last we arrived at C767U, which was just as cozy as it sounds. The HR rep gave me a professional smile and sent me into the room with assurances that Chad would be there in a few minutes, and in the meantime I could enjoy the bottle of water she'd provided and stare at the clean whiteboards.

"Great," I said, and she vanished.

Chad. I had no idea if he was someone I'd be reporting to or someone who'd be reporting to me. Or possibly neither. I opened the water and sipped self-consciously, wondering if there were hidden cameras on me, observing how I behaved when unobserved. I was trying to decide if it would look bad for me to subtly adjust my interview outfit (sober black Donna Karan skirt and perfectly tailored Thomas Pink blouse) when the door opened.

A preppy young executive type appeared, wearing khakis and a blue Oxford shirt with a discreet PlanetCom logo over his heart. He had that intentionally harried look that people wear around an office, the one that says "God, I'm busy and important" and was calculated to make you feel grateful for five minutes of his time.

"Becks Mansfield? I'm Chad Barlow. I've heard so much about you!"

I heard the faint sound of a starter pistol, and we were off.

I WAS FABULOUS. I know I was fabulous because people kept saying things like "Really? That's fabulous!" I was amazing. I'm sure I was amazing because there was more than one instance of someone saying, "Gosh, that's amazing!"

I might not have found my dream job in the past few years, but I had damn well learned how to kill in an interview.

I was three people into the process before I had a glimmer

of understanding of what exactly PlanetCom did and what precisely they'd like me to do for them. That understanding came with the realization that I'd have to shelve any feelings I had about the protection of individual privacy rights and somehow embrace the beauty of point-to-point wireless communication, but for the right salary I could probably do that.

Suffice it to say, things went well.

Particularly with one Mr. Chad Barlow. I'd spent five hours talking to five people and thought I was finished when Chad came back for seconds.

"Exhausted yet?"

I was, but I grinned in an I'm-game-for-anything way. "Hell no. Bring it on."

He came in and closed the door behind him. "I don't think you'll be surprised to know we're all pretty excited about you."

Not surprised, no. But relieved anyway. "Thanks."

He sat and gave me an endearingly shy smile. "Speaking for myself, I'm very excited."

Okay, he clearly expected me to say something. "So what brings you back, Chad?"

"Oh." His eyes widened. "Someone else wants to chat with you, just for a minute, if that's okay."

"Sure, no problem."

"So I thought I'd grab the chance to spend a little more time with you myself." There was that smile again.

"Do you mind telling me who I'll be seeing?"

"It's such a coincidence. She couldn't believe it when I mentioned your name earlier. Said she'd worked with you back— Oh, here she is now!"

The door opened again to reveal a small thirtyish gnome.

She wore a floaty gray dress and had a seriously bad dye job. The long red hair parted in the middle and hanging over her face, paired with the hideous dress, indicated that she was going for some sort of Druid priestess look. I remembered her instantly. Everything except her name and where I'd worked with her. But the hair was etched in my memory. And, if the pieces were coming together correctly, she'd had a habit of knitting in meetings. *Madame Defarge*, I thought, but knew I was wrong. So I did what any other self-respecting marketing professional would. I faked it.

"Oh my God! It's so great to see you!"

She smiled a tight smile that triggered a little something, but no name popped magically to the forefront of my brain.

"Becks." She dropped my name on the table like a gauntlet.

"Wow, I had no idea you were here!"

She turned to Chad. "Could you give us a minute?"

"Sure." He turned to me with another smile, this one less shy and possibly inappropriate. "I'm sure I'll be talking to you again, Becks."

And he winked. Definitely inappropriate, but I didn't care because the next thing he said was "See you, Rita" before he left.

"Rita!" I gushed. "How long have you been at PlanetCom?"

She gave me a look that could have frozen lava in its tracks. "Since you fired me, you bitch."

"SHE DIDN'T!" Max's jaw actually dropped, which is exactly why I'd called him to meet me for drinks the instant

I'd gotten out of PlanetCom. You could always count on Max to provide a gratifying audience for life's little disasters.

"She did," I affirmed. "'You bitch,' she said."

"And did you remember firing her?"

"I didn't *fire* her." I downed the last of my lemon drop and looked meaningfully at the empty glass. Max, bless him, made the universal "another round" gesture at the bartender. "It was when I was a manager for a minute and a half at WiredGlobe and I got stuck doing a bunch of layoffs before I got laid off myself. She called me a bitch then, too."

"Well, given the circumstances, I suppose that might have been expected."

"But, come on!" I protested. "She still hasn't gotten over it?"

Max patted my arm. "Not everyone is as used to it as you are. Now, take it from the top. Tell me everything she said."

I nodded and reached for my new drink. "First"—I sipped—"she told me she'd see me in hell before she'd let me get a job at PlanetCom."

"Ouch."

"Then she just started shouting at me. That I was—again—a bitch, and that everyone at WiredGlobe had hated me and—" It was too much. I had to stop for vodka. "She said I was a corporate machine," I told him. "She said I didn't care about anything but getting promoted."

This was the point at which Max was required to murmur "That's complete nonsense" or something equally reassuring. I looked at him expectantly.

He suddenly found the stem of his glass completely fascinating.

"Max?"

"Was that all she said? Becks, she's just a sad, bitter woman. You shouldn't spend one more minute thinking about her. Life's too short."

I nodded glumly. "Life's too short," I agreed. "Assuming you have a life."

And by a life, I meant a job.

Five

After a few days of licking my Rita-induced wounds, I decided I'd better keep my day job. That is, I'd better keep vanquishing the evil foes of Vladima, Defender of the Night. Meaning, I'd better go see Josh.

The studio where he and a small but dedicated band of artists and animators created Vladima's bloodthirsty world was located in a low brick building on Folsom, in a neighborhood where electrical supply houses and auto repair shops were giving way to trendy bars and industrial lofts. They were pretty nice digs, considering the fact that I couldn't figure out how Josh managed to fund the whole enterprise.

There was no reception desk, just an electronic keypad where you could enter your security code and come in off the street to a minuscule lobby containing a staircase to the business upstairs (which I suspected was some sort of shady enterprise, since nobody ever seemed to come or go there) and the door leading to Vladima's inner sanctum.

I keyed my code into that door, entered the bat cave, and let my eyes adjust to the gloom. The décor of the place was undoubtedly inspired by the subject matter created there.

The walls were painted dark gray, and I wasn't sure if the mottled concrete floor was a pricey interior designer's reference to an oil slick or evidence that the building had once actually been a garage. There were posters of Vladima everywhere, alongside various other superheroes and assorted children of the night. Pride of place was given to an original movie poster of the silent classic *Nosferatu*, autographed by the director F. W. Murnau himself. It was kept under glass, and more than once when deadlines had been close I'd seen candles burning under it. The staff took their work very seriously.

The office area was barely big enough to contain twelve cubicles for Vladima's minions (their term, not mine) and one glass-walled office for Josh. The cubicles were constructed out of something that looked like gray burlap. The only windows letting a little natural light into the place were made of a thick wire-reinforced glass that left the place pretty murky, which is just how the inhabitants liked it. I'd once commented on how dismal it was and had been given a lengthy lecture on eyestrain suffered by computer artists and how soft indirect light was best for them.

It certainly didn't do much for anyone's complexion.

I could see Josh was on the phone, so I wandered through the aisle of cubicles, heading for the break room at the opposite end of the building. The minions all wore headphones and were pretty much glued to their monitors, pushing pixels with intense concentration. It would take more than one mild-mannered voiceover artist to disturb their concentration.

And that's what I was in Vladima's world. My role in the process was to show up when the script was written and record Vladima's dialogue. Other people, most of them actual professional actors, came in at different times to record the rest of the characters.

Josh wrote the scripts and created the storyboards for the animation. He'd started out with Vladima by drawing her in comic book format, and that's what the storyboards still looked like. After the voices—audio assets—were recorded, he farmed out the production of the animated films to the minions. Some did backgrounds, some did characters' illustrations, some did the actual programming of the animation and coding of the Web site.

When the whole thing was put together, it was usually necessary to come in and rerecord some of the dialogue. That's where we were with our latest offering, *Daemons of the Night*.

In the break room, a large wall-mounted plasma screen was running the most recent version of the feature. I entered in hopes of making a nice cup of tea and was confronted with my animated alter-ego sinking her pointy teeth into a very nasty-looking creature in a red velvet cape. Then she looked up, and I heard myself say "*Mmmm.* There's nothing I like more than French food."

Uh-huh. So the creature must have been the murderous Richelieu, who was a sort of right-wing time-traveling political assassin. Lovely. I watched as the battle between good (me—um, Vladima) and evil (Richelieu) drew to its predictable conclusion.

"What do you think?" Josh stood in the doorway behind me, his attention on the screen. He was dressed unsurprisingly in black jeans and a black dress shirt with the tails out. He was just over six feet tall and needed to put on a few pounds. If the shadows under his dark eyes were any indication, he also needed to get more sleep. Onscreen there was a sort of slurpy sound. He winced and ran a hand distractedly through his mess of dark hair. “I’m still not happy with the sucking.” He shifted his gaze to me. “How are you?”

I resisted the urge to say “sucking” and opted for “peachy.”

He gave me a critical look. “Things that bad?”

“You don’t even want to know.”

His eyes met mine for a minute, then he looked down at the floor and nodded as if he was deep in thought. “Cup of tea before we get started?”

“You read my mind.”

We caught up for a while before heading for the sound booth. Josh had been working too hard (not unusual) and trying to recover from some staffing changes. He’d lost the woman who specialized in sound effects a few weeks ago and wasn’t happy with her replacement.

“It’s not just the bloodsucking,” he told me, stirring a cup of Darjeeling. “It’s everything. The footsteps on gravel sound too hollow now, and the *thwannng* of the crossbow is just lame.”

“There’s nothing lamer than a lame *thwannng*,” I commiserated.

“And I still don’t get why Amy left like that,” Josh went on. “No notice or anything. Just that e-mail.”

“Amy got a call from George Lucas,” I reminded him. What I didn’t say was that it was stunningly obvious to everyone else in the studio that Amy had been in love with Josh for at least two years. Two years is a long time to go unnoticed by a dark brooding poet of the undead. “Shall we get started?”

"Might as well." He led me down the hall, away from the cubicle farm, past a horrifically cluttered conference room to the small sound booth at the back of the building. I stepped into the booth and thanked heaven once more that I wasn't claustrophobic.

The room was about the size of a small walk-in closet, with walls covered in (surprise) gray foam that looked as if it had once had giant eggs packed in it. There was a thirteen-inch monitor where I could watch the movie play. Aside from that, we're talking a stool, a microphone, and a set of headphones.

The actual recording wasn't hard work. It was even kind of fun, now that the animations were complete and I could see them on the monitor as I spoke the lines. For the most part, Vladima's speech was synced to what I'd already done. But script rewrites and other minor changes always made it necessary for me to redo some bits.

Josh was stationed at a mixing board in a slightly larger walk-in closet next door, separated from the sound booth by a window. He could flip a switch and talk into my headphones to give me direction. It always surprised me how intimate it felt to have his voice in my head.

"Okay, let's go." He waited until I'd gotten as comfortable as a person can get on a wooden stool. "Take it from 'Hello, Cardinal,' okay?"

I gave him the thumbs-up and waited for the video playback. Then I sneered "Hello, Cardinal. It's been a long time. Nice to see you haven't lost your fashion sense."

And for this I get paid. Kind of a lot.

. . .

I LOST TRACK of the time after a while and was a little surprised when Josh said, "That's it, Becks. Let's call it a day." He was rubbing his eyes.

"Josh," I said into the mike, "excuse me for saying so, but you look like hell."

He gave me a tired grin and shrugged. "Then you should buy me a drink."

Emerging from the booth, I was surprised to find that all the minions were gone; then I realized it was after ten on a Friday night. Josh locked the place up and we walked down Folsom to Wilde Oscar's, a sort of hip-SOMA-club-meets-cool-Irish-pub kind of place where they know how to pour a proper Guinness.

We took a corner booth, and the minute I sat down I regretted taking Josh up on his drink suggestion. Every woman in the place had checked him out as we'd made our way through the crowd. I was still stinging from the hostility I'd caught from Rita the other day. The last thing I needed was to feel brutally assessed by a collection of bar Bettys who all figured they'd look better sitting across from Josh than I did.

I knew that on a good day I can hold my own in the looks department. I wear my darkish hair in a low-maintenance but reasonably fashionable cut, and I work out often enough to be able to pull off most styles that didn't insist on bare hip bones. So on a good day I had no complaints.

This was not a good day. I'd been wallowing in self-pity since the disaster at PlanetCom, and to be honest I wasn't even sure I'd brushed my hair that morning. Let alone suited up in the combat gear necessary for Friday night drinks at a

South of Market bar. I decided I'd have a quick pint and get out of there.

But Guinness isn't really a quick sort of drink. So eventually I just sat back in the booth, warmed by the stout and the sound of Josh's voice. If I didn't really pay attention to what he was saying, it was all rather pleasant.

Of course he was discussing Vladima. Vladima's latest adventure and what remained to be done to finalize it. Vladima's next storyline, where she'd meet an archenemy who was finally worthy of her skills. The whole Vladima world that he'd constructed and apparently lived in.

In case I haven't made it clear, I should mention that Vladima is a good guy. Sure, she's a bloodsucker, but she kills only really bad types. In effect, she's a vampire with a social conscience. She may not suck for truth, justice, and the American way, but she does suck with a strict moral code.

From a marketing standpoint, it was brilliant. Josh had tapped into the whole Goth, disaffected youth demographic with a heroine who is very much an outcast (what with being undead and all) but who still cares enough about society's ills to rise above her own pain and save humanity's sorry ass in each and every Webisode. Sometimes twice. The fact that she wears a black leather body suit and is stacked as only a cartoon character can be stacked doesn't hurt her download statistics either.

I caught the tail end of what Josh was saying. ". . . I'm boring you to death, aren't I?"

I made a face. "I may be just the tiniest bit over Vladima for the night."

He scrunched his hair with both hands. "God, I need to get a life."

Now, that caught my interest. "What did you say?"

He shrugged. "I'm sick of spending all day sitting around in the dark getting deeper and deeper into a mythology that has no real point."

"You're kidding."

He gave me a lame grin. "Becks, I hope you don't think I'm so deluded that I don't realize Vladima's chief appeal is to fifteen-year-old boys who have a very small chance of ever getting laid."

Wow. "Actually," I told him, "I did think you were that delusional."

He laughed. "There!" he said. "Just there, did you hear that? Do you have any idea how long it's been since I laughed?"

"I guess there's not a lot to laugh about when you're hanging out in graveyards all the time. Even cartoon graveyards."

He nodded and took a drink.

"Josh, what exactly do you mean when you say you need to get a life? Because when I say it I usually mean I need to get a job—not that Vladima isn't fun and everything but . . ."

"You have a degree from Stanford," he finished for me. He'd heard it before.

"Right. So when I say it, I mean I need to get my life back on track."

He was regarding me with curiosity. I plunged ahead.

"But you have a job, one that seems to be your life, so when you say you need to get a life . . . I wonder what you mean?"

He kept looking at me and seemed to be thinking carefully about what he wanted to say. I started to get a little uncomfortable with the suddenly intense mood. I'd given up hope that he'd actually answer by the time he finally spoke.

"I mean I'd like a reason to come out of the graveyard."

Right. I nodded as if I understood what was going on behind those dark eyes.

Six

It was a week later, and Vida and I had been drinking. About the time we ordered our third round of mojitos, I wondered aloud if perhaps we'd been drinking rather a lot lately.

"It's the damn wedding!" Vida wailed.

"The damn wedding!" I agreed.

We'd had our final fittings for the bridesmaid dresses that afternoon. The dresses themselves were supremely tasteful creations in a sort of café latte–colored silk. Almost Edwardian looking, they were strapless with a little drape across the breasts. The skirts were straight in front, with another little drape across the hips pulled back into something that I don't know if we're calling a bustle anymore. They were elegant. They were sumptuous. They were not comfortable.

Connie came to supervise the fitting, and she brought her hairdresser with her. She didn't trust anyone in England to do her hair, so she was flying Roger over to take care of her. It was his job to make Connie look fabulous for the onslaught of cocktail parties, afternoon tea parties, formal dinner parties, the "hen" party (which I'd found out was the

British equivalent of a bachelorette party) and, um, the wedding. His curling iron wouldn't have a chance to cool off for the entire two weeks.

In the dressing room, Roger cast his professional eye over Vida and me as we were tugged and tucked by a collection of women holding pins in their mouths.

"What do you think?" Connie looked at us as if she was afraid our friendship had blinded her to the reality of just how awful our hair was.

Roger moved closer to Vida's sun-bleached head and made a clicking sound with his tongue. "It's very straight, isn't it?"

Vida sent me a "help me" look in the mirror.

"But the color is exquisite," Roger relented. "And the length gives us a lot of flexibility."

Connie briefly looked relieved. Then she eyed me apprehensively. "What about . . ."

Roger approached with eyebrows raised. He blinked quickly a few times, then said one word: "Extensions."

"Excuse me?"

His smile was an attempt to reassure me. "Nothing permanent, don't worry. I'll just bring some extra bits of hair in that . . . brown color . . . and we'll be able to make it look like . . . it will be fine." He turned to Connie and gave her his professional word. "It will be fine."

Connie beamed at us. We'd passed. We'd be able to advance to the next level in the tournament of bridesmaids. I studied my reflection and began to rethink my stand on highlights.

"Becks," Vida whispered out of the side of her mouth, "we are so going for drinks the minute we're unpinned."

I nodded my . . . brown . . . head. It seemed like the only sensible thing to do.

NOW, AT THE BAR, Vida was swaying slightly. Or maybe it was me. "Do you know what's really not fair?" she demanded.

"What's not fair?"

She brought her palm down on the table. "Max!"

"Max!" I agreed. "What's not fair about Max?"

"Where the hell is he?"

I checked my watch. "It's nine on a Wednesday. He's probably watching a TiVo of *Queer Eye for the Straight Guy*."

"Exactly!" she trumpeted.

"Exactly what?" As far as I knew, it was still legal to watch excessively fabulous makeover shows.

"We're off getting criticized and jabbed with pins while he's snug on his couch in perfect comfort. And why? I ask you—why us and not him?"

"I'm just guessing here, but I think it may have something to do with the fact that he's a guy."

"Exactly!" She hit the table again. "One damn Y chromosome and he gets out of being a bridesmaid for his entire life!"

I saw her point. "Let's get a cab."

MAX WAS LESS THAN THRILLED to see us on his doorstep. It was subtle, but I picked up on it when he said, "Good God, what are you two trollops doing in my respectable neighborhood at this hour of the night?"

"Seething with resentment," I told him.

He stepped back so we could come in. "What have I done now?"

"You were born with a Y chromosome," Vida said as she paused to rest on his shoulder.

Max looked at me over the top of her head. "I'm making coffee, aren't I?"

"You are."

Max lived in a newish condo in Dolores Heights, with a view of the park as well as the old Mission Dolores that had given the neighborhood its name. The front door opened into a big living/dining room with an open kitchen, so it was no trouble to pull Vida away from our host and plunk her down on a couch. "I don't want coffee," she said. "I want gender equality!"

Max gave me raised eyebrows.

"She wants you in a bridesmaid dress," I explained.

"Sorry, sweetness. I haven't done drag since college," he grinned. "Not that it wouldn't be fun to see the look on Ian's face as I came traipsing down the aisle in pink organdy."

"Café au lait silk," Vida corrected him.

"Is it café au lait?" I asked her. "I thought it was café latte."

"This is a color?" Max asked.

"You just make the coffee," I told him.

"Café au—"

"Shut up!" we yelled.

AS IT TURNED OUT, Max had little sympathy for our bridal complaints.

"Oh, come on," he scoffed when we told him about the fitting. "Big deal. So you have to wear a dress and be fawned over by seamstresses and hairdressers. *Boo hoo.*"

I turned to Vida. "Remind me again why we came here?"

"At least you get to be in the wedding," he said.

"What do you mean?"

He rolled his eyes. "Connie wanted Ian to ask me to be a groomsman."

"You're kidding!" Vida said. "That's so cool! When"—then she saw the look on his face—"oh, I mean . . . um."

"Right." Max nodded. "It seems Ian isn't really a member of my core fan base."

"Connie told you he said no?" I asked. I hadn't heard anything about this.

He shook his head. "Of course not. I wouldn't have known a thing if Ian hadn't gotten all British with me at the engagement party. He said he was sure I would understand that 'it just wasn't on,' whatever the hell that's supposed to mean."

"He's a jerk," Vida said.

We stared at her.

"Oh, come on. Don't pretend you like him. I mean, it's one thing to support Connie, but we don't need to lie about the guy when it's just us here."

Max cleared his throat. "Ian's not a jerk," he said firmly. He paused. "Being a jerk requires having a personality."

"I so don't get it," Vida said. "She could do so much better than him."

I was hugely relieved to find I wasn't the only one who harbored doubts about Ian, even if I couldn't quite put my finger on the source of the doubts. "I can't even say what it is about him . . ."

"I know," Max agreed. "I mean he's perfectly pleasant on the surface."

"There's just nothing much below the surface, as far as I can tell." I sipped my coffee and thought about it. "I mean, has he ever expressed an opinion?"

"Only about me being in his wedding," Max said.

Vida patted him on the arm. "You really wouldn't want to hang out with him anyway, Maxie. Think about what his friends must be like. I mean, the only reason to be a bridesmaid is because you can usually count on getting lucky with a groomsman. But in this case"—she made a face—"I'm not optimistic."

"Maybe Connie likes bland," I suggested. "Or maybe it was the English accent. I mean, she went after Ian, didn't she? It wasn't a case of her being date lazy."

"Date what?" Max asked.

"Something I've recently been accused of." I ignored his baffled look and went on. "She must have seen something in him to pursue him, right?"

"Maybe," Max said delicately, "she saw a wedding."

Vida groaned. "Not Connie. She's not just in it for the dress."

"Maybe some women," I protested, "but not Connie. I mean, how many weddings does she handle for her clients every year? She's more likely to be sick of them than to be lusting after her own."

"And yet . . ." Max said.

"And yet." Vida sounded as if she was considering it. "There is the whole Princess for a Day syndrome to consider . . . or, in this case, Princess for Two Weeks."

"No," I said firmly. "We're talking about Connie. She's a

princess every day. I don't think it's that." I paused. "Maybe it's the dying alone thing."

"That's not Connie's thing, Becks, that's my thing." Vida looked a little embarrassed.

"That's everyone's thing," Max said.

"Really?" Maybe I was a freak after all. "Not me. I'm much more afraid of spending my next thirty years with the wrong guy than I am of spending my last thirty days on my own."

"That's because your fear of commitment thing is stronger than your dying alone thing," Max told me. "Commitment, however, is clearly not a problem for Connie."

"No," Vida agreed.

"Trust me," Max continued. "She just sees her 'sell by' date getting closer, and Ian looks like he'll do."

"Ugh," I groaned. "I won't believe that of Connie."

"Happens every day," Max said breezily. "Usually ends in divorce."

"Max!" Vida and I both protested.

"She isn't even married yet!" I said.

"What?" Max said innocently. "That doesn't mean we don't love the pants off the girl. And it doesn't mean we won't have a very good time at the wedding."

After quite a bit more speculation we decided to call it a night, and Max gallantly offered to drive us both home. He dropped Vida off first, and when he pulled up outside my loft, he offered me a peck on the cheek and a promise.

"In our next session we'll deal with your fear of commitment."

"Please," I said. "I've had plenty of discussions about what's wrong with me lately. I don't need your sham analysis on top of it."

And so what if I was afraid? As I unlocked my door, I remembered my grandmother's advice, offered when my eight-year-old heart had been broken by Dean Hitzelburger in an inexcusable display of playground infidelity.

"Becks, there's something every girl should realize and realize early." She'd lifted my chin so I could look straight into her bright violet eyes. "It's better to *be* single than to wish you were."

Good for Grandma.

Seven

I returned home to a blinking light on my answering machine, which I ignored until morning. It wasn't until the sun was fully up and the slice of cheesecake I'd hidden in my freezer started mentally announcing itself as a perfectly reasonable breakfast choice that I rolled over and hit the Play button.

"Becks? Hi! It's Chad Barlow. From PlanetCom."

Yikes! Had Rita not torpedoed me after all? I sat up and paid attention.

"Look, I'm really sorry about what happened the other day."

The other week. Closer to two weeks, in fact. But I forgave him.

"I couldn't believe it when I heard what Rita said. Um . . . anyway, I'd like the chance to make it up to you. Are you free for dinner sometime? Maybe Thursday? Let me know, okay? I'd hate for you to get the wrong impression about everyone at PlanetCom."

A nervous laugh. *Beep*.

Yes! Hope was not lost! Maybe the powers that be had decided my obvious marketing brilliance outweighed Rita's overt hostility. They were wooing me! I mean, it wasn't a request for a second round of interviews—it was a dinner meeting. Yes!

ZUNI CAFÉ, NO LESS. When I'd called Chad back, he'd even offered to pick me up. Since I didn't want to make it too social, I told him I'd meet him there.

I loved Zuni. Aside from having amazing food, it was right down the street from one of my favorite bars in town, Martuni's. If it had been a night out with friends, a nightcap at the Martuni's back room piano bar would have been inevitable. But I didn't think I'd be making that suggestion to Chad. This was business, after all. Business and drunken renditions of show tunes rarely mix.

Chad was waiting at the bar when I came in, looking very sharp in a silky deep-blue striped shirt that he wore out, with the sleeves unbuttoned, over black leather jeans.

Leather jeans? I hadn't done the corporate dress thing either, opting for a lightweight cashmere sweater and simple A-line skirt, but I couldn't imagine wearing leather jeans to a business dinner.

"Becks!" His face lit up when he saw me, and as I got within range, he stood up and kissed me on the cheek.

Kissed me on the cheek? What the hell was that about? Then I tuned in to what he was saying: ". . . really happy you didn't let that stupid thing at work get in the way of going out with me."

Holy shit. Vida was right. I do need to be conked over the head before I realize someone is interested in me. And Chad Barlow had just conked me.

I probably responded with something like "Um . . . hi" before the hostess saved my clueless ass by telling us our table was ready. As we walked around the open-fire oven toward the brick wall at the rear of the restaurant, I felt Chad's hand resting proprietarily on the small of my back.

Yep. This was a date.

IT WASN'T HORRIBLE. Once I adjusted to the fact that this was a personal thing, I said a mental "Oh, what the hell" and ordered a martini.

I spent some time kicking myself for being such an idiot, but it turned out I could do that while paying enough attention to Chad's conversation to be polite. It was standard first date patter. How much he liked this place, had I been there before, what he liked to do, *blah, blah, blah*.

But the oysters—I had said "what the hell," after all—were amazing, and the wine Chad ordered with our roast chicken was quite nice, and after a while I found myself nodding and smiling and answering and chatting without even having to tell myself to.

Okay, so it wasn't fireworks and symphonies, but he was, when all was said and done, a nice guy. Good-looking even, in a prep school sort of way. And he had interests in things like art and music and movies.

"But I have to admit," he said over a shared slice of chocolate hazelnut cake, "I'm really a geek at heart."

"Big surprise," I told him. "Let me guess, computer games?"

He grinned. "Even worse. Comic books."

I felt a faint stirring of apprehension. "Could be worse. You could have an Internet gambling problem."

He laughed. "It's not that bad. But I do spend a lot of time online. A lot of the best comics are Web-based these days."

Okay, definitely time to change the subject. "Gosh, this cake is good."

Not my best effort, I know. And it didn't work. Chad blundered right out onto the minefield. "It's the weirdest thing, but when I first saw you I thought we'd met somewhere before."

"Oh, that happens to me a lot," I babbled. "I have one of those faces. People always think I used to be in a sitcom—"

"No," he marched on, "it's not just your face—it's your voice. It took me a while, but I finally figured out who you remind me of. Have you ever heard of an online comic, well, more of an animation, I guess—anyway, a superhero vampire named Vladima Cross?"

I swallowed and gave him a completely blank look. "Vladima?"

"It's funny." He forked the last bite of frosting. "Because I'd swear the guy who draws her must know you."

"Weird." I wasn't going to give him a single inch more. The last thing I needed was the news getting back to PlanetCom, and by extension everywhere else in the business world, that I was a cartoon blood drinker. My chances for a professional comeback would get a serious stake through the heart.

Chad shot me a look from beneath his lashes. "I don't suppose I could talk you into giving me a little bite on the neck?"

I gulped the last of my wine. "Never on the first date." I think I managed a smile.

. . .

CHAD WALKED ME TO MY CAR. I knew what was coming. I just didn't know how I should handle it. But as it turned out, Chad moved so fast I didn't have time to plan anything anyway. Before I could get out a breezy little "well, this was fun," I was being kissed. And rather well.

He started with his hands lightly on my shoulders, then drew me closer when it was pretty clear I wasn't going to back away and slap him. Things progressed until I was leaning against my passenger door and felt the tip of my tongue reaching out for him.

Oops.

He pulled back just enough to look searchingly into my eyes, and I knew. I knew I wasn't interested. I knew he was a perfectly pleasant, good-on-paper sort of guy and that if I didn't do something about it I'd probably end up making out with him tonight, and going out with him again, and sleeping with him on the third date, and probably taking him to Connie's going-away party next week and introducing him to all my friends. And I knew I wouldn't miss him in London, and I'd start looking for his flaws the minute I got back.

If I didn't stop this right now, I'd be just as date lazy as I'd always been. I'd be seeing him because he was into me, not because I was into him. And he wasn't really into me anyway. He was into Vladima. And that would only get worse if he found out the truth. So I took a deep breath and did the decent thing.

"Chad, I had a really nice time tonight, and you seem like a really great guy, but I just don't think this is something I want to pursue."

I gazed up at him confidently, sure I'd done the right thing.

He took a step back. He blinked and, I have to say, looked kind of stupid.

"What?"

Okay, I realized he'd lost some of the blood supply to his brain with that kiss, but really.

"I just don't think we're right for each other," I explained.

"Are you serious? Did you really just say that?"

"Yes, well . . . don't get me wrong. I'm sure you're a great guy, but . . ." I waited. It seemed to be taking him an awfully long time to get it.

"Chad?"

"I don't believe you." He seemed dazed. "I mean, Rita told me you were a bitch, but . . ."

"Hey—"

"She was right." He shook his head, then looked at me again with narrowed eyes. "You're such a bitch."

Surely the man had been rejected before? But something in his increasingly pissed-off expression convinced me that I might have been better off telling him something more tried and true. Something like "It's not you—it's me" or "I'm just getting over a really bad breakup."

Someone who says those things probably never gets called a bitch.

"POOR BABY," Max sympathized over the phone. "You do seem to be getting the bad reviews these days."

"Tell me about it."

"And he couldn't come up with anything more descriptive than 'such a bitch'?"

"You see why it would never have worked between us."

"No conversational skills," Max agreed. "Still . . ."

"I did the right thing!" I protested. "I was just shorthanding the whole affair. I saw the future, I didn't want to spend my time there, and I thought we should leave it at that!"

"Is that what you told him?"

"More or less."

"What did you say?"

"I told him it wasn't something I wanted to pursue."

"Hmmm."

"You think that was the problem?"

"It might be a little harsh."

"Don't be ridiculous. It wasn't harsh, it was just direct. Honest. Harsh would have been 'I can tell we're doomed to a short-term mediocre relationship, and I'd rather cut my losses now than indulge in yet another pointless time-waster.'"

"Yes, well, that relies a bit too much on your faith that you can actually see the future."

"Believe me, I could. It looked remarkably like the past." I groaned with the hideous unfairness of it all. "I thought I'd get points for this! I broke the date-laziness cycle!"

"You get points from me, sweetie, and I'm sure you'll get points from Con and Vee."

I sighed. "Yeah."

"But it's probably a bit much to expect points from the guy you've decided to break the cycle with. Especially when you do it so . . . directly."

"Maybe."

"Anyway," he suggested, his tone brightening, "why don't we have lunch with the girls tomorrow? We'll shower you with points."

"I can't," I moaned.

"What? Have you got another date?"

"Sort of." I looked over at my coffee table and the script Josh had sent by messenger. "With a vampire."

Eight

At the studio the next day it was business as usual. Except for the sword fight in the break room.

I strolled up behind Josh, who was standing at the rear of the gathered crowd of minions. I hadn't seen him since our talk at Wilde Oscar's. He looked slightly better than usual. As if he'd managed to remember to both eat and sleep on the same day.

Josh was absorbed in the battle currently raging between two of his senior staff members. Malcolm, one of the animators, was wearing his usual skateboard fashions and brandishing a medieval-looking broadsword. Alex, Vladima's Web master, gave the action some class with his J. Crew shirt and a shiny new saber. I tapped Josh's shoulder. "Who's winning?"

He jumped a little. "Hey, Becks. You're early. We're listening to the swords."

"Oh, darn. I thought maybe they were dueling over my besmirched honor."

Malcolm landed a seriously clanging swat on his opponent's weapon. A small woman close to the action clapped. "That's it!"

"Let me guess—she's your new sound effects person?"

Josh nodded, not taking his eyes off the action. "As of two days ago. I fired Amy's replacement. This is Raven. She's great. Her sucking is classic."

In other offices that comment might be considered sexual harassment. "I can't wait to meet her."

"Who besmirched your honor?" he asked.

"Who hasn't?"

He shot me a look. "You're suitably despondent today."

"I'm just trying to fit in with the cool kids."

The new sound effects artist yelled something, and the fight was over. Everyone applauded and headed back to their cubicles.

"Raven," Josh called. "Come meet Vladima's voice."

The small woman approached, her face flushed with pleasure. "I think we've cracked it," she announced, then gave her attention to me. "You're very good when you're very bitchy."

"Succinctly put, Raven," Josh said. "This is Becks Mansfield. Becks, Raven Nightly."

I considered becoming very bitchy on the spot but decided it wasn't worth the effort. Raven was older than I'd thought from a distance, and there was something about the enthusiastic grin beaming from her weather-worn face that made it impossible to be offended by her calling me a bitch.

Either that or I was getting used to it.

JOSH AND I HEADED for the sound booth. I was there to work on a couple of promotional spots Josh was planning to place with some of the bigger Web sites and possibly run as commercials on a few cable TV stations.

He'd pulled most of the vocals from previous features, but I still needed to record things like "Check it out" and "AOL users click on keyword Vladima." It only took an hour or so.

"That was great." Josh's voice sounded in my headphones. "I think we're done."

"Hey, Josh, have you got a minute?" I spoke into the mike and looked over at him through the glass that separated the control room from the recording booth.

"Sure. Come on over." He took off his headset and motioned me into his studio.

I wasn't sure I should be doing this, but I figured it was now or never. I hadn't realized I'd be so nervous about it.

Josh looked apprehensive as I came in. "You're not going to quit, are you?"

My eyebrows went up. "Quit? What makes you think I'd quit?"

He gave me a look.

"Okay, so maybe I'm not Vladima's biggest fan, but I wouldn't walk out on you, Josh."

"You wouldn't?"

I was probably as surprised as he was, but I realized it was true. At least until my real career came back from the undead. "Where else would I get paid to hang out and say ridiculous things in a tiny dark room all day?"

"Well, when you put it like that." He sank back into his chair and made a gesture for me to pull up the other one.

It was pretty close quarters in there. Most of the room was taken up by the big mixing board that Josh manned when we were recording. Aside from that there was just enough space for the two chairs and some miscellaneous piles of junk—cords and extra microphones and assorted other hardware that I'd be hard-pressed to identify.

Suddenly, this close to Josh, I felt completely awkward about what I was going to say. "Josh," I began, "I really don't know how to put this . . ."

He looked away and began fiddling with some switches on the board. "Put what?"

"It's about the promotional spots."

He stopped fiddling. "The what?"

I decided if he could avoid my eyes, I could avoid his. I picked up a piece of speaker wire and tried to make it into a neat coil. "I've been thinking about them."

"You have?"

At least I'd managed to surprise him again. "The thing is, Josh . . ."

"Yeah?"

I could feel him watching me. There was nothing else to do but plunge ahead. I looked him in the eye. "They suck, Josh."

It had become clear to me as I'd been looking over the copy he'd sent the night before that, despite being a creative genius and everything, Josh was lousy at promotion.

The question was, should I say anything about it? I'd never gotten involved with the business end of Josh's enterprise. I'd just said my lines and scampered out of there as fast as I could. But he was a friend—sort of—and clearly he was awful at advertising. I could help. The question was, would he want me to?

He was completely still for a minute, then a huge grin

spread across his face. “Rebecca Mansfield, are you offering to help me with my marketing?”

God help me, I blushed.

“Do you want help?”

Josh got his grin under control. “I’d be honored,” he said.

I let out a huge breath. I hadn’t realized how nervous I’d been about whether Josh would be willing to listen to my opinions.

He reached under the mixing board and pulled out a backpack, then rummaged in it until he eventually found a legal pad and pencil. He looked at me expectantly. “Tell me what to do.”

Music to my ears.

THREE HOURS LATER Josh was beginning to get a clue. They were possibly the most gratifying three hours of my life. I knew I missed having a real job, but I hadn’t realized how much I’d missed the actual work. Figuring out problems, identifying concrete goals, and planning strategies to meet them. The more we talked, the more I realized that I knew almost nothing about Josh’s business. I had no statistics to cite, no demographic data to turn to, no market analysis. The sheer volume of what we’d have to do if we were serious about broadening Vladima’s viewer base was enormous.

Finally, I could sink my teeth into something other than cartoon necks.

When we finally ran out of steam, Josh started flipping through the pages of notes he’d taken. “Becks, I don’t know what I was thinking all this time just using your voice when I could have been exploiting so much more.”

"Exploit away. I'm happy to do it. Besides, as far as I can tell, the major qualification for using my voice is my overall level of bitchiness." I made a face. "And apparently I have other outlets for that these days."

"It's not just the bitchiness," Josh corrected me. "It's also the obvious disdain you have for the material. That comes across as a nice little snobbishness when you record. It makes Vladima superior to the rest of the characters."

"Seriously?"

"Seriously. But don't worry. You're still a great bitch."

Okay, I had started it, but it stung a little anyway. "Josh?"

"Yeah." He was packing up his backpack.

"Am I really a bitch?"

Something in my voice must have told him I wasn't joking anymore. He didn't look at me, but I could tell he was thinking because his eyebrows came together and sort of vibrated. It's a thing he has. "No," he finally said, "you're just old school."

"Old school?"

"You know, like Katharine Hepburn or Rosalind Russell or Joan Crawford. You talk fast and sound smart and you say what you mean."

"So I'm a diva," I said, deflated. "Which is pretty much a bitch in good shoes. Thanks." At least he was honest with me.

"No." Josh seemed bothered by the fact that I wasn't getting it. "You're just old school. It's like you expect to be taken seriously while at the same time you're this great-looking babe. No!"

I was just beginning to like the sound of things when he corrected himself.

"I'm not a babe?"

He shook his head. "You're not a babe or a fox or a chick or anything like that. You're a grown-up. You're"—a light dawned—"you're a dame." He seemed pleased with himself. "Yeah, you're a dame."

"A dame." This is how he saw me. This is why I should never ask his opinion about anything again.

"You know," he went on, "Bette Davis had this great line. She said that if a man asks for what he wants, he's a man, but if a woman asks for what she wants, she's a bitch."

Bette had a point. "So you do think I'm a bitch."

"I think you're not listening."

"I'm asking, Josh. Does everybody think I'm a bitch? Is that why I'm Vladima?"

He mumbled something.

"What?"

"You're Vladima because you kick ass." He looked up from the console. "You have power and you're decisive and you know what you want and you don't take anyone's bullshit and you expect a lot out of people and you don't suffer fools and you're . . ." He'd started out sounding angry, but something in my reaction must have cooled him down because he sort of trailed off and looked down at the wires again.

Wow. It may take a lot to get him going, but it was worth it.

He finished packing up his things and he spoke again, quietly this time. "Becks, a lot of those things will get you called a bitch, but in my mind and in this world"—he gestured at the console and the sound booth beyond—"they're what make you a hero."

I stood up. I blinked at him. "Really?"

"Really." He looked away and cleared his throat. "I wonder what you'd say if I asked you what you think about me."

Warning signs started flashing. This was all getting a little too intense. I mean, he'd just said . . . and I wasn't used to compliment . . . and he'd actually spoken more than five words at a time on a subject other than the undead. It was all getting way too real. He expected an answer from me.

"I think . . ." I gulped. "I think for a straight guy you know an awful lot about old movie stars."

Disappointment flickered across his face, then he nodded.

And I got the hell out of there.

Nine

The countdown to the wedding had begun. The night before we left for London Connie's parents threw a simple little going-away party for all of her friends who wouldn't be able to make it to the actual event. And, of course, all of Ian's friends who were in the same boat. And while they were at it, everyone who would be going to the wedding, too.

When your living room resembles a tastefully decorated airplane hangar, why not?

There was a three-piece jazz combo called Hi Neighbor, a swan carved out of ice, a plenitude of eerily similar-looking waiters passing champagne and nibbles, and a buffet that stretched on for about a mile.

"How does Connie expect us to fit into the damn bridesmaid dresses if we're going to be fed like this at every damn party for the next two weeks?" Vida asked in dismay.

"Didn't you get her instructions?" I asked.

"What instructions?"

I pulled a neatly typed 3 x 5 card out of my evening bag. "Number One: Eat a large salad with no-cal dressing before the party. Number Two: Drink one 8-ounce glass of mineral water between each alcoholic beverage. Number Three: Limit alcoholic beverages to—"

Vida snatched the paper from my hand. "You have so got to be kidding me!"

I so wasn't. "It's what she gives her clients before a big party. I mean, not the socialite clients, but the nervous ones who want to be told how to behave. Apparently lots of brides appreciate it."

Vida tore the card neatly in two and dropped the pieces to the floor. "I do not"—she punctuated her statement with a gulp of champagne—"want to be told"—here she grabbed a passing waiter by the arm and exchanged her empty flute for a full one— "how to behave." She polished off the contents of the new glass. "Let's hit this buffet."

Something told me the party had just gotten interesting.

Max joined me as Vida went foraging. "What's the green stuff?" He gestured to an unappetizing platter.

"Something expensive," I guessed.

"You know, I always forget how loaded Connie's parents are. I really should schmooze them more."

"Please. Half the people here are your clients." I looked around the room and saw evidence of Max's skill with the Botox needle everywhere.

"There's always room for more. And I must drop a discreet hint to Con's mom about a friend of mine who could take care of her neck." He gave me a knowing look.

Vida joined us for the tail end of the conversation. "Max! Connie's mother is at least sixty, and she barely looks forty-five. Leave her alone!"

"Honey, if she was left alone, she'd look sixty." Max sipped complacently. "What's up with you two?"

Before I could say “Nothing” and glide away, Vida blabbed. “Becks had a date!”

“Yes, I heard. The native drums were all over it.”

“Heard what?” Connie appeared out of nowhere, which was her favorite party trick. “What’s going on? How is everybody?” She party-hugged each of us in turn. When she got to Vida, she whispered something in her ear.

“No, I’m not wearing a sports bra!” Vida extracted herself from Connie’s embrace. “I’m wearing the thing you had sent over from Nordstrom.”

“Vida!” Connie’s the only person I know who can yell in a whisper.

“Well, come on! I can’t help it if I’ve got the tits of a twelve-year-old.” Vida tugged at the ice blue silk of her neckline.

Max opened his mouth to speak and Vida turned on him. “And if you tell me you know a guy who can turn me into a D-cup, I swear I’ll push your face into the crab dip.”

Max turned his expression into a smile. “I think I’ll go explore the buffet.”

“Get me another slab of pâté,” Vida called after him.

AN HOUR LATER I was shivering on the terrace with Max and Vida. Connie’s parents lived in a Pacific Heights mansion with a stunning view of the bay. We’d slipped away to watch the lights of the Golden Gate through the fog and try to pinpoint when Connie had lost her last semblance of sanity.

“She seriously sent you a bra?” I asked.

Vida made a noise that an uncharitable friend might have called a snort. “It came with attachments.”

Max gave a low whistle. “Dare I ask?”

Vida sat on the steps and put her chin in her hand. "I can't wait until this wedding is over and we can have our normal old Connie back."

"Don't worry," Max sat next to her. "The bridal demon is usually exorcized as part of the wedding ceremony."

"Can we not talk about demons?" I joined them on the cold stone stairs. "I get enough of that at work."

Two heads swiveled to stare at me.

"What?"

"You've never called the Vladima thing work before," Vida said.

Max agreed. "You always call it the Vladima thing."

I shrugged. "Well, since the little nuclear meltdown masquerading as an interview at PlanetCom, I'm starting to think the Vladima thing isn't that bad."

They digested this. Eventually Vida giggled.

"What?"

"If we're talking nuclear meltdowns, I think the date with Chad wins out over the interview."

"Can you believe her?" Max asked Vida. He raised his voice in mockery. "'I thought it was a business meeting!'"

"I hope you two are having fun," I said.

"Oh, yeah." Vida finished another glass of champagne, and I started wondering if perhaps we should have heeded Connie's 3 x 5 card.

"What I don't get," she continued, "is why you didn't at least sleep with the man."

"Who?"

Vida and Max exchanged looks. "'Who?'" Max mimicked.

"Chad!" Vida practically shouted. "This allegedly good-looking guy who was allegedly totally hot for you!"

"Hang on," I protested. "Aren't you the one who called me date lazy for dating guys just because they're hot for me?"

Vida shook her head. "I said you shouldn't get into a whole relationship with them. I didn't say you shouldn't sleep with them."

Stunned. I was absolutely stunned.

"Why would I sleep with them?"

"I think I may cry," Max said hollowly. "That's the saddest thing I've ever heard."

"Becks, are you honestly saying that you don't see the point of sleeping with a cute guy?"

"Of course I see the point! Geez, I have been known to have a good time in bed now and then!" I thought about it. "I have. Several times."

"All right then," Max said. "So what was stopping you with Chad?"

I gave them a blank look. "He didn't want sex."

Howls of derisive laughter.

"Seriously! I could tell he wanted to get all involved," I explained. "Besides, he had a Vladima thing—how creepy is that?"

"Honey, if I were a sexy cartoon vampire, I would play that card for all it was worth," Max assured me.

"Becks"—Vida got her giggles under control—"have you ever considered whether you might be a lesbian?"

"Sister!" Max threw open his arms. "Welcome to the family!"

"I'd love to be a lesbian," I told him. "Except they have to sleep with women."

"That is a definite downside," Max agreed.

"And despite what you may have gathered from this conversation, I enjoy sleeping with men. Usually. In the right circumstances." Really.

"So do I," Vida said wistfully. "If memory serves."

"Been a while, sweetie?" Max inquired.

"Please. If I uncrossed my legs, moths would fly out."

The French door opened behind us, sending out party noises and Connie's voice. "There you are—get back in here!"

AFTER WHAT FELT like several years, the party was over. Connie sent her future husband home and dragged Vida and me up to her old bedroom, which her parents had kept as a sort of living museum dedicated to their daughter. She was using the space as a staging area for the vast wardrobe she was taking to England.

Max had once again cited the Y chromosome and gotten out of the dirty work, so it was just the three of us girls. We decided to attack the problem by peeling off our party dresses in favor of some comfy pajamas of Connie's and sprawling on her fluffy pink bed.

Vida summed up the situation. "That's one shitload of clothes, Miss Bride."

We regarded the clothes rack Connie's mother had provided for the assortment of evening dresses, cocktail dresses, tea dresses, and brunch outfits that Connie had meticulously planned out for each event leading up to the wedding.

"What are those?" I nodded in the general direction of what looked like a clear box full of photos placed on top of a stack of many, many shoeboxes.

"Polaroids," Connie said. "I laid out every outfit I'm going to wear—complete with accessories, jewelry, and shoes—and took a picture of it. Then I listed the event and the date I'd wear it on the back. The pictures are arranged by date and cross-indexed on a spreadsheet I've got on my laptop."

She saw the looks on our faces. "What? I didn't want to repeat an outfit."

"Wow," I said.

Connie got a little huffy. "It's very complicated. Different people are going to be at different parties, so I had to figure out who I was going to see where and make sure that, for example, Ian's Great Aunt Penelope wouldn't see me at three different things wearing the same earrings."

"Because that would be grounds for calling off the wedding?" Vida asked.

I headed Connie off before she could respond. "It must be hard to get everything right," I said sympathetically. "I guess men have it a lot easier than we do."

Connie gave me a puzzled look. "I did the same thing for Ian."

Their relationship was starting to become a little clearer to me.

"You laid out his clothes?" Vida squeaked.

"I do it all the time," Connie said briskly. "He wouldn't have a clue how to dress himself. And unlike most men, he realizes that and appreciates my help."

I said it again. "Wow."

Connie sighed with something very like pity for us, her spinster friends. "Someday you'll meet a guy and you'll understand," she said in that bridal-superior way. "People think relationships are supposed to be fifty-fifty. That's just denying the reality."

"What's the reality?" Vida dared to ask.

"It's the same in every relationship." She got up and opened a suitcase. "With clients, with employees, with boyfriends, it's all the same. You simply have to seize control from the very beginning." She looked critically at the rack of clothes. "And never for one instant let go." She turned to us. "Do you think the ostrich feather on that hat is just a little too much?"

Vida was too busy blinking really really fast to answer, so I did.

"Way too much."

AS I STAGGERED HOME in the wee hours of the morning, I kept thinking about Connie's massively organized approach to all aspects of her life, and whether that approach was responsible for her getting pretty much everything she's ever wanted.

I had always been something of a control freak myself when it came to work, but I had to admit that I had a tendency to let the other aspects of my life just drift by. Maybe that was the key to my failure with relationships. Maybe I could overcome my date-laziness if I put sufficient planning and organization into the task of finding someone. Okay, I wasn't willing to call it a Man Plan, but maybe if I had a clear picture of who I wanted, I wouldn't end up with some guy who made my eye start twitching whenever he started talking about his collection of vintage G.I. Joes.

Or maybe I should just invest in a Polaroid camera.

Ten

I'd been to London before, but this wasn't the Shakespeare-and-the-Houses-of-Parliament vacation I'd had after my senior year. Nor was it one of the insides-of-hotels-and-conference-rooms business trips I'd taken. This was Wedding London, where apparently every person who had ever met Ian or any member of his family was required by the code of British etiquette to throw a party.

I'd toasted Connie and Ian in grand hotels and intimate restaurants. I'd drunk to their health in the dining rooms of the wealthy and the tea rooms of the traditionalists. I'd wished for their first child to be a son (actually, I'd raised my glass while others wished for that particular joy) on no fewer than three occasions.

And we'd only been in town four days.

Tonight the celebration was in someone's dining room, on the second floor of a house I was sure I'd seen on an episode of *Masterpiece Theatre*. Maybe it was Ian's Great Aunt Penelope's house, maybe not. I'd lost track. I just smiled and nodded and said, "Yes, they *are* a lovely couple," and tried to keep Vida from grumbling too loudly.

In another three days we'd head to Sussex or Surrey or someplace in the countryside, and then the social whirlwind would give way to escalating plans for the Big Day.

Vida and I were carrying the bulk of the party burden. Because Max wasn't officially a member of the wedding party (damn him), he hadn't been invited to several of the bashes that we girls had been duty-bound to enjoy. We kept coming back to our hotel to find Max with some engaging Irishman he'd met at a little out-of-the-way pub or a fierce Scotsman he'd encountered during intermission at a West End musical.

It just wasn't fair.

When the three of us did manage to sneak off to the Tate Modern or a Covent Garden pub, we amused ourselves by placing bets on when exactly Connie's head was going to explode. The bride was lovely at all times, enchanting in all ways, and headed for a complete mental breakdown. Meanwhile, the parties went on.

"HOW MANY TIMES have we eaten poached salmon in the past four days?" Vida hissed under her breath as plates of pink fish were placed before us.

"Think of it this way," I whispered back. "With all the Omega 3 we're getting, we'll probably never grow old."

Vida glanced around the table at her fellow diners. "I don't think it's working."

She had a point. The crowd was leaning fairly heavily toward the dowager set. I had hoped Ian might number among his friends a handsome young duke or two, but so far I'd met nothing but elderly couples who were friends of his parents and a staggering uniformity of vapid people with whom he'd been either "at school" or "at university." The only good news was that I hadn't met one person who seemed likely to have ever heard of Vladima Cross, Defender of the Night.

Vida landed a discreet elbow to my ribs. "We have to make an early break for it."

The dining room, with its acres of white linen, glittering silver, and sparkling crystal, was a setting worthy of a spread in *Town & Country* entitled "How the Better Half Lives." But Vida, sick to death of panty hose and party frocks—don't even get her started on high-heeled sandals—was planning an escape worthy of Steve McQueen's best movie.

She'd announced her strategy at the hotel as we were getting dressed. "I'm making a break for it between the dessert and the after-dinner drinks," she'd said with defiance. "Are you in?"

Max, who was keeping us company while perusing a copy of *Time Out*, offered a suggestion. "Why don't you just blow off the whole thing and come with me? I've decided to visit every pub within a two-mile radius that has the word *Queen* in the name. You'd be amazed how many there are."

Vida ignored him. "Becks, are you with me?"

I shrugged. "Unless I meet the LOTM. What's the plan?"

"Look at this," Max spoke half to himself. "The Queen's Arms, The Queen's Banner, The Queen's Head—oh, I like the sound of that one . . ."

"I won't know the plan until I get the lay of the land," Vida said. "I just know I can't spend one more night dressed up like a goddamn girl."

I looked at her. "That comment would carry more weight if you weren't wearing a push-up bra and thigh-highs."

"Hey," Max spoke up. "What the hell is an LOTM?"

"Lord of the Manor," we both told him.

He squinted. "Have you two been holding out on me?"

"Never," I promised. "He's a mythical beast. The modern woman's version of the unicorn. A single, stable, straight man with chiseled good looks and a certain boyish charm. He's often reported but rarely seen, and approachable only by the pure of heart."

"But you don't have to be a virgin." Vida's muffled voice emerged from a tangle of lavender chiffon that would theoretically resolve itself into something like a dress shape once she had it on right.

"Thank heaven for that," Max said. "And have you seen this creature?"

Vida's head popped out. "Not unless he's been disguised as a gin-swilling, polo-playing, middle-aged barrister with bad teeth and no conversation."

Max snorted. "I knew Ian's friends would be hideous."

"We haven't met them all yet." I turned my back on him so he could zip up my navy blue sheath (which I knew Connie would think was frumpy, but I'd run out of acceptable wedding-attendant wear). "And the barrister is a completely different person from the polo player."

"We're meeting the brother and sister at the thing tonight," Vida told him, twisting around to see if the dress covered everything in the back.

Ian's brother, Phillip, was slated to be his best man, and his sister Trinny, despite the fact that Connie had never met her, was the maid of honor.

"So, Becks," Max asked, "you're actually looking for a man at these parties?"

"Try not to sound so amazed."

"It's just so unlike you. I mean, I'd have no trouble believing you were cruising for an executive position, but cruising for an executive?" His eyebrows went up.

"Not just an executive," I clarified. "A Lord of the Manor. Someone who wears bespoke shirts and rides to hounds and belongs to a gentleman's club."

"Well, I'll say this for you, when you create a fantasy figure, you go all the way."

Vida looked at me proudly. "Becks is cultivating her love life." She leaned forward and gave her breasts a tug, then straightened up to view the effect in the mirror. "And I'm going to kick-start my sex life if it kills me. Which, if these parties are anything to go by, it might. We're going to have to dine and ditch if we want to make any progress." She held up her hand for a high five.

"I'm with you."

I'D DECIDED THE TRIP to England would be just what I needed to recover from my chronic case of date laziness. I'd taken as much of Connie's example as I could stand and spent the time on the plane identifying and cataloguing the salient characteristics of my dream man. In detail. We're talking college degrees and majors, knowledge of wines, credit rating, and physical appearance right down to the length of his fingernails. As well as some other vital measurements. Since making the list, I had studiously ignored anyone who didn't meet 85 percent of my criteria. Back at the room each night, I updated a spreadsheet where I kept my statistics.

The highest score so far had been a disappointing 62 percent.

At one point Vida made a comment along the lines of "You might be going a little overboard with this," but she was wrong.

I was a woman with a plan.

I was not, however, a woman with a particularly successful plan. The LOTM had yet to show his face.

Speaking of plans, Vida abandoned the one about a quick escape from Great Aunt Penelope's—assuming it was Great Aunt Penelope's—the instant she met Ian's brother, Phillip.

I WAS WAITING FOR HER as arranged in the cloakroom. This was the kind of house that had a cloakroom. I'd slipped away on schedule and was beginning to worry that Vida had gotten into trouble when she flung herself into the room and slammed the door.

"He's here!" I don't think it's an exaggeration to say Vida's bosom (such as it was) heaved.

"Who's here?"

"The man I'm going to sleep with before this week of wedding hell is over."

"Mazol tov. Does that mean we're not leaving?" I had my jacket in my hands.

"Leaving?" She grabbed my arm. "Didn't you hear me? Do you know who Ian's brother is? Do you have any idea?" She started pacing in the confines of the glorified closet. "I mean, I knew his name was Phillip, and I knew Ian's last name was Hastings, but I had no idea—" She turned to me wildly. "No idea Ian's brother was Phillip Hastings!"

"And he is . . . ?" As long as we were going to stay, I fished my compact out of my glittery little evening bag (on loan from Connie's collection) and checked my makeup.

"You're joking!" Vida stared at me in disbelief.

I gave her my attention. "Okay. Phillip Hastings?" Then I realized who I was talking to. "Oh, let me guess, he's a sports guy."

"You're hopeless, you know that? He's not just a 'sports guy,' he's . . . he's Phillip Hastings!" The bosom started heaving again. "British Olympic champion? Star soccer player?" Then apparently she remembered who she was talking to. "He does the commercials for WorldWired."

My jaw dropped. "*That* guy is Ian's brother?"

Vida grinned. "Pass me your lipstick. What we have here is a whole new ball game."

I STAYED IN THE CLOAKROOM after Vida dashed out to follow her sexual destiny. Without her to whisper disgruntled comments to me, I felt all alone at the party. I'd had more than I should have had to drink (again) and I dreaded approaching any of the people whose names I'd already forgotten and trying to make small talk. I particularly dreaded the inevitable question "And what do you do?"

At a previous party I'd answered one well-meaning elderly man with "Being Connie's bridesmaid is a full-time job," but I'd had the distinct feeling that when he wandered away, he started telling everyone I was weird.

Oh, well. I took a deep breath, opened the door, and walked right into Connie.

"Becks!" She shoved me back into the closet. "Thank God it's you!"

It was quite an evening for heaving bosoms.

"Connie, what's wrong?" Despite the fact that her dress was perfect, her hair was perfect, and from what I could tell her shoes were perfect, Connie's eyes were welling with tears. They threatened the perfection of her makeup. I grabbed a scarf off of somebody's coat and started dabbing.

"Look up," I ordered her. "Calm down. What's the matter?"

Connie made a visible effort at self-control. "My necklace." Her voice was shaking.

I stepped back. "You're not wearing a necklace."

The tears threatened again. "It broke!" she wailed. She grabbed the scarf and shoved her evening bag into my hands. "The pearls Ian gave me when we got engaged! His grandmother's pearls!"

I opened the tasteful satin purse and saw dozens of loose pearls. "It's all right," I assured her. "I'm sure you got them all. Where did it break?"

"Just now." She took a deep breath. "When I was in the loo."

She'd started spouting Britishisms the moment the plane had landed. "The loo? You mean the bathroom?" A horrible thought struck. "Connie—where did they fall?"

Her eyes widened. She nodded. "I had to fish them out."

I closed the bag and held it a little farther away. "Yuck."

Okay, so that wasn't the most supportive thing I could have done, but really—yuck.

"Don't be a baby!" she snapped. "I rinsed them off." Then the tears threatened again. "You have to help me," she begged. "You have to get them restrung."

"All right, fine." I took the bag back. "I'll take care of it in the morning."

"No!" She dug her nails into my arm. "Tonight! I have to wear them to brunch tomorrow morning."

"First of all," I said, prying her off me, "*ow.* And second, just where do you expect me to find an all-night jeweler in this town?"

"Please, Becks!" She bit her lip.

Good God. "Fine," I agreed. "Now, anything else?"

She missed my sarcasm entirely as she threw her arms around me. "Thank you!" And she was gone.

I never really planned any sort of imaginary wedding when I was growing up. I wasn't that kind of girl. And I've never spent time fantasizing about my big day one way or another as an adult. But at that moment I knew, beyond a shadow of a doubt, that if I ever did get married, I'd make Connie my maid of honor and I'd put her through absolute hell.

I WAS HALFWAY DOWN the marble staircase when the bag started dripping. "Yuck." I shook it a little, holding it away from me.

And it opened.

And all the pearls came spilling out.

I may have yelped. I probably did. I know I lunged for the beads as they started clattering down the stairs. I know I lunged because spectators to the event later told me I made a spectacular effort before I tumbled down the stairs.

At the bottom, there was more embarrassment than pain, which was a good thing. But there was still considerable pain. I kept my eyes closed longer than I needed to, listening to the dull buzzing in my ears and the warm sound of a man's voice murmuring pleasant things to me.

Murmuring . . . "I think she needs a doctor."

I opened my eyes and looked for the source. Either there was a light behind his head or he was sporting a snazzy halo. I only saw the silhouette of a sleek figure in a well-cut suit.

I looked up at him, and at this point I admit to being dazed because I said, "You're the Lord of the Manor."

He patted my hand comfortingly. "Do you know—I rather think I am."

Eleven

Sir Charles Shipley. I kept saying the name to myself as I was taken to an urgent care ward, pronounced fine (except for a bump on the head, a twisted ankle, and a dress torn beyond repair), and discharged. Sir Charles Shipley. He was a friend of Ian's family. It was at Sir Charles Shipley's estate in the country, Lakewood, that Connie and Ian were to be married. Sir Charles Shipley was—in a very real sense—the Lord of the Manor.

He was perfect.

He had been the one to pack me off to the emergency room. It was against his tall, trim, impeccably tailored frame that I leaned for support as I hobbled to the waiting car. His car, with his driver. Sir Charles Shipley's.

Sadly, it was Vida who greeted me when I came back out to the waiting room after my examination. She's my best friend, but she's no knight in shining Armani. "Where is he?"

"How are you?"

"Where is he?"

"Who?"

"Where is he?"

"Becks!" Vida started to look a little freaked. "How bad is the bump on your head? What are you talking about?"

For the first time, I said the magic words out loud. "Sir Charles Shipley."

"Oh, he's gone. He . . ." Her voice trailed off as she took in the look on my face. "*Oh.*"

VIDA TOOK ME BACK to the hotel and tucked me in. She'd been with Ian and the famous Phillip when I'd taken the tumble. Ian's first thought had been to keep Connie from finding out.

"Gee, thanks," I said. "It's not like I was hurt or anything." I rubbed the golf ball–sized lump behind my left ear. "I wouldn't want to spoil her good time."

Vida fluffed my pillows and made a clucking sound. "It wasn't that," she said. "Ian's just as afraid as we are that Connie's going to lose it before the wedding. If you'd been really hurt, I was supposed to call him, but since it's just a little bump—"

I gave her an injured look.

"—there's no reason to give Connie anything more to stress about."

I sighed. "Fine. She was in the middle of a meltdown anyway—" I froze.

"What's wrong?"

"The pearls!"

"What pearls? Oh, the pearls you dropped." Vida said. "What were you carrying them around for anyway?"

"Where are they?"

"I don't know. Someone probably picked them up."

I groaned. "Connie's going to kill me."

"Oh my God." Vida's eyes widened. "They were Connie's pearls."

I winced, and not because of my head. "Ian's grandmother's pearls," I corrected.

Vida spent about three seconds looking worried, then she dismissed the problem. "It doesn't matter," she said firmly. "Connie won't be mad when she finds out what happened."

I leaned back into the pillows. "Yeah, right. It's been nice knowing you."

"Meanwhile." Vida ignored my melodrama. "Phillip Hastings." She gave me a highly significant look.

I arched my eyebrow, not without a little pain. "I'll see your Phillip Hastings," I said. "And I'll raise you one Sir Charles Shipley."

WE SLEPT IN to the decadent hour of eight A.M. That's when Connie started banging on the door. Vida let her in with a stoic sigh and was practically trampled to death by a size-six bride in a marabou-trimmed dressing gown trailing her bleary-eyed intended behind her.

"Becks!" she shrieked. "Ian just this minute told me what happened to you last night! Are you all right? Where are you hurt? How bad is it? Where did you fall? What happened? Why didn't you tell me?" The last was barked somewhat viciously to her beloved. Then back to me. "What's broken? Can you walk? You're not going to have to limp down the aisle, are you? Oh, God, you're going to limp down the aisle. You won't be able to wear the shoes, and the dress will be too long. And I don't know a seamstress here, and the dresses are already at Lakewood anyway, so I wouldn't know what to do about the measurements, and it's just going to be a disaster, a complete disaster!"

"Con, hang on a minute—"

But she was incapable. "And what about your head?" She grabbed my face and started an examination. "Where's the lump? Oh, God, it's big. Can you wear your hair the way Roger wants you to? Will he be able to use the extensions? Where's Roger?" Again she turned on Ian. "We need Roger here right now and—"

"Hold it!" I yelled.

At least I got her attention.

"Connie, calm down for one minute, will you? I'm fine. It's a tiny twist to the ankle and a little bump on the head, both of which will be fine by the wedding. We've got more than a week, for heaven's sake." She was still verging on hysteria, so I took both her hands in mine. "Everything will be fine. I'll be fine. The wedding will be perfect."

She took a deep breath, nodded, and burst into tears.

"Um," Ian said hesitantly. "Tea. I think I'll go sort out a pot of tea."

He fled.

Vida rolled her eyes and sat on the bed. We spent a while saying things like "There, there" and "Let it out, sweetie," but we were worried. Either this was just a good cry that would leave Connie feeling better once it was over, or it was the beginning of the end.

"Connie?" Vida said after a while. "Do you want to talk about it?"

She did.

"Everything's falling apart." She sniffed. "Everything.

Trinny got in from Lakewood last night and she says the flowers aren't in bloom yet." Trinny, Ian's sister and the missing maid of honor. Presumably she'd been doing reconnaissance work at Sir Charles Shipley's estate. I allowed myself one brief tingle of excitement at the thought of Sir Charles Shipley, then tuned back in to Connie's anxiety attack.

"And I haven't even met the stupid English wedding planner who's down there, but so far she's completely useless. I mean, her brilliant suggestion was to just have masses and masses of cut flowers—which is so not the point of a country wedding—and on top of everything else, it may *rain*." The tragedy of that possibility was etched into her face. "Can you think of anything worse in the world? I got a huge tent, just in case, because I'm not an idiot." She sounded momentarily like the old on-top-of-everything Connie. "But I never really thought it would happen. I mean, my wedding in a soggy old tent, everything smelling musty, and God—what if there's a leak? I handled a wedding once where the tent leaked and buckets of water came in and ruined the cake and it was a disaster, a complete disaster, and I'm a wedding planner, for God's sake!"

Now she was starting to get angry. "I throw the most fabulous parties on the entire West Coast and now I'm stuck in some stupid town where I don't even know the caterer and I'm expected to pull off the social event of the damn season? I mean, I'm good." She wiped her eyes defiantly. "I'm very good. Am I not the woman who found the single bridesmaid dress in the world that flattered a pregnant woman, a dwarf, and an androgynous lesbian?"

I nodded seriously. I'd seen the wedding pictures. The dress had been amazing.

"Am I not the woman who had Chinese acrobats tumbling *down the center of the tables* when WiredGlobe threw the party to announce its new Beijing offices?"

Vida squeezed her hand. "You are. It was fabulous."

"So why the *hell* can't I organize one fucking English country wedding?" she demanded. "I mean, it shouldn't be hard. A few flowers, a string quartet, and you're done, right? So what's my fucking problem?"

"Connie," I said, as gently as I could, "it's *your* fucking wedding."

She stared at me.

Vida put it more diplomatically. "Look, Con, how many times during the course of a wedding does the bride go totally nuts on you? Like once a week, right?"

Connie sniffed. "More." She wiped her eyes. "I hate brides."

Vida nodded. "Well, this time you're the bride. And you've got no one to go nuts on except yourself."

Connie took a deep breath. "I guess I am going a little nuts."

A little?

"It's just all these stupid parties. I shouldn't even be taking time to have a meltdown because I have to get ready for brunch and— Oh!"

She stopped. I should have been grateful, but I saw the look in her eye and knew what was coming.

"Where are the pearls?"

At this point all I can say is that Trinny Hastings is an angel sent from God. Seriously. Because at that exact moment there was a knock on the door.

Vida opened it and the angel sent from God stuck her head in. "Is this a private party or can any bridesmaid join in?"

She was poised and polished, with honey-colored hair pulled back into a simple neat twist and one of those classic English beauty kinds of faces.

Connie instantly began using my sheets to dab at her eyes while she made the necessary introductions.

Trinny's good breeding showed. She ignored the evidence of Connie's recent crying jag and perched primly on Vida's unmade bed.

"Normally I wouldn't dream of intruding this early, but I saw Ian down in the breakfast room and he told me where you were." She looked brightly from Vida to me. "Are you coming to Aunt Phoebe's brunch?"

I felt the lump on my head. "I think I'll have to skip it." I grimaced for good measure.

Trinny smiled impishly. "You must be the bridesmaid who fell. I hope you're feeling better because it's you I came to see." She opened her purse and pulled out a long velvet box. "I think you dropped these."

Connie snatched the box and opened it. "The pearls! They're fixed." She hugged them to her chest.

It happened so quickly that I might have imagined it, but I swear Trinny winked at me. She was an angel sent from God. Or possibly Mary Poppins.

VIDA AND I WENT BACK TO BED after they left. I woke up around noon and found a note.

> !!!I've gone rollerblading in Regent's Park with Phillip Hastings!!!
>
> —V!!!

"Well done, Vida." I applauded, and headed for the shower. When I got out, I took a good hard look at myself in the mirror. Then I pictured Sir Charles Shipley standing next to me. Then I picked up the phone and dialed another room in the hotel.

"Roger? It's Becks. I need you to make me gorgeous."

Twelve

I'm a terrible flirt.

When some women say that, they mean they're incorrigible, batting their eyes and tossing their hair at anything in pants. But I mean I flirt terribly. Badly. Really. I understand that to some extent it's a skill, and therefore like any other skill it can be learned—at least to a reasonable level of proficiency. I'd just never made the effort to learn it.

But then, I'd never had Sir Charles Shipley supplying the motivation.

I quickly formed my plan. I'd use my twisted ankle as an excuse to skip whatever parties I could for the next couple of days in London and get Max and Vida to teach me everything they knew. Connie would actually be a better coach, but I hardly thought I'd be able to talk her into joining us. By the time I arrived at Lakewood I'd be an old hand at the hair toss, the half-smile, the "I want you" look, and whatever else might be required to make a knight of the realm fall madly in love with me.

But first things first—I had to get gorgeous.

. . .

"BECKS!" ROGER GREETED ME. "You've made me so happy!"

In the ten minutes since I'd called him, Connie's hairdresser had been burning up the phone lines. Now he sailed into my room, clipboard in hand.

"You're getting waxed first. Then you have a facial at one-thirty, a sea salt scrub after that, and then a mani-pedi," he said triumphantly. "You have no idea how many names I had to drop in order to get you in. Seriously, Becks, you'll be a new woman!"

I had one question. "Waxed?"

"You won't feel a thing," he assured me, "and, oh, do you need it." This was added after a brief inspection of my upper lip. "It's not too bad," he said in a tone that clearly indicated he was lying. "I've seen worse, but oh . . ."

"What about my hair?" I asked. "I was really thinking in terms of a haircut—"

"Don't think." He held up his hand. "Just relax and trust me."

"I may not be too good at the relaxing part."

He waved away my apprehensions. "I've sent Shayla out for supplies. Have you met Shayla yet? No, I didn't think so. I know you've been avoiding me, but that's all about to change, isn't it Becks?" He beamed. "I'm just so happy!"

"I'm happy for you, Roger," I told him. "Who's Shayla?"

"My assistant." He seemed slightly embarrassed. "She's here to help out because on the big day I won't be able to deal with Connie and the three of you and the mother of the bride and Ian . . ." His eyes widened. "Forget I said that. Connie didn't mention Shayla?"

"I suspect Connie didn't want me to use the word *entourage*."

"Probably not. But I really did need someone. She's also doing the makeup for those of you who need help." He moved in for another inspection of my face.

"It's okay, Roger. I know I need help." For anything beyond slapping on tinted moisturizer and a quick swipe of lipstick, anyway.

He beamed again. "Becks, this day is going to change your life!"

It certainly changed my understanding of what beauty queens go through.

ROGER HURRIED ME to the hotel spa, where I discovered billowing white curtains, fluffy white towels, comfy white robes, and a kind of pain I had never dreamed existed.

To start things off, my eyebrows, upper lip, chin, underarms, and legs were forcibly denuded of hair. At first my eyes stung with tears, but then the pain leveled out and it was the humiliation that bothered me.

When I thought I was done, the sadist in charge of the wax gave me an inquiring look.

"Bikini?"

I closed my eyes, thought of England, and nodded.

The facial, on the other hand, was actually rather pleasant. Lots of yummy-smelling creams being massaged into my ready and willing pores while I reclined comfortably. I was just starting to love being a girl when someone began poking my face with a sharp needle.

"Ow!"

"Extractions," muttered the aesthetician, a woman whom I'd been (wrongly) thinking of as a kindly Eastern-European aunt. "So many blackheads." She clicked her tongue in profound disappointment and kept poking.

The sea salt scrub had something of an I'm-naked-and-stretched-out-in-front-of-a-stranger aspect to it, but the procedure itself was limited to a massage with bits of grit in the lotion. Not bad.

"Now you're beautiful," the therapist said when it was done. Then she hosed me off and sent me on my way.

I MET ROGER in the salon, where I was scheduled for a manicure and pedicure. These treatments were no strangers to me, and I was actually sporting a cheerful cherry red on my toenails already.

"Do you really think this needs to be redone?" I asked my spa Sherpa.

Roger recoiled. "Becks." He rubbed his brow. "You can't seriously want the feet of a Spanish harlot on Connie's wedding day."

"Oh." I looked at my cheerful Spanish harlot feet. "Of course not."

Roger brightened. "Look who's here!"

Vida. And not happy to be in a salon. "I can keep my fingernails clean without an intervention from you," she announced loudly in Roger's direction, rather disrupting the whole blissed-out spa vibe. Vida turned to me. "He booked me an appointment without even asking, can—what the hell happened to you?" She had just taken in my spa attire and presumably glowing skin.

"I'm getting gorgeous," I told her, keeping my voice low. "It's Phase One of my Sir Charles Shipley plan." I barely breathed the name, fearful that one of the women currently being filed, clipped, or painted might overhear. Vida had already drawn their attention and not a small amount of disapproval.

"You're already gorgeous." Vida was perfectly matter-of-fact. "You don't need to spend a fortune on this junk." She picked up a bottle of hot pink polish and set it down again dismissively. "I mean, look at me."

I looked at her. She glowed with health. Her blond hair was held back in a clip, and she was wearing what for Vida passed as a good outfit—yoga pants, a T-shirt, and a zippered hooded jacket that all matched. She looked like the surfer and athlete she was, and like she didn't give a damn about nail polish.

However. "How are things going with Ian's brother?" I asked.

She opened her mouth to speak, then closed it. She looked at Roger, whose eyebrows went up in hope. She compressed her lips and nodded in grim determination. "Okay, but no pink."

She made Roger's day.

IT BECAME OBVIOUS in the time it took to soak our feet that in the theory and practice of flirting, Vida and I were the blind leading the blind.

"Have Max take you out tonight," she suggested. "He's good at it."

"Won't you come with us?"

"Ow!" Vida snatched her hand away from the manicurist and sent a look of loathing toward Roger, who was flipping obliviously through a magazine in a chair near the door. "No, I'm going to the cocktail party. The plan is for Connie and Ian to go on to some chamber music thing afterward, with this guy who has a box. If Phillip ends up going with them, I'm tagging along."

"Chamber music? You must really be crazy about this guy."

"Seriously, Becks." Her eyes lit up. "We had so much fun blading today. It was just the best time I've had with a guy in *ages*."

"Do you think he's interested?"

"I think he likes me." She winced, and I wasn't sure if it was from the nail file or the conversation. "But I'm not sure if he *likes me* likes me."

I wondered if women who know how to flirt also know how to talk about men without resorting to junior high school phraseology. "What kind of woman does he usually date?"

She shrugged. "I don't know. That's not the sort of thing *Sports Illustrated* usually covers."

"Try *People*. Better yet, Google him on my laptop."

"Have you Googled"—she looked around to make sure nobody was listening, then mouthed the words—"Sir Charles Shipley?"

"Not yet. He's only been on my radar for sixteen hours, and what with the hospital and the spa and all—"

Vida nodded. "I understand. You've been busy."

"IT'S NOT LIKE I'm some sort of troll, Max, I mean, I do take care of my personal hygiene on a regular basis." I had just met Max in the hotel lobby, and he was making entirely too much fuss over my new look.

"I'm sure you do, Becks, but if I can just say something?"

"What?" I prepared for the inevitable mockery.

He stepped back and considered me, put a thoughtful finger to his lips, and pronounced "Yowza."

"You think?" I touched my caramel-and-honey highlighted hair, which was now "hip and swingy" instead of "hanging down pathetically."

"I think Roger is a genius and you are a goddess."

"I like the last part," I told him. "Did you see my eyelashes? I'm wearing false eyelashes." I closed my eyes so he could get a better look.

"Yeah," Max said. "Now we just have to teach you how to use them." He slung his arm around me and propelled me to the door. "I just hope you appreciate the sacrifices I make in the name of friendship."

"I do," I assured him. "Teach me everything."

"You're in good hands, Becks. After all, if you're going to be a princess, you might as well learn from a queen."

AT FIRST I WAS HOPELESS. Max took me to a nearby bar—not a cozy, comfortable pub sort of place but a loud-music-and-hipsters bar—and made me sit at a high table out in the open instead of in a corner booth. Just instructing me on the proper way to perch on a tall stool took the better part of half an hour. Then we moved on to distance flirting.

"Okay," Max said. "Now, when I'm at the bar, I want you to look across the room and give me your best 'I'm interested' smile."

I nodded. No problem.

He returned with two martinis and a pained look on his face.

"What?"

"Becks, are you suffering from gastric problems? You can tell me, I'm a doctor."

"You're a dermatologist."

"True, but that fleeting grimace that passed across your face seems like a clear indication that you need to consult an internist."

"It was a grimace?"

He rolled his eyes.

"How's this?" I produced another hopefully seductive expression.

Max held up his hands. "You're scaring me."

I had to admit, it hurt. I had assumed I'd just need to learn a few techniques, but now Max had me thinking I might inadvertently frighten small children in my attempts to attract the LOTM.

I thought I knew what the problem was. I'd spent my entire adult life trying to be taken seriously in the business world, always worried that male colleagues would think of me as a "marketing bimbo" or "booth bunny." So I'd made it a point to never give them any reason to. Everything from the way I dressed to the way I carried myself had been part of a plan to look professional, intelligent, and competent. Not sexy.

Now I looked at Max helplessly. "Have I turned it all off for good?"

He took pity on me. "First, drink this." He slid a martini toward me and I obeyed. "Trust me, that will help." He put his elbows on the table and leaned forward. "Here's the thing. We need to forget about the boardroom and get to the bedroom. How are you in bed?"

I blinked. "Reasonably competent."

Max signaled for more drinks. "This may be harder than I thought."

"Max—"

"No." He stopped my protest. "Hang on. You're in marketing, right?"

"Yes. I mean, I was . . ."

"Okay." He stopped me before I got into the whole career thing again. "So if you were marketing some hot babe, would you say she's 'reasonably competent' in bed?"

I saw his point. I nodded and focused on the message my target market would want to hear. Then I spoke. "I'm phenomenal in bed."

"Good!"

"Would I really say that to a guy?"

"Probably not. But you need to be thinking it while you talk about the weather. Now go."

I did my best. "I know tricks you haven't even seen on the in-room porn channel."

The waiter, who had approached me from behind, gave me a huge grin as he deposited the fresh round.

"Max," I exclaimed when he'd gone, "I said something sexy and he didn't get scared away!"

"Well done, Becks, now drink that up like a good girl and we'll work on the smile. Oh, and how do you feel about a little shopping tomorrow?"

"For what?"

"God give me strength," he muttered. "For clothes."

I thought about my wardrobe. Then I thought about my credit limit. Then I thought about Sir Charles Shipley.

"Let's make a list."

Thirteen

- Fabulous new hairstyle. *Check.*
- All new makeup employing all the latest beauty breakthroughs. *Check.*
- A vast number of brushes with which to apply makeup. *Check.*
- Hair care products, skin care products, nail care products. *Check.*
- Slinky little dresses and flirty little skirts. *Check.*
- Selection of tops with plunging necklines. *Check.*
- Lingerie. *Double check.*
- Shoes and bags. *Oh my God, Check.*

Everything that could be purchased had been purchased and it gave me an increasing sense of confidence as the piles of shopping bags grew. Whether Max's lessons in womanly wiles would prove effective was still open to question, but after two days of intensive training, I was as ready as I'd ever be for an English country wedding.

I HELD MY BREATH as we approached the grounds. I was Jane Eyre, getting her first glimpse of Thornfield Hall. I was Maxim de Winter's new bride, seeing Manderley for the first time. I may even have been Miss Elizabeth Bennet, viewing Mr. Darcy's Pemberley.

All right, I was more than a little carried away.

But Lakewood lived up to expectations. The first thing anyone said when we rounded a corner and the house came into view was "Oh, thank God!"

The speaker was Connie.

She turned to Ian's brother, seated across from her in the vast silver limousine that had been waiting for us at the station. "Phillip—it's wonderful! I can't believe you talked Sir Charles into letting us have the wedding here. It's just . . ." She began waving her hands in front of her face in an I-can't-spoil-my-mascara sort of way.

Phillip looked slightly puzzled. "Oh, but he does it—"

"He does it out of friendship for the family," Ian cut him off. "Our families have been close for generations."

The house was an enormous structure, all gray stone and glittering windows. It had a turret. It had a cupola. It had any number of flourishes for which I had no name. Parapets? I cursed myself for not boning up on nineteenth-century architecture as fodder for discussion with Sir Charles Shipley.

As we got closer, Connie grabbed Trinny's arm. "You told me the flowers weren't out yet. Look—there are flowers everywhere!"

Trinny extracted herself from Connie's grip. "I thought you were worried about the roses," she explained smoothly. "Of course the rhododendrons are out, and the spring flowers in the back around the fountain."

Very briefly, it looked like Connie might pass out. Then she recovered and began explaining things to those of us whose families hadn't been coming to Lakewood for generations.

"There are several fountains, as well as a Victorian-era folly overlooking the lake. But the fountain that Lakewood is famous for was brought over from Italy around 1850. It's a stunning example of baroque architecture, and the wedding ceremony will be held in front of it."

And she wasn't even referring to her notes.

She went on in a tour-guide voice. I learned that Lakewood was the name of the estate, and that Lakewood House was . . . well, what it sounds like. I got a little distracted by the somewhat unsettling way Vida was looking at Phillip Hastings as he followed Connie's lecture. I had to admit, he was worth looking at. He had the compact, graceful body of an athlete, and the same flawless bone structure and honey-colored hair as his sister, Trinny.

Connie was still going on. "There's also a beautiful walled garden with masses of rhododendrons and a rose trellis. We'll have a reception there the evening before the wedding."

I could tell Connie was mentally drafting the society page's account of her wedding. *A reception was held in the walled garden . . .*

"And if the weather gets dicey, we can move it indoors to the conservatory," Ian added helpfully. "Which might be very nice as well. It's enormous and filled with palm trees and so on that Charles's family had sent from the West Indies a hundred years or so ago."

I had a fleeting mental image of Sir Charles Shipley bending to kiss me by moonlight in his tropical conservatory. It left me the instant the car pulled up to Lakewood's massive front steps. Because standing at the top of them was the Lord of the Manor himself.

"I'M AN IDIOT and I don't deserve to live."

It was an hour later and we'd all been shown to our rooms to freshen up before tea in the Red Drawing Room.

"It wasn't that bad," Max told me unconvincingly.

Vida and Max and I had been assigned rooms along the same hallway—"Spinster's Alley," as Vida had named it when it became apparent we were in a separate wing from everyone else. But she was just bitter because Phillip and Trinny, although technically among the ranks of the spinsters, had been situated closer to the host. Vida and Max had waited until the somewhat scary housekeeper had gotten out of sight before they'd both come to my room to comfort me.

It had been that bad.

"Maybe you should avoid slippery shoes," Vida suggested gently.

"Maybe I should ask the gardener for some quick-acting poison." I spoke into a throw pillow. I had to. I'd fallen face-down onto the bed in humiliation and couldn't bring myself to get up.

I had tripped. I'd managed to get out of the car and make it up the stairs fine, rejoicing that my ankle had healed to the extent that I didn't have an ungraceful limp. I'd even made it inside the house. Then, just as I'd been approaching the LOTM, wearing my new Prada heels and rehearsing the witty little quip I'd make when greeting him, I'd gone sprawling—sliding—across the Italian marble floor of the central rotunda until I had come to rest inelegantly at the feet of Sir Charles Shipley.

He'd smiled in a "What can be wrong with this woman?" kind of way as Max had hoisted me up. Then he'd turned us all over to the slightly scary housekeeper.

"Becks, if you stay facedown like that, your eyes will get all puffy," Max cautioned.

I sat up. "There's no recovering from this," I told them. "I mean, at the party it was one thing. It would have been the funny story we told our grandchildren about how we met. But a second time?" I hugged the pillow to my chest.

"Grandchildren?" Max asked.

"You can recover," Vida assured me. "And you have to. I fully intend on throwing myself wantonly at Phillip Hastings, and I'll be damned if I'll be the only one making an exhibition of myself."

"Wantonly?" Max echoed.

"Don't worry. I think I've got the exhibitionism covered." I rubbed my aching butt. "Vida, how am I supposed to face him after that? I mean, he probably dates princesses or something, and I'm this crazy woman who's already displayed her panties to him in disturbingly similar circumstances both times I've seen the man. Does this sound like the behavior of someone who's likely to prompt a guy into declarations of undying love? I don't think so."

"Undying love?" Max exclaimed. "Wanton exhibitionism? Grandchildren? Who are you people? What has this wedding done to you?"

Vida ignored him. "Look, I've asked Phillip to give me some pointers with a soccer ball on the east lawn. You do what you like, but if I were you, I'd ask Sir Charles to take you on a tour of the house immediately after the stupid tea party." She paused on her way out the door. "Seriously,

Becks, do you want the man? Or are you going to give up on day one?" She gave me a last firm look before leaving.

"I think that's what you call 'tough love,'" I told Max.

"What are you going to do?" he asked.

I sighed. "I'm going to put on whatever outfit you tell me to and ask for a tour of the damn house."

ACTUALLY, the house was fabulous. It was a castle decorated in Early Fairy Tale. And Vida had been right. I'd recovered. What I'd not managed to do was get my personal Prince Charming alone. Following the lengthy afternoon tea, Field Marshal Connie had pulled her bridesmaids and assorted attendants aside for a leading-up-to-the-wedding-day strategy session. It was ages before we rejoined the men, and by that time Sir Charles was at the center of a conversation about local politics.

But maybe it was better that way. It gave me an opportunity to study him in a group setting, which could only improve my ability to tailor my romantic overtures to suit him. After all, you can never know too much about your target market.

And he was so nice to study.

He was as tall as I'd remembered, and had one of those elegant English physiques that seem to belong in white linen shirts and khaki trousers—very *Brideshead Revisited*, with possibly the tiniest bit of *Out of Africa* thrown in.

He had light hair, almost blond, and while I usually don't go for fair men, on Sir Charles Shipley it just seemed to work. Particularly when it flopped down a little on his forehead and he had to run his long tapered fingers through it to get it out of his sparkling blue eyes. The man was perfect.

I was determined to make him mine.

And the vision of perfection was heading in my direction.

"Well," he greeted me with a charming smile, "you look fully recovered."

I didn't ask him which of my spectacular falls he thought I'd recovered from. Instead I returned the smile, hopefully with equal charm rather than a horrible grimace. I trusted that Max had worked wonders with my technique when Sir Charles Shipley didn't cringe and back away.

"In fact," he moved closer, and his voice took on a low conspiratorial tone, "you look absolutely gorgeous."

I was never letting anyone but Max tell me what to wear ever again. Thankfully—because I didn't have a quick comeback—he didn't wait for me to respond.

"I do hope I'll be seeing a lot of you this week." Was it my imagination, or was that smile just the slightest bit suggestive? "Hopefully not flat on my back," I responded. Then I died a thousand deaths as I realized what I'd said.

"I mean, not falling down. I mean, standing up, I mean—"

I was saved by the bell. Or at least by a very loud gong.

"Ah," Sir Charles Shipley made a sort of strangling sound, "yes. That means we dine in an hour. Perhaps we should dress. Can you find your way to your room?"

"Of course," I said automatically. Then I mentally kicked myself for passing on the opportunity for him to escort me through all those long hallways.

There was that smile again and, amazingly, it was still suggestive. Was there the possibility that he was attracted to incoherent babbling?

"Until tonight, then." He sauntered away.

"Tonight," I managed to reply to his retreating back.

Vida appeared in front of me. "How did it go?"

"Honestly?" I watched Sir Charles leave the room. "I have no idea."

Fourteen

I was back on track, or at least not completely out of the running, and I figured the sensible thing was to come up with a plan. Also a schedule. We were going to be at Lakewood for six days. That didn't leave much time to make Sir Charles Shipley mine, so I had to make every minute count.

Max had already chosen the outfit I was supposed to wear to dinner—a sort of silky sweatery ruby-colored dress with a daring halter top. I had some reservations about it. If I slipped again, there was no telling what might fall out.

Luckily, Roger's assistant Shayla showed up to help with my hair and makeup. Roger had instructed her to make Vida and me presentable for all public appearances, so we'd seen a lot of her lately. She was cute and round and bubbly and bouncy, which I'm ashamed to say had made me assume she was also stupid. But she'd proven me wrong. At least in terms of style, the woman was a genius.

I expressed my concerns about the dangers of the dress.

"We could use tape," she suggested.

"You mean on the bottom of my shoes?" An alarming pair of Manolo Blahnik evening sandals.

Shayla did her best not to laugh at me, but I could tell it was an effort. "No, I mean on your breasts."

I think my mouth fell open because she did laugh this time.

"Don't worry," she giggled. "People use it all the time. It's double-sided so it sticks to both your skin and the dress." She pulled a roll of the stuff out of her bag of tricks and demonstrated the technique using her forearm and sleeve.

There was so much I didn't know about being a siren. "If you say so."

She said so.

She did my makeup quickly, then turned to the serious business of tugging my hair into a style she promised would be sexy and chic. While she was at it, I grabbed a legal pad and pencil. It was time to draft my Sir Charles Shipley plan of attack.

- DAY ONE: Get LOTM aside after dinner for an intimate conversation. Impress him with wit and charm. Avoid embarrassing declarations. Do not slip. Do not pop out of dress.
- DAY TWO: Request a Lakewood tour. Suggest conservatory, grounds, or stables. Mention love of riding and wait for him to take the bait. In the evening, exploit opportunities for romance at scheduled club dinner dance.
- DAY THREE: Possibilities: trip to nearby town for sightseeing, exploration of island on the lake, picnic. Again, don't miss chance for after-dinner romance. Think conservatory.
- DAY FOUR: Challenging, as he'll have many host

duties having to do with wedding preparations. Try to be of assistance to him. Make things easier. Make him realize how lucky he'd be to have you around all the time. At evening garden reception, be devastatingly attractive and flirt with other men. (Verify this tactic with Max.)

- DAY FIVE: Wedding Day. Perfect scene for romance. Be fabulous. Drive him crazy.
- DAY SIX: *Do Not Go* without sealing the deal. Obtain invitation for follow-up visit or statement of his intention to come see you. Also possible, a romantic vacation together. But *Do Not Go* without knowing where you stand.

I reviewed my plan with satisfaction as I heard the gong sound again. The writing was barely legible, due to Shayla's efforts, but that was all right. And I had left unwritten the most important guiding principle of all, but that was all right too. Because there was no way I was going to forget my new personal mantra. *Don't fall down. Don't be a bitch. Don't fall down. Don't be a bitch.*

Shayla allowed me to peek in the mirror, and—miraculously—I looked the part of a chic, sexy dinner guest. It was good to be in the hands of a professional.

I met Vida in the hallway and tried not to gasp. Shayla had visited her before taking care of me, and the transformation was amazing. Her blond hair sort of shimmered up into a glittery clip and her dress made the absolute most of her square shoulders and defined arms.

"Do you know how much gunk I have in my hair?" she asked me.

"Don't talk to me. I've got tape on my tits."

We were both a little giddy. The game was afoot.

I WAS THWARTED almost immediately.

The plan called for cutting Sir Charles Shipley off from the rest of the pack after dinner, but it soon became glaringly apparent that this was not going to happen.

It was all Phillip's fault. "Charles, you must show Ian your new pool table. He tells me he's gotten quite good in America."

That's all it took. We left the Chinese Dining Room and headed for the Turquoise Parlor, which opened up to the Billiard Room. I felt as if I'd wandered into a game of Clue. The men went off to play pool, but Vida and I got stuck talking wedding talk with Connie and her mother, Ian's mother, and the rest of the girls.

Except for Trinny. For some reason she seemed to be exempt from normal bridesmaid duties. She was in playing pool with the boys. How did she get away with it?

"Do you believe her?" Vida mouthed to me across the sea of women. She nodded toward the other room, where Trinny was just accepting a light of her cigar from the LOTM himself.

Damn—he should be lighting my cigar, not hers! Well, all right, if he did light a cigar for me, I'd probably go into watery-eyed coughing spasms, and heaven only knew if my double-sided tape would be equal to the strain. But still.

I made my way around the crowd to Vida. "This was all your stupid Phillip's idea."

"I know," she agreed darkly. "Do you think we can make a break for it?"

But at that exact moment, Ian's mother turned to us and demanded to have a description of the dresses we'd be wearing on the Big Day. By the time we had fully discussed every last tuck and seam, Sir Charles Shipley was excusing himself, citing some phone calls he had to make to Tokyo.

The party broke up after that. The only thing further I have to report is that double-sided tape is a bitch to take off.

DAY TWO. Another opportunity for romantic success. However . . .

Connie woke me up early, having already roused Vida, and dragged us both to the florist. We spent hours looking at more varieties of white, off-white, cream, and ivory blooms than I had ever dreamed existed. The flowers had all been ordered months before, and the designs had been agreed on weeks before, but that didn't stop Connie from endless discussions with the florist about durability versus elegant presentation, referring often to illustrations and reference materials she had brought with her. Vida and I kept checking our watches.

We got back to Lakewood in time for lunch, but not in time to meet up with a certain elusive soccer star and his aristocratic friend.

"Where are the guys?" Vida asked Trinny with all the nonchalance she could produce.

And why the hell hadn't Trinny come to the florist with us?

"They took Ian off somewhere to do manly things." She allowed herself an indulgent smile. "Max went with them."

"Then they can't be too manly," I told her, and pinned all

my hopes on the dinner dance some friends were throwing in Connie and Ian's honor at a nearby country club.

SHAYLA DID MY HAIR and makeup wearing a strapless vintage Dior that she told me she'd picked up in a thrift shop on Haight Street back home.

"Good for you," I'd greeted her. "It's about time you and Roger got to go to a party."

She giggled. "I feel just like Cinderella."

She may have felt like it, but I looked the part. Max had insisted on what I can only describe as a ball gown for this party. Apparently he'd been paying attention during one of Connie's many social briefings, where my mind tended to wander. It was a good thing because when the gang all gathered in the French Room for pre-party cocktails, the scene was more glam than Oscar night.

"Where did you get that?" I asked Vida. She was in a full-length crimson thing that had criss-cross ruffles at the bust and hugged her perfectly.

"Do you like it?" She looked down at herself. "Max bought it for me in London. He said I'd cause an international fashion incident if I wore the same dress to every party." She looked around at our glittery companions. "I hate it when he's right."

The fashion guru himself sidled up to us, looking nothing short of dashing in a white dinner jacket à la James Bond.

"Hi, guys. Listen, I was thinking I could give you a little Botox in your underarms so you wouldn't have to worry about perspiration."

He read the looks on our faces.

"Never mind. Just a thought."

Connie joined us out of thin air. "Max, did you tell them about the Botox?"

"Connie, you didn't!" Vida said.

She looked at us as though we were crazy. "I have a twelve-thousand-dollar Richard Tyler wedding gown upstairs. Damn right I did it." And she was gone.

Just as well, because I finally found *him* in the crowd. I doubt there was really a sort of glowing light all around him, but there might just as well have been. The first time I'd seen him in a tux I'd just had a bump on the head, so I might have been imagining things. But this time, clear-eyed and sober—relatively sober, anyway—I was able to confirm that Sir Charles Shipley was the most perfect man I'd ever seen.

"Make your move, tiger," Max muttered as he gently propelled me toward the vision of masculine perfection. "Remember what I told you—shoulders back, natural smile, you've got it, now chin up—you're ready." I felt his hand leave my back, and I was reminded of the very first time my father let go of my bike without training wheels.

"Sir Charles," I said smoothly, when I came within his sightline.

"Rebecca," he responded, and I loved the fact that he didn't use my boyish nickname. "You look lovely." It would have been nice if there hadn't been a definite tang of surprise in his voice, but I ignored it as he stepped closer, looked down at me with a decidedly wicked smile, and murmured, "You must save a dance for me."

It was at that precise moment that I understood why people in musicals sing.

. . .

THERE WAS ONLY one problem.

"It's a *ball*," I hissed to Max.

The evidence was all around us: the orchestra playing what I could only assume were waltzes or fox-trots or polkas or something, the couples moving together in a complex series of patterns that clearly had some meaning, the polite applause after each dance ended.

"What did you think?" Max hissed back. "Wasn't the fact that you're wearing a ball gown any sort of a clue?"

Vida joined us with a look of panic on her face and identified the central problem. "I don't know how to do these goddamn dances!"

"Where's Phillip?" I asked her.

"Dancing," she moaned. "And of course he's great at it."

"Who's he with?" Max asked.

"That's the only good news." Vida nodded her head in the direction of her sexual holy grail. "He's with Trinny."

The brother and sister moved flawlessly across the dance floor.

"They probably took lessons when they were kids," I said.

"Looks like Ian missed out on that," Max observed. I followed his gaze in time to see Connie wincing as Ian stepped on her foot for probably not the first time.

"Becks," Vida spoke with dread in her voice. "You'd better think of something. You've got the LOTM on approach at six o'clock."

I braced myself. I smiled charmingly when he tapped me lightly on the shoulder. I made polite conversation with him as Max and Vida faded away. I considered reminding him of my twisted ankle but didn't want to promote the whole klutz image I was trying to overcome. So I made delighted sounds when Sir Charles Shipley asked me to dance, and I faked it.

"SERIOUSLY, it wasn't that bad." The next morning Vida spent a good half hour trying to convince me I could come down to breakfast without the risk of people snickering behind their napkins.

"I would never have known you didn't know what you were doing," Shayla offered. She'd decided Vida and I were a lot more fun to hang out with than Connie the Compulsive, and had come by to lend her support. "I mean, until . . ."

Until the incident. With the cellist.

I closed my eyes. "You go on without me. I'd rather starve than face them all."

Vida didn't give up. "You really were pretty good out there, Becks. How'd you do it?"

I tried to summon the feeling I'd had on the dance floor with Sir Charles Shipley's masterful arms around me. "There's a lot to be said for a guy who can lead," I told them.

Max spoke from the doorway. "If only you hadn't gotten goosed by that cello player's bow."

I moaned. Max continued. "I blame him. Or maybe Sir Chuck for backing you into him. Anyway, I really don't think this one was your fault." He took a sip from a teacup he'd brought with him. "Why haven't you guys come down for breakfast?"

"I'm not leaving this room until the ceremony," I told

him. "I'll do my bridesmaidenly duty for Connie and then I'm coming straight back to this room. I mean it."

"Oh." Max sipped again. "Then I shouldn't bother telling you that the LOTM is going riding this morning. Alone."

I was dressed and downstairs in five minutes flat. After all, horseback riding was clearly listed as a Day Two event on my plan, and here it was Day Three already. I had some catching up to do.

And I'm an excellent rider.

"YOU'RE QUITE AN EXCELLENT RIDER," he complimented me. We'd just jumped a small fence, and I was feeling fully redeemed from the incident of the cello. We came to the top of a hill, and I realized we'd made a big circle because after riding for an hour or so we were coming back toward Lakewood House again. The lake itself was to our left. "What's that building out on the island?" I asked him.

"Oh that? Just the folly." He dismissed it.

Of course, just the folly. Don't we all have a folly on our private island? I took a moment to imagine him by moonlight in front of it. Leaning over me, closer, gazing deep into my eyes, lips parting slightly . . .

"Damn!" he said forcefully. His horse had made some sort of misstep. Did I mention that it was a white horse? Well, light gray anyway. Still—I was out on a date with a real-life, actual knight on a white horse.

"What's the matter?"

"This damn beast might not have been as good an investment as I thought." He shook the reins. "Still"—he flashed me a grin—"he's rather lovely to look at, isn't he?"

Rather.

I tore my gaze away to take in the scenery. "Is all of this yours?"

"More or less." He looked toward the house. "My father is still living, and I'm guardian to two nephews. Their parents died in a boating accident."

I looked at the lake. "Here?"

"Lord no." He shook his head. "Somewhere in the Pacific between Tahiti and somewhere else." He shrugged.

So they hadn't been a close family. A movement down by the water's edge caught my eye. "Who's that?" I pointed to a figure who was struggling toward what was probably a boathouse because it was next to a small dock. He was swaying under a load of what looked like lumber.

A flash of distaste crossed Sir Charles Shipley's perfect features. "An old gardener." He sniffed and seemed bothered by something.

Okay. Not a good subject. "What's that town in the distance?" I asked. "Is that where the train station is?"

"That?" He squinted. "No, that's the village. The town is over there." He maneuvered his horse close to mine, and we both came to a stop. Then he reached out and placed one hand on my back, extending his other arm over my shoulder so I could follow as he pointed to the town. This put his head close to mine, and his mouth just behind my right ear. I have no idea what he said, but I nodded at whatever he was pointing at and tried to resist melting against his chest.

His hand moved down my back and began making its way around my waist. I was trying to decide whether I should turn my head toward him, in a "kiss me" sort of way, or keep pretending to pay attention to his guided tour of the area. Should I wait for him to take the lead? Maybe he'd say something like "Rebecca, I must have you here. I must have you now." Or maybe I wasn't going to get that clear a message. Maybe he was waiting for me to indicate a certain willingness in some way. Maybe . . .

"Damn!" His beautiful horse kicked at mine and we were parted. Sir Charles gave me an angry look, possibly meant for his mount. "I'm going to have to give him a good gallop. Can you find your way back on your own?"

I wanted to say, "Hell, no—get off the stupid horse and come over here and kiss me." But that might be interpreted as bitchy. So I nodded.

"Good. I'll see you this afternoon." The horse reared as he dug his heels in. "Damn," he said as he turned away.

And then he was gone.

Damn, indeed.

Fifteen

I spent the ride back analyzing the exchange and came to the conclusion that it had gone well. I barged into Vida's room the instant I returned. "Success!"

"Me too!"

The gong sounded as Shayla appeared behind me. "Oh," she said, "this I've got to hear."

It was a little like being sixteen again, only not like being me at sixteen—like being some popular-girl-who-was-into-boys at sixteen. Anyway, between getting our dinner dresses on and getting our hair and makeup done, there was a whole lot of giggling going on.

Vida had spent the day playing tennis with Phillip. It had been his suggestion, which would have been cause enough for celebration, but it also turned out he was just taking up the game, whereas Vida was a fairly serious player.

"So there we were," Vida told us, "and Phillip Hastings was asking for pointers from me, and being great about it—not like a guy at all, you know? I mean, I hate it when some guy tries to show me how to do something that I've been doing better than him for years—"

This threatened to turn into a rant, so I steered her back on course. "So what happened after tennis?"

Vida beamed. "Well, we got started talking, and he was really impressed by my upper-body strength, and I told him it was the surfing. And it turns out he's always wanted to try surfing." She studied her fingernail in an attempt at nonchalance. "So he may plan a trip to California this summer."

Fine, but in my mind that couldn't compare to having Sir Charles Shipley's lips within inches of my neck.

"Okay, so what's your plan for dinner tonight?" I asked Vida. "I'm going to do my damnedest to get my guy out in the moonlight. I don't care if it's the terrace or the fountain or whatever."

"I think it's going to rain," Shayla said doubtfully.

"Have him take you to the conservatory instead," Vida suggested. "At least it's got a glass roof. And I've got my evening under control. I've asked Phillip to teach me how to play snooker."

"You guys are so complicated," Shayla said. "If I want a guy, I just have a couple of drinks and jump him."

Vida and I exchanged looks. I don't think the direct approach had occurred to either one of us.

"What if he's not interested?" Vida asked.

Shayla made a broad gesture encompassing her hair, her face, her impressive chest, her hips.

We got it. He'd be interested.

"If you want my opinion, and you're both probably a lot smarter than me—" We protested, but she waved a hairbrush dismissively. "If you want my opinion, nothing works like pushing a guy up against a wall and planting one on him."

. . .

EVEN IF WE'D DARED take Shayla's advice—and we probably wouldn't have—we never got the chance. When we went down to the Chinese Dining Room, we were greeted by a winking Trinny, who informed us that Sir Charles Shipley had arranged something called a "lad's night" in Ian's honor. All the men were gone.

"They'll probably come back legless in the wee hours of the morning and sit around uselessly all day tomorrow, but boys will be boys," she said. "They need their little indulgences, and we must keep them happy."

They do? We must?

"Why don't we all go out somewhere?" Vida proposed. But it was not to be.

"Becks, Vida." Connie materialized at my elbow. "Come sit by me. We need to go over some of the things I'll need you to take care of tomorrow at the garden reception."

Resistance was futile. Day Three was lost.

ON DAY FOUR, Sir Charles Shipley disappeared. Some "unavoidable commitments" took him to London. The slightly scary housekeeper mentioned that he might not even show up in time for that evening's reception in the walled garden—at which Vida and I would monitor the guest book, alert the staff if the canapés were running low, make sure the volume of the music suited the level of conversation, and carry out all the other duties on Connie's lengthy and Trinny-free list.

After lunch, I stood at my bedroom window and glumly

watched Vida and Phillip set off for a jog around the grounds. We were both supposed to be meeting Connie at the fountain to help supervise the people setting things up for the next day, but Vida hadn't needed much encouragement to bail on that in favor of a sweaty run with her dream man.

Oh, well. At least one of us was happy. I gave myself five minutes to wallow in LOTM-induced self-pity, then set off to help Connie.

Two enormous trucks had arrived, and a gigantic white tent was being spread out on the open lawn behind the famous baroque fountain. Rows of immaculate white chairs were being placed in precise, angled lines facing the rose-covered arch that had been positioned in front of the fountain.

Swarms of efficient-looking workers seemed to have the situation completely under control. Connie was nowhere in sight.

"Excuse me." I spotted a tall woman in a silk blouse and tailored trousers wearing a telephone headset and appearing to be in charge.

"What?" she snapped at me. "Do you work for me? What are you supposed to be doing?"

Wow. I expected snakes to leap out of her eyes. "I'm a bridesmaid. I'm supposed to meet the bride here."

"You bloody fucking bastard!" she shouted. "No, that's not good enough! I said fucking white silk organza ribbons and you'll bloody well bring me fucking white silk organza ribbons!"

She was shouting into the headset, I realized, but I still took a step back. Her gaze flicked to me. "The bride's in the house. I sent her away to take a bubble bath and think pretty thoughts or whatever the fuck brides do. What they do *not* do is tell me my business, thank you very much, or get in my way while I'm trying to prevent a *bloody fucking catastrophe!*"

The last three words seemed to be for the benefit of her staff, who continued to rush around efficiently. I realized who she had to be.

"You're the wedding planner."

Connie had spoken in dismissive terms about someone she'd been faxing and e-mailing on this end. She hadn't mentioned anything about the woman's ability to breathe fire.

"That's right. And unless you've got twenty pounds of *pâté de* fucking *foie gras* down your shirt I'll thank you to let me get on with this *fucking disaster!*"

I fled in the direction of the lake.

I PROBABLY SHOULD HAVE TRIED to find Connie, but the thought of getting between her and the creature with the headset terrified me. Instead, I set off for the little dock I'd seen the day before with some sort of vague idea of finding a rowboat and investigating the island folly as a potential romantic backdrop.

But as I got closer to the dock, I heard a sort of clanging, banging sound coming from the boathouse. The door was open, so I stuck my head in to see what was going on.

I was greeted by the sight of a six-foot-tall white swan in the process of having its neck wrung by an elderly English gentleman.

"Hullo," he huffed when he saw me. "What extraordinary timing. Could you please hold this in place for a moment while I try to find the right size spanner?"

"Um. Sure." As my eyes adjusted to the gloom of the interior, I realized the swan was in fact some sort of sculpture in the final stages of construction. The man, I assumed, was the old gardener I'd seen from horseback the day before, struggling under his load of equipment.

I reached out and steadied the swan's neck. "Here?"

"Lovely." He stepped back to check the angle of the head. "Very nice." He rooted around in a pile of tools on a shelf behind him and emerged triumphant. "Ah! Here you are!"

He reached into an open flap at the swan's shoulder and began tightening something.

"Um, I'm one of the wedding guests."

"Oh?" He squinted in concentration.

"Actually, I'm a bridesmaid."

"How nice," he grunted conversationally. "There! I think we've got it!"

He stepped back and motioned that I should let go. When I did, the whole structure groaned forward slightly but held.

"Brilliant! Can you help me get her outside?" The gardener placed a shoulder under one wing, and not knowing exactly why this had become my responsibility, I did the same on the other side. The structure was light. "Fiberglass," he explained. "Weighs next to nothing and should float like a charm."

Oh. It was a boat. Of course. When we got it to the dock and I could look at it in the sunlight, I realized it was one of those bicycle-pedal boats people can rent at ponds, to take the kids out and feed the ducks or something.

"Isn't she lovely?" my companion asked. "I got her on eBay."

Where else? "It certainly is . . . big," I offered.

"Oh, well, a lot of her will be underwater, you know. Just like the real thing. Furious activity underneath while up top we see only white, smooth, serene beauty."

Much like a wedding, I reflected.

He held out his hand. "My name's George," he said.

"Becks." I shook his hand.

He took a large white handkerchief out of his trouser pocket and wiped his brow. Then he glanced up toward the mansion, where the tent was beginning to rise. "I expect that place is a madhouse by now."

"Pretty much."

We both thought our own thoughts for a moment. Then I asked a question. "Why did you buy a swan pedal-boat on eBay?"

He let out a surprisingly ringing laugh. "Yes, I suppose it does look a bit eccentric at that. But I got it for the boys, you see."

I looked around. Maybe George had been in the boathouse too long.

He waved away my confusion. "My grandsons. I thought it would be rather jolly for them, but then . . . perhaps they're getting a bit old for pedal-boats." He shrugged. "In any case, they got an invitation from a school chum to go to Cannes or Nice or someplace for the end of their hols, and well . . . she's lovely, but she can't really compete with topless French girls, can she?" He patted the swan's neck affectionately.

"How old are the boys?"

"Fifteen and seventeen."

I looked at the swan. "She didn't have a chance."

George laughed again. "Ah, well, since I've retired, I need to do things to stay busy myself, so there you have it.

I'm sure you understand, a bright young lady like you. You must work?"

How had I walked into that dreaded topic?

"Well, yes, of course."

His expectant gaze asked the follow-up question. And for the first time in eighteen months I thought "screw it" and answered truthfully.

"I'm a voiceover artist for a cartoon vampire." As soon as the words were out, I felt like a complete idiot.

"Really?" He seemed impressed, which for some reason made me feel like even more of an idiot. "On American television?"

How soon could we stop talking about this? "On the Internet," I explained.

"Oh, good heavens." He clapped. "You're not that Vladima person, are you?"

I wouldn't have thought eccentric English gardeners of advancing years were the demographic Josh was looking for, but there it was. "Yes."

"Oh, but the boys love you!"

Right, that explained it. Fifteen- and seventeen-year-old boys who'd ditched gramps to go ogle French girls—that sounded more like my public.

"They'll be so sorry to have missed you."

"Yeah, well, gosh . . ." I had no idea how to have this conversation. Suddenly I longed for Connie and her wedding-dragon accomplice. This was my reward for running out on my bridesmaid responsibilities. Talking Vladima next to a giant swan.

"Well, this has been an exciting day," George enthused. He gave the swan an absentminded pat on the rump. "I tell you what"—his eyes sparkled—"come back tomorrow when I've got her hull sealed and I'll give you a spin on the lake. You can tell me all about your delightful vampire work. The boys will be so impressed."

Tempting. But my plans called for moonlight passion with the LOTM after the wedding, not pedal-boats and Vladima with the retired gardener, however cheerful he might be.

"I'm going to be a little tied up," I explained.

"Of course, of course," he said. "Silly of me. In fact, is that someone trying to get your attention now?"

I followed his gaze toward the house and saw Connie on fast approach. "That's the bride," I told George. "I think I'd better go."

"Yes, I think you better had," he agreed. We could now hear Connie's voice on the breeze. And she was not saying, "Oh, what a pretty swan."

Sixteen

Day Five. Wedding Day. The ceremony was scheduled to begin at six that evening. The panic began at dawn.

I'd stumbled to my room only five hours earlier, after a day filled with anxiety (Connie's), obscenities (the wedding planner's, whose name was Mona and whose voice I heard in my dreams that night), frustrations (Vida's, caused by the consistently friendly-yet-unromantic behavior of Phillip Hastings), and despair (mine, fueled by the continued absence of one Sir Charles Shipley).

"Becks!" Connie banged on the door and barged in. "Get up! The florist will be here in an hour, and the caterer will be setting up in the kitchen at nine, and the rehearsal is at noon, and we all need to be getting hair and makeup taken care of by two!"

I looked blearily at the bedside clock. "That's eight hours from now. I think I'll make it."

Max appeared in the doorway. "What's all the fuss? Connie, did you cancel the wedding?"

She gave him a look that singed his eyebrows. "Don't even joke about it." Then she whacked me over the head with a pillow and yelled "Get up!" once more before heading off to Vida's room to give her the same treatment.

"Max, can you drug her or something?" I asked when she'd gone. Then I took a good look at him. "What are you doing dressed at this hour?"

He put a finger to his lips and slipped into the room, closing the door behind him. "Don't tell anyone. I'm just getting in."

"Just . . . did you guys go out drinking again last night?" And did the LOTM meet up with you? I wanted to ask but didn't.

"Some of us. Look, Becks, I need your advice about something." He sat on the bed and took a deep breath.

"Max!" Connie flung the door open and stood with hands on hips. "Would you leave her alone? She has a lot to do today. Becks, for the love of God, get up!"

Max rose and saluted the bride. "Yes ma'am." Then he winked at me. "Talk later?"

"Sure." I immediately forgot about him.

THE FLOWERS WERE PERFECT. The food was perfect. The cake was beyond perfect. Only Connie was a mess. Vida and I tag-teamed her all morning, doing our best to calm her down every ten seconds while also keeping her out of Mona-the-fire-breathing-wedding-planner's way. We merely carried the messages between the two, until even that became too dangerous.

"Look." Mona threw down the orchid corsage she was inspecting and turned on me with a pair of the florist's shears. "If that bloody bride doesn't think I can handle one bloody country wedding, she can fire me, right? Otherwise, keep her the fuck out of my face and let me do my fucking job!"

When I translated this diplomatically to Connie as "I really do think Mona has a handle on it, Con. Really, you can relax," I was answered with "I can *relax* on the most important day of my *life*? Don't you understand *anything*?" At which point she burst into tears and I turned her over to Roger and Shayla for makeup damage control.

The only break came during the noon rehearsal. All three bridesmaids had been able to walk down the aisle and stand in our assigned positions to everyone's satisfaction, so we got to sit for a while as Connie and Ian went over the intricacies of the ceremony in excruciating detail.

After a few minutes of this, Max plopped down next to me, earning a basilisk stare from Mona.

"Don't crush the ribbon," I warned him in a whisper. Each of the two hundred white chairs had been decorated with a large white silk organza ribbon tied in a floppy bow. It was Connie's belief that each bow should flop identically, and hours had been spent on the task already. Max didn't need to earn a death threat by messing one up.

"I need to talk to you," Max said softly. "When are you done here?"

I gave him a "You have no idea" look. "Around midnight, probably. What's going on?"

He glanced beyond me. Vida was looking our way. "What's up?" she mouthed.

"Never mind." Max sat back and crossed his legs, brushing against the bow of the chair in front of him and causing Mona to start toward him with narrowed eyes.

Max clearly felt a strategic retreat was called for. He

stood. "Tell Hitler she shouldn't wear pink," he said, nodding toward Mona. Then he fled.

THEY SAY MOTHERS forget the discomfort of pregnancy and the pain of childbirth as soon as their new baby is placed in their arms. It was a little like that with me and Connie. She'd driven me crazy for weeks leading up to the ceremony, but when I saw her walking down the aisle looking regal and impossibly serene and more beautiful than I could ever have imagined, I forgot and forgave everything. And I wasn't even the groom.

The weather was ideal, the music was flawless, the vicar was eloquent, and the guests were suitably moved. I didn't cry. I never cry. But I think mine were probably among the very few dry eyes in the house.

Walking back up the aisle after the ceremony in a shower of rose petals, Vida and I were each on the arm of a smiling and proper groomsman. But I knew Vida was wishing hers were Phillip—he and Trinny, as best man and maid of honor, were together ahead of us—and I was checking the crowd in vain for Sir Charles Shipley.

While the guests scattered around on the lawns and were offered champagne and lovely little bits to nibble on, those of us in the wedding party were situated on the grand staircase for photographs. We were ordered into formation after formation, instructed where to look and how to smile, and generally browbeaten into panoramic splendor.

Toward the end of the ordeal, Phillip approached Vida somewhat hesitantly and asked if she had a moment for a quiet word.

She did. As he led her off toward the conservatory, she turned around to give me an "Oh my God" look. I held up crossed fingers.

Connie appeared at my side. "Do you think they're going to get together?"

My jaw dropped. "You mean you know about them?"

She gave me a squeeze around the shoulders. "I may have been a little preoccupied lately, but I'm not blind."

A little preoccupied?

"And what about you and . . ." She nodded her head in the direction of the terrace.

I followed her glance and stopped breathing. I'd seen him dressed formally on several occasions by now, but the vision of Sir Charles Shipley in a tux still made me reel.

"Go for it," Connie whispered.

"I have every intention," I assured her.

I GAVE IT A GOOD TRY. But as I approached him on the terrace, Mona ordered the wedding party to assemble into a reception line. Then, as I moved toward him during the designated milling-around-munching-prawn-thingies period, Ian's father slapped him on the back and propelled him to the bar. Later, as I followed on the heels of a waiter bearing champagne, Trinny cut me off by asking his opinion of the toast she would give. Finally, as I was within inches of him inside the tent, he was swept away by an agitated Phillip.

Phillip? Then where the hell was Vida? I looked around the tent and saw only Max, trying frantically to get my attention. I hoisted my skirts and made for him.

"What—?"

"This way." He shoved me out of the tent. "Vida's in her room and I can't get her to come out. She won't talk to me. She won't listen to reason."

"What the hell did Phillip do to her?" I picked up the pace and we arrived breathless at Spinster Alley.

"Vida? It's Becks." I tried the door. "Let me in. Vee, what's wrong?"

The door opened a crack to reveal Vida's furious facc. "You can come in, but that backstabbing bastard who used to be my friend can't."

Max held up his hands in surrender. I went in. "Vee—"

"He's *gay*!" she announced. Which was a little confusing, since Max had been out of the closet since roughly the age of nine.

"Of course he's—" Then I stopped. Because I got it. "Phillip?"

She flopped on her bed and was all but swallowed by the yards and yards of coffee-colored satin that made up her dress. "Max knew."

"Max?" I needed a minute to catch up. "Max and Phillip?"

"I didn't sleep with him," I heard Max yell through the door. "I'm the one who insisted he tell you."

"Vida, I'm opening the door," I said.

"Vida," Max pleaded when he came in. "Please. He's not out—his career would be over. Nobody knows. You couldn't have known."

Vida stared at him. "You seemed to figure it out."

"We were drinking," Max said, "at the stupid lad's night thing. And I just knew all of a sudden, and—"

"You don't need to draw us a picture!" Vida snapped.

"Vida, I swear," Max insisted. "I told him I wouldn't do anything to hurt you, and that he had to tell you. We were up all night talking—"

"I'll just bet you were—"

"Look, I'm your friend, you moron"—he cut her off—"and I love you, and he's actually a very decent guy who likes you a lot, and neither of us intended to hurt you."

There was a silence as Vida seemed to digest what Max had said. Then she took the only reasonable course of action. She started to cry.

"Vida," Max said gently. He sat on the bed and put his arms around her.

"I expect this in San Francisco, you know." She took the handkerchief from his breast pocket. "But I thought we'd be on safer ground in England."

"Oh, my dear, you know nothing about Englishmen," Max said.

"Clearly."

There was a polite tap at the door. Shayla peered in. "Something told me it might be time for a little repair work." She held up her makeup case. "What's the drama?"

"Nothing much." Vida blew her nose. "Max has found true love and I've got a new tennis buddy and that's just the way things go."

"Uh huh." Shayla seemed unfazed. She turned to me. "What about you and the duke?"

"After dinner," I promised her.

I MADE EYE CONTACT with him all through the long formal meal. I was trapped at the head table and he was over at another with a bunch of people I didn't know, but we definitely made eye contact. Which made it all the more frustrating that he disappeared as soon as the dancing started.

"You really didn't have very good luck with him dancing, though," a newly philosophical Vida pointed out. "Maybe you'd be better off lurking by the bar until he needs a drink."

We lurked. The only problem with the plan is that we drank while we lurked, and after a while we realized we should lurk no more.

"I need some fresh air," Vida said. "It's been a long day."

We stepped out of the tent and found the stars had come out, the fountain and house were lit up like a fairy tale, and it was just so romantic I wanted to kick something.

Vida sighed.

"Are you really all right?" I asked her.

She shrugged. "Like I could ever have been happy with someone who calls soccer football. God, my feet hurt."

I had a brilliant idea. "Let's go down to the dock and stick our feet in the lake."

"That's a brilliant idea," Vida told me, which should demonstrate how much we'd had to drink. "I was going to jump in the fountain, but we're much less likely to get yelled at down by the lake."

We came around the side of the tent and nearly ran into Mona, but she wouldn't have noticed anyway because she was arm in arm with Connie.

"You're absolutely the best fucking bride I've ever worked with, Mrs. Hastings, and I bloody well mean that."

"No, Mona, you're the best. You're the best wedding planner in the whole world—better than me."

Vida and I had to run away before they heard us laughing.

"Hey," I said, grabbing her wrist as we got closer to the dock. "Someone's beaten us to it."

The music was drifting down the hill, and there were two figures, silhouetted by the moonlight on the water, swaying gently to the song. It was the most perfectly romantic thing I'd seen all the long romantic day.

"Are you okay?" I asked Vida, who was staring at the couple with an unreadable expression. "You're not thinking it should be you?"

She shook her head. "They look good together, don't they?"

We left before Phillip and Max even knew we'd been there.

SHAYLA MET UP WITH US as we got back to the party. "Becks!" she called in a loud whisper. "Get over here!"

"What?"

She grabbed me and turned me toward the fountain. Once again I stopped breathing. Because the only sight that could possibly top that of Sir Charles Shipley in a tux was Sir Charles Shipley by moonlight, in front of the floodlit fountain, with his tie undone and his collar open.

"That's the sexiest man I've ever seen in my life," Shayla said seriously. "And if you don't do something about it right this minute, I swear to God I will."

She pushed me forward with her fingertips, and as if I were drawn by his orbital pull, I approached the Lord of the Manor.

"Rebecca," he said as I got closer, "you do look lovely in that dress."

I went straight up to him, locked my eyes on his, reached up to run my hands through his hair, pulled him toward me, and kissed him as if my life depended on it.

It was right about then that the fireworks started.

"THIS WAY," HE GASPED, pulling me toward him and kissing me again as we turned down another hallway. "Quickly!" He put his arm around my waist and pulled me after him, pausing every few steps so we could lock lips again or pull urgently at each other's clothes.

"Here!" he said suddenly, and propelled me through a door to a dimly lit chamber that seemed to be all velvet furniture and tapestries.

"This is your room?" I asked.

"My room," he agreed. His jacket was off, then his shirt. I'd pulled off his tie somewhere on the stairs. "My bed," he swept me forward. "And I want you in it."

After that it was a matter of hot hands working swiftly to rid me of my bridesmaid regalia. "Oh, yes," he said, his eyes lighting up, as the dress slid down to reveal the strapless corset Connie had insisted on underneath. He opened the top hook with his teeth. God bless Connie.

His hands were everywhere, and I could feel him straining to get to me. I reached for his zipper and heard him groan. When I wrapped my hand around him, he gasped. Then his fingers found me, and I stopped breathing entirely for a while.

The corset was a distant memory, and my breasts were filling his hands, then his mouth, as I dug my fingers into his shoulders and held on. Then he suddenly pulled away from me, raising himself up to change position, and our eyes locked.

Sir Charles Shipley, naked in the moonlight, smiled slowly at me. And it wasn't at all what I'd imagined.

It was better.

Seventeen

The movies are so right about so many things. They're right about how one night can change everything. About how the memory of that night can make your blood sing and your heart race and your whole life look candy-colored and new. The movies are right about birds warbling and flowers blooming and the sun shining and the whole damn thing.

Here's where the movies are wrong:

In the movies, there is inevitably a simple misunderstanding that causes the lovers to break up. This happens two-thirds of the way into the show. Long enough from the beginning that we can't stand the thought that the two stars won't end up together, and long enough from the end that we have time to watch them flail around like idiots until that perfect meant-to-be final shot.

The basic flaw in all of this is the initial breakup. Because no real woman would walk out on her man just because of something she suspects, or something she's found, or something she overhears, without giving him absolutely every opportunity in the world to clear it all up and make her happy again.

Women—and by women I mean myself—need to be conked over the head before they realize it's over. Our capacity for denial is so vast, and the stubborn refusal to admit defeat so strong, that sometimes even a moderate conk (for example, finding another naked bridesmaid in your new boyfriend's bedroom) won't do the trick. If he won't explain it away, fine. A resourceful woman—again, me—can do that for him.

Maybe she got lost and fell asleep in the wrong room.

Maybe he was just on the point of fending her off . . .

Maybe they used to be lovers, and now she wants him back, but it's too late because he's fallen for me!

Maybe he's a jerk and I'm an idiot. But that one doesn't cross a real woman's mind until later.

BEFORE THE DISASTER, there was the wedding breakfast.

Everybody was once again in nice clothes and there were mimosas and pastries and assorted miniature foods and it was in the Morning Room, rather than the Breakfast Room, which meant there wasn't a table, so we had to balance the delicate little china plates and cups and things on our laps while we all talked about what a beautiful ceremony it had been and what a lovely bride Connie had been and how the band had been delightful and the food delicious and, in general, how splendid it was to have played a part in the whole thing.

There was no discussion about who had hooked up with whom, and which beds had remained unslept in. That would have been bad form. But if the remoteness with which they greeted each other and the distance they maintained were any indications, there were two couples who'd had hot, sweaty sex the night before. And I'm not talking about Connie and Ian. Those two sat sipping, nibbling, and opening presents while the two couples in question discreetly ignored each other.

The two couples that any idiot could have pegged if they'd taken a moment to think about it were Phillip and Max, and—miraculously—myself and Sir Charles Shipley.

He was the model of decorum. I caught the occasional sly glance passing between Phillip and Max (I'm sure Vida did too), but from the LOTM there was not the slightest hint of a suggestion of an intimation that he had anything but the most proper host-guest relationship with any person present.

Only I knew differently.

"I just don't get it." Vida made this attempt at small talk.

"Uh huh," I said. Sir Charles Shipley was speaking with Connie's parents. He looked good talking to parents. I pictured him talking to my parents. Yep, it looked good.

"I mean, look at him," Vida went on. "How the hell can he be gay?"

I looked over at Phillip. He plucked a small rosebud from a vase and placed it in his buttonhole. "I don't see it either, Vida," I assured her.

Ian now stood and said something funny that I missed. I was a little sad about that because I didn't think I'd ever heard Ian say anything funny, and now it was possible I never would. Then he placed a hand on Sir Charles Shipley's shoulder, and they excused themselves and left the room.

"I wonder what that's about," I said.

"Probably settling the bill," Max spoke from behind me and I jumped.

Vida turned away. "I'm back to never speaking to you again." She headed for the pastry cart.

"I hope she gets over this," Max said tiredly.

"What do you mean, 'settling the bill'?"

His eyes widened. "Whoops. I wasn't supposed to say anything."

"But you did, so what do you mean?"

Max cast a furtive glance around to make sure we weren't being overheard. "Phillip told me about it last night. He's not a friend of your Prince Charming at all. Ian just asked them to pretend to be old chums because he didn't want Connie and her parents to know he'd rented out this shack for the wedding."

"What?"

Max elaborated. "Ian wanted Connie to have this whole dream wedding thing, but he actually doesn't have any old family friends who managed to hang on to their old family houses."

"What?" It seemed to be the only comment I was capable of.

"But Trinny knew about Lakewood, and when Ian mentioned he was looking for a castle for his princess's wedding, she arranged with your boy toy to lease the place out for the week."

"You're kidding!"

Max shook his head. "So the whole family-being-friends-for-generations thing is a sham, and Ian is probably writing out an enormous check as we speak."

Wow. The LOTM was certainly better at keeping secrets than Phillip was. I had a moment's flare of jealousy that Max had gotten better pillow-talk scoop than I had, but then I remembered that Sir Charles Shipley's mouth had been engaged in pursuits other than conversation in the night, and I melted a little.

"Connie doesn't suspect a thing?" I asked Max.

"And Ian doesn't want her to, so—shhhh." He cut himself off. "They're leaving."

Ian had returned to the party and the bride and groom were saying their good-byes. There was a tremendous flurry of activity involving rose petals being tossed and bouquets being thrown (nowhere near me or Vida), and then they were gone. Out through the garden gate and off to Paris.

Which meant I had exactly three hours in which to close the deal with Sir Charles Shipley before the cars came to take us to the station. I was already packed, but I had major unfinished business. I hadn't forgotten my five-day plan. "DO NOT GO without knowing where you stand" was the last item on the list, and it was time to find out.

I didn't see him anywhere in the crowd, so I looked in various drawing rooms and studies in the general vicinity. Then I wondered if he'd gone back to his room to change (having observed that's what the English upper classes do between meals), so I tracked him to his lair.

I knocked quietly on what I vaguely remembered as his door and thought I heard his voice inside, so I took a quick look around to make sure I wasn't observed and scooted in, a smile on my face caused by the knowledge that we could have a lot of fun in our three remaining hours.

My LOTM was already in bed. And already naked. Which would have been great, except he was already having sex. With Trinny.

I think I wasted a lot of time blinking because he was out

of bed and wrapped in a paisley dressing gown before I could say anything. Even then, what I came up with wasn't brilliant.

"What—"

"Rebecca, are you still here?" he asked me.

"What—"

Trinny cleared her throat softly. "Shouldn't you be packing or something, Becks?"

"What?"

This is the point at which the maybe-this-is-just-a-horrible-mistake possibilities were presenting themselves in my mind. But it wasn't. It became clear with Sir Bastard Shipley's next words that this wasn't a mistake at all.

Last night sure as hell had been.

"Look." he attempted one last charming smile. "As fun as last night was, I hope you didn't think it was anything more than . . ." He brushed that damn lock of hair out of his eyes and shrugged. "Well, part of the wedding package."

I stared at him until he spoke again.

"Isn't it time for you to go home now?"

I ran.

THE HALLWAYS SEEMED to close in on me as I took random turns trying to find my way out to somewhere I might possibly be able to breathe. I eventually staggered outside and away from the house.

I don't know how long I wandered around in the gardens, stunned at my own stupidity. And I don't know at what point I started muttering at the birds and flowers, cursing the Bastard Lord of the Bastard Manor as well as the Conniving Blond Bitch who'd been in his bed.

Eventually I found myself out of breath on the hill by the lake. I saw George in the distance struggling to pull the enormous white swan across the lawn, and suddenly I wanted nothing more than to exhaust myself in some pointless physical labor.

"Hey, George!" I yelled. To hell with behaving like a lady. I was a brash Yank, and I'd yell to the gardener if I felt like it. Take that, Sir Snobby British Shipley.

I gave George a hand, relieved that he didn't ask if I'd had a good time at the wedding. With much huffing and puffing, and after tearing several satisfactory gouges in the immaculate lawn, we got the completed swan boat into the water. It bobbed a bit and leaned a little drunkenly to the left at first but eventually evened out and floated just like you'd expect a swan-shaped pedal-boat to float.

George turned to me, rubbing his hands in anticipation. "Shall we take her out?"

Now that the work was over, I wasn't really interested anymore. "Will it hold us both?" I asked doubtfully.

"She"—George stressed the pronoun, reminding me we were talking about a ship here—"should be able to hold a family of four. So unless you weigh more than the equivalent of a mother and two children, we should be just fine."

"Fine. Whatever." It's not as though I had a lot to live for anyway.

"Splendid!" The old man beamed.

He held my hand rather gallantly until I was safely seated, and then we began to pedal, and wonder of wonders, the silly thing worked.

We moved across the water to the tune of George's delighted mutterings and the soft *splish-splish* of the paddles. It wasn't until George gave me a slightly puzzled smile and said, "Is something troubling you, my dear?" that I deteriorated into the most pathetic woman on the planet. And to make the humiliation complete, I started to cry.

I would have expected a proper old Englishman to be flustered by a woman's tears, but George wasn't. He simply produced a clean white handkerchief and made the occasional soothing comment such as "There's a good girl" and "Mustn't worry about it" as I choked out the whole sordid story between sobs.

I'll say this for myself—once I let go, I really let go. I didn't stop with the tale of the night before. I told George all about my stalled career, my many recent layoffs, and my inability to get my life back under control. I even gave him a semi-hysterical version of Connie's date-laziness theory.

Some might say my complete breakdown was overdue, and what better place to have it than on a floating swan with a complete stranger that I'd never have to see again?

Eventually I took a huge sniff and the tears dried up. I realized we were at the center of the lake, and George had stopped pedaling. The water was like silk around us, and the view of Lakewood House in the distance still had that damned fairy-tale quality.

"There. You feel better now, don't you, poppet?" George asked.

"I feel like an idiot," I told him. "I never cry."

"Never? Not even at American movies? Personally, I can't get through that scene in *Casablanca* where they start singing 'La Marseillaise.' But I'm just a sentimental old fool. Always have been."

I looked at Lakewood, dancing in the shadows as clouds passed quickly overhead. We were silent for a while as a dis-

turbing thought took root in my mind. It had to do
Prince Charmings and knights on white horses—now a h
ribly real image for me—and being rescued. Had this ju
been some incredibly predictable Cinderella thing? Was my
can't-get-a-decent-job, can't-recognize-a-decent-guy, stuck-making-cartoon-vampire-noises life back home so bad that I'd been seduced by a standard escapist take-me-away-from-it-all scenario?

God, what a depressing thought. And with it, inevitably, the rain began.

I looked over at George. "How seaworthy is this swan?"

"I suggest we don't find out," he responded. "How do you feel about pedaling?"

We made it to the dock as the downpour really started. I worried about the old man getting soaked as we hauled the swan to safety, but I suspect he was in better shape than I was.

"There," he said briskly, as we made it to the boathouse. "That's all right, then." He extended a dripping hand. "My dear, I shall think of you always whenever I see a swan."

"Thank you." I stood on tiptoe to kiss his rainy cheek, then went back to the house, back to London, and finally back home.

Thank God.

Eighteen

I wasn't the only one who'd had an eventful twenty-four hours. Vida had news.

"You slept with the vicar?"

She had sprung this on me as soon as we'd taken our seats for the flight home. "Maybe I shouldn't have said anything yet, with you being so upset about . . . But I've been dying to tell you all day and this is the first time we've been away from Max—and I don't want him to know yet because I'm not finished making him feel like shit about Phillip." She gave me a bright smile.

"You slept with the vicar?"

"He isn't really a vicar. He was just a sham, like everything else about the wedding. He's a friend of Ian's cousin or something and got one of those Church of the Internet ordinations so he could perform the ceremony. Didn't you think he was cute?"

"You slept with the vicar?"

"Becks, are you all right?" A little worry line appeared on Vida's brow.

I stared at her. "I thought you were heartbroken about Phillip."

She grinned. "I got over it. But don't tell Max." She settled back in her seat and told me all about it. About wandering away from Shayla after I'd pounced on Sir Biggest Bastard on the Face of the Planet. About running into the vicar and pouring her heart out to him about Phillip (who remained nameless in her story, to protect his career—Vida was still a fan, after all). About a quiet stroll through the conservatory where the vicar came up with delightfully creative ways to comfort her. About his confession that he wasn't bound by any actual religious oaths to be a good boy, and about their subsequent steamy interlude.

"Right under a palm tree," she concluded. "We might as well have been on a desert island."

"Vee!" I couldn't believe she didn't realize what had happened. "He took advantage of you!"

"Yeah," she agreed happily. "I know. And it was just what I needed."

WHEN I GOT BACK HOME, the following three messages were not on my answering machine:

> "Darling, I'm so sorry. Can you ever forgive me? Trinny had a revolver under the covers and threatened to kill me if I told you my true feelings, but I've turned her over to the police now, and I can tell you it was always you . . ."

> "Becks? It's Trinny. I'm so sorry. The truth is I've been committed to a mental institution for years. I'm a hopeless nymphomaniac and Charles was just being supportive of my therapy by having sex with me. But I'm institutional-

ized again now, and I can tell you that for Charles it was always you . . ."

"Hey, Becks, it's Chad. I'm so sorry about that crazy misunderstanding the night we went out. Of course it was a business meeting, not a date. PlanetCom wants to offer you a gigantic salary and complete free rein with the department. We're not talking to any other candidates until you call us. Becks, it was always you . . ."

At least that last one sounded like my old irrational fantasy life instead of the new, and disturbingly romantic, irrational fantasy life.

I did have three messages on my answering machine when I got back. They were just a very different three messages.

"Hi, this is Sunny Kirk calling from Western Pacific Family Mutual Finance company. As you know, mortgage rates are at an all-time low, and we here at Western Pacific Family Mutual Finance would like to offer you an incredible opportunity to save money on your monthly house payment. Call me today . . ."

"This call is for Rebecca Mansfield. Rebecca, this is Sneak Preview Video calling. The movie *Four Weddings and a Funeral* is seriously overdue. I'm afraid we're going to have to charge your credit card for the full price. Thanks for renting with Sneak Preview."

"Hey, Becks, it's Josh. I saw something in the paper about a bridesmaid who went berserk and bludgeoned the bride to death with a bouquet because she said the phrase 'seed pearl embroidery' one too many times. Figured it was you. Call if you need bail money."

Good old Josh. I didn't call. I didn't even unpack. I just found my oldest, comfiest set of jammies and crawled into bed. And didn't get out for three days.

"I'M NOT DEPRESSED," I insisted. The fact that I insisted it while back in bed after a solitary dash to the corner market for five pints of Häagen-Dazs and a bottle of tequila might have undercut my defense, but since Vida didn't know about that, she couldn't reproach me.

"Tell me the truth, Becks." She was calling from her cell phone on her way back into the city from her peninsula office. "Are you sitting in your PJs eating ice cream right now?"

"Of course not! That's such a cliché!" But it was hard to be properly indignant with a mouthful of mocha almond fudge.

"This has gone on long enough," she said. "I'm coming over and I'm going to drag you out of your house if I have to. If I can get over the fact that my soccer star plays for Max's team, you can get over one lousy English bastard."

She hung up, and I admitted she was right. It wasn't as though Sir I Hate Your Guts Shipley had actually broken my heart. I mean, when it came down to it, I barely knew the man. We probably spent more time together naked that one night than we'd spent in the entirety of the two weeks before that. So it wasn't that. It wasn't him. It was me.

. . .

"I DON'T EVEN KNOW myself anymore," I told Vida. "I mean, how can I be the same person I was before this damn trip when faced with the fact that I started caring about whether my makeup had crossed the line from appropriately 'dewy' to inappropriately 'shiny'? I mean, what kind of person gives a damn, and when did I become one?"

I speared my salad angrily. Vida had gotten me out of bed and out of my house with a promise to take me to the nearest bar, but instead we were in a healthy-fresh-veggies and whole-wheat-crepes place on Valencia that didn't even have a liquor license. I couldn't trust anybody these days.

"Yeah, well," Vida said. "I got pretty swept up in things too. I mean, I started out just wanting to get laid on my vacation, and I ended up fixated on the most unattainable man in Britain." She shrugged.

"At least you made a comeback." I shook my head. "I've never behaved like that in my life," I told her. "It was like I was in high school or something."

"Maybe you *should* have behaved like that in high school. Maybe there's been this giddy teenaged girl inside you all the time, lurking beneath the business suit, just waiting for the glasses to come off—"

"I don't wear glasses."

"You know what I mean," Vida sipped her iced chai dismissively.

"I do know that with all the wedding paraphernalia, I've never been exposed to so much girly stuff in my life," I admitted.

"Maybe it was too much for you," Vida suggested.

"Maybe we both OD'd on it. All that silk and lace and everything."

"Yeah, well." I sighed. "What I Did on My Summer Vacation: I dreamed, I danced, I loved, I cried. I got made over and got rejected. I wore a tiara and set sail in a swan. I got in touch with my feminine side."

"Is setting sail in a swan a euphemism for something kinky Sir Lying Scumbag does in bed?"

"Sadly, no."

"BECKS, YOU'RE NOT a traitor to the entire women's movement just because you had a crush on a cute rich guy," Max insisted. It was two days later and he was buying me Tiffany Blue martinis at his favorite new hangout.

"I know."

"Besides, I think you're spending too much time kicking yourself over the whole thing when it would be so much more entertaining if you just placed all the blame on the bastard knight and his British ho."

"Are you rapping these days?"

He grinned. "No, I'm just feeling particularly alliterative."

"In any case, I can't in all fairness blame Sir Screw Anything That Walks when I'm the one who stuck my tongue down his throat first."

"I'm told it was a beautiful sight," Max assured me. He brightened. "Can we blame Trinny?"

I raised my glass. "It's open season on Trinny." I drained the blue martini. "Trinny Hastings," I told him, "is a demon sent from hell."

"I thought you didn't like to talk about demons," Max said. "What with the Defender of the Night and all."

"I'll take Vladima Cross over Trinny Hastings any day. In fact, I'd like to sic Vladima on her bony British ass."

Max looked thoughtful. "I wonder if Josh could arrange that."

"As satisfying as it might be, it wouldn't make me feel any better. I mean, what really bothers me is what an obsessive freak all the gushy romantic stuff turned me into."

"Ah, well, I won't say you haven't always been an obsessive freak . . ."

"Hey!"

"But," he added, "you've always been an obsessive freak about your career, not your love life."

There was a certain truth to that.

"Which leads me to my theory." He paused.

I sighed. "All right, but if it's about Cinderella, I've already gone there."

Max shook his head. "Becks," he said sorrowfully, "a statistical analysis of ideal male qualities? A tracking spreadsheet for romantic progress? A five-day phased plan for nailing the guy?"

"You have a problem with an organized approach?"

"I have a problem with the fact that you took more interest in the planning than in the actual guy."

"Ouch."

"Which brings me to my theory . . ."

"All right, tell me your damned theory," I snapped.

He took a breath. "This whole unfortunate series of events was not about you needing a man to fill some void in your life. It was about you needing a project to fill some void in your life."

I blinked. Several times. "You're saying this was all about wanting a job?"

"Didn't you realize, about the time you started plotting your romantic future on a gantt chart, that you might be sublimating an urge to sink your teeth into a project?"

I shook my head, dazed. "No."

Max put his arm around me. "Don't worry," he said philosophically, "you're not the only one who's still reeling from that trip. I met what may have been the love of my life, and I left him there."

I looked over at him. "You don't think you and Phillip have a future?"

He gave me a look that spoke volumes. "I know myself. I could be in a long-distance relationship, and I could be in a discreet relationship, and I could maybe even be in a relationship with someone who isn't out." He finished his drink. "But I can't see myself in a discreet long-distance relationship with a closeted sports star."

We looked at our empty glasses. "What should we do?" I asked.

"There's only one thing to do." Max stood and held out his hand to me. "We need to go to the piano bar at Martuni's and request Cole Porter songs. I suggest we start with 'Just One of Those Things,' followed by 'So Near and Yet So Far.'" He led me toward the door. "And, please, 'Let's Not Talk About Love.'"

"Can I ask for Elton John?" On the street, I twined my arm through his as we began looking for a cab. "Maybe 'Love Lies Bleeding'?"

"How about 'Madman Across the Water'?" Max suggested. "We could dedicate it to Sir Charles."

"Absolutely. But no Elton after 1975. And if anyone suggests 'Can You Feel the Love Tonight,' we're leaving."

"Agreed."

"Max," I stopped, and I realized I felt better than I had in days. "I think I really need to hear 'The Bitch Is Back.'"

Max grinned. "Thank heaven for that."

Nineteen

All right. Fine. If I was so starved for employment that I'd turned the courtship of a philandering Englishman into a project, there was no reason I couldn't turn the promotional needs of a bloodsucking heroine into one. I was going to make Vladima a star.

"YOU'RE LATE," Josh greeted me. "And you look different."

I'd just joined him in his office, the minions working feverishly in the cubicles on the other side of the glass walls, the latest cut of *Daemons of the Night* playing silently on the wall-mounted plasma screen over Josh's desk.

"It's my new image," I told him. "And sorry I'm late." I pointed at my animated counterpart. "How's she doing?"

"She'll come out all right in the end." He was still looking at me curiously. "You changed your hair."

Was that an observation or a compliment? Whatever. "I got highlights for Connie's wedding. Honey and caramel." He was still looking at me. "What?"

"Honey and caramel." His gaze shifted from my hair to my eyes. "Tasty."

There was a flicker of . . . something across his face. Sometimes I don't know when Josh is mocking me. It's very irritating.

Especially when I'm about to make him an offer he can't refuse.

"YOU WANT TO BE IN CHARGE of Vladima's marketing?"

"It makes perfect sense," I told him. "Look how much I was able to help you out on the advertising spots before I went to London. How much has your audience increased since you've been running them?"

He looked vaguely embarrassed. "I don't know."

"That's my point, Josh. You don't have any idea how successful you are, or whether you're successful at all. You need someone who can monitor your fan base and channel their feedback into your work. You need someone who can find out what the competition is and how we can beat it. You need someone who can help you take Vladima to the next level."

In the silence that followed I thought I heard muffled sounds from the mystery office upstairs, but I couldn't be sure.

Josh was regarding me with an expression I couldn't read. I hate it when he does that. He finally asked the obvious question. "What's the next level?"

I spread my hands. "Whatever you want it to be. A cable TV show, merchandising, maybe a movie."

He leaned back and ran his hands through his unruly dark hair.

"But," I cautioned him, "we can't get any of that until we find out where we are now. I mean, do you even pay attention to how many page hits you get in a day?"

He crossed his arms and shrugged. Dressed in his typical black, he looked a little like a hip gunslinger who was reluctant to go out onto Main Street and draw.

"I didn't really get into this to make money. I mean"—he looked out into the office behind me—"it just sort of snowballed."

"Think about how much bigger it could get if someone was taking care of the business end," I used my most persuasive voice.

He looked me straight in the eye. "You really want to get that involved with Vladima?"

I really wanted to get that involved with *something*, and Vladima seemed to be the only game in town.

"Yes."

"And you'll still record her voice? You know the new script is ready."

I nodded. "I'll still record her voice." Small price to pay.

"I suppose you'll need a raise."

I was stunned to realize that hadn't even occurred to me. I blinked. "Thirty percent."

He held my eyes with his. Then slowly he grinned. "Deal."

"Deal." For better or for worse, I was Vladima's new best friend.

I BEGAN BY LOOKING over everything Josh had ever written about Vladima. I took home a filing box full of back issues of the original printed comic books he had begun with and half a dozen CDs of her later incarnation on the Web site, first as a Web-based comic and then as an animated cartoon.

It was very enlightening.

I was already familiar with some of Vladima's lore. I knew Josh had originally based Vladima on his ex-girlfriend. She had broken off their engagement two weeks before the wedding—right after Josh's Internet startup lost approximately 75 percent of its value overnight in the dot-com crash.

So it's safe to say the theme of betrayal had played a large part in the birth of a certain vampire. The first issue of *Vladima Cross*, produced crudely in black and white, was titled "Scar Around His Finger." The plotline revolved around this nice guy and the spawn of hell who was planning to marry him for his money. When he lost the money she decided to settle for drinking his blood and laughing as she walked away from his dry corpse. The titular scar, on the victim's ring finger, was featured in close-up on the last panel.

Bitter? Yes. Dark? Yes. Subtle? Um, no. But apparently it had made him feel better, so he kept drawing. It gave him something to do while he tried to figure out how to put his life back together.

So Vladima drank her way through more innocent victims. Josh put out a new issue about once a month, at first just photocopying them for his friends.

After the sixth issue, Vladima got her first minion. Donovan was a laid-off graphic artist who knocked on Josh's door one day. He was a friend of a friend who'd seen the comic. The next day he started inking the upcoming issue. He added color, and that's when I found out Josh's ex had been a redhead.

Donovan lightened Vladima's mood a little. She still tore her way through an unsuspecting world of blameless bachelors, but Donovan's pen added a touch of camp humor to Josh's dark pencil. Eventually, as Josh got tired of his own bitterness, the scripts began to change as well. Vladima began going after the blood of crooked politicians and gang leaders rather than hapless geeks.

The move from printed book to Web site had been a pragmatic one. Josh had simply gotten tired of photocopying, and as more and more people asked for copies and the costs added up, he decided a Web site would just be easier. Enter the second minion, Alex, who became Vladima's Web master.

But at that point it was still just an online comic book. The big change didn't come until Jeremy joined up. He was a disgruntled tech support guru with a passion for computer animation.

Jeremy used animation software called AniSplash to bring Vladima alive. Suddenly, instead of simple panels showing still images, she moved. She hit, she kicked, she dug her fangs in, and the blood of the evildoers poured out. It was hideous. Josh's growing collection of fans loved it.

Under Jeremy's influence, Vladima also sprouted enormous breasts and started wearing stiletto-heeled boots. I think it's safe to say the animator didn't have a girlfriend.

It was at about this point that I first heard about Vladima. Because it was at about this point that I first met Josh.

I had been the product marketing associate for a company called Megaware at the time, and I was manning their booth at some trade show in the Moscone Center. Megaware was the proud purveyor of AniSplash, and I was there to give demonstrations of the product on a small stage in front of the booth every forty-five minutes.

I wouldn't have noticed Josh hovering at the edge of the crowd if it hadn't been for the booth girls discussing who the dishy guy in black might be.

"He looks like a rock star," one of them said.

"No, I think he's an artist," the other one sighed. "Or maybe an independent filmmaker."

What drivel. I glared at them in hopes they'd remember why they were collecting their paychecks, then glanced up to see what all the fuss was about.

The first impression I had of Josh was stillness. The show floor was crazy—computers blaring from every station, multimedia demonstrations on every screen, stressed-out vendors calling from every booth to stressed-out conventioneers storming the aisles in a frenzy of freebie-collecting—but Josh just let it all swirl around him. He was the only fixed point in the entire flashing, throbbing, pulsing hall.

He met my gaze and moved toward me. When he reached the booth, he handed me his card, and when he spoke, it wasn't in the show-floor yell that everyone else used. He simply said, "I'm Josh Fielding and I love your voice."

Now, almost two years later, sitting on my living room floor and watching the last of the pre-sound Vladima movies play on my laptop, I remembered the day.

"I'm Josh Fielding, and I love your voice."

The only reason he'd heard my voice is that some stupid actress we'd hired to record the spoken copy about what cool things you could do with AniSplash hadn't shown up on the day she was supposed to. So in order to hit our deadline I'd recorded the damn stuff myself.

And, apparently, a star had been born.

I'd turned Josh down flat when, a few days later, he asked me to voice Vladima. But six months later it had been a different story. Josh was persistent, and I'd been laid off yet again. I didn't understand how he could afford to pay me what he was offering, but I was in no position to turn it down.

Vladima's appearance had changed again over the course of the animations I'd worked on. The breasts still defied any semblance of gravity, but the sneer of the still images was replaced by a mocking smile when she began to speak, and the hair completed its transformation from red to something just short of raven.

I'd been so busy being embarrassed about my connection with Vladima over the past eighteen months that I'd never really paid much attention to her. Now that I'd just read her life story, I had to admit there was something endearing about the old girl. She'd been through a lot in her three-hundred-year life, and her lipstick was still perfect. You had to give it to her for that, if for nothing else.

And as the monitor of Josh's psyche over the past few years, she showed he'd come a long way, baby, himself. As far as I knew he hadn't had a serious relationship since the fiancée from hell had broken his heart, but I'd heard that he did go out on the occasional date, so that was something. He was perfectly acceptable company these days. Good company, in fact.

And, unlike all my other bosses, he hadn't fired me yet.

Twenty

Okay, now dig, really DIG!"

Vida was yelling at me again. Apparently my upper-body strength was a disappointment to her. Which was only fair—my first taste of surfing was proving a disappointment to me.

I'd gotten fairly jazzed about the whole thing after Vida had made me watch a double feature of *Blue Crush* and *Step into Liquid*. I'd had expectations of a visceral thrill and a rush of excitement and everything else that had been advertised.

Instead I was crammed into a humiliating rented (don't even think about that aspect of it) wet suit, working like a madwoman just to get far enough out to turn around and surf back in. I also noticed that the beach at Pillar Point, while it had the advantage of being only about half an hour south of the city, didn't exactly feature the crystal blue waters of those tropical beaches in the movies.

I was belly-down on the board, using my already-aching arms to paddle my way out past the breakers, and apparently not digging deep enough.

I'd been at it for quite some time.

"Come on, dude!" another surfer called in encouragement. There were maybe five of them, all safely out where they should be, sitting up on their boards, dangling their legs in the water, observing my lack of progress. They'd already paddled out to the line-up. Friends of Vida's, applauding my minuscule efforts and shouting out advice.

Nice guys. I hated them.

I took a moment to catch my breath, tried not to think of the black-suited surfers as a passing shark would ("seals on crackers—yum!"), and I dug.

This time I made it. Out past the breakers—"mushy" today, thank God—and to the smoothly swelling surface where we'd wait for the perfect wave.

And wait.

"What do you do while you're waiting?" I finally asked Vida.

"If I were by myself, I'd be trying to work out this bug that's been driving me crazy," she said. The software Vida was coding was nearing its ship date, and that always made her a little work-obsessed. This had been her only free morning in a week. I was so jealous.

"Or if I were just here with Tim, we'd be talking about code and bugs and office politics." She nodded in the direction of the other surfers, bobbing in a line and waiting for a wave. Tim, I knew, was someone Vida worked with as well as surfed with. He may have been the one who'd called me "dude."

"But since it's you and me, I thought I'd ask how the I'm-never-going-to-think-about-Sir-Charles-again plan is going."

I suppose I'd walked right into that. "I'm never going to think about Sir Charles again," I told her. "Max has a lunatic theory that I've decided to accept, so I've relegated the whole episode to the status of learning experience."

"What exactly did you learn?"

I made a face. "Well, among other things, the corollary to my need to be conked over the head when someone likes me is a need to be conked over the head when someone doesn't."

"That's useful. I mean, you've always been oblivious, but now you know you're oblivious, so that's got to be a step in the right direction."

"And apparently I sublimate my need for productive employment with elaborate sexual fantasies."

"Okay, that one's weird. Is that Max's theory?"

I took my eyes off the water long enough to glance at her. "He's probably right. And speaking of Max, have you two made up?"

She laughed. "I came clean about the vicar yesterday. Max pretended to be totally outraged that I'd let him grovel for so long, but I took him out for sushi and he got over it."

"Thank God I don't have to keep secrets anymore." I watched as two of the surfers at the other end of the line both went for the same wave and both caught it. It didn't look that hard, really. And it did seem like they were having fun.

"He says Phillip's coming over in a month or so." Vida mentioned this very casually.

"Are you okay with that?"

She shrugged. "I'm over it. I mean, we really did have fun together, and I still think he's a great guy, so I wouldn't want to let one little thing—"

"Like his preference for hairy chests?" I suggested.

"One little thing," she insisted, "keep us from being friends. I mean, I did say I'd teach him to surf."

"Oh, I get it. I'm just your surfing-student guinea pig. Great."

"You're my proof of concept. And you'd better get ready because it's your turn next."

Vida had made me practice my pop-up technique on the beach before hitting the water, so in theory I knew I was supposed to turn myself to catch the wave while on my belly, then grip the sides of the board and raise my chest, then hop into a crouch—left foot forward—still holding onto the board, then stand. And surf.

What I didn't have a clear understanding of was when, exactly, I was supposed to execute the three major moves in relation to when the wave would be passing under my board. Or, as events unfolded, over my board.

It was probably only seconds later that I came up for air, and by that time the board—strapped to my ankle for just such contingencies—had dragged me close enough to the shore that I could stand while I sputtered and gasped and verified that I was still alive.

"Dude!" one of the surfers called to me gleefully. "You got worked!"

If "worked" meant being tossed to the bottom of the sea, getting a mouthful of sand and ocean, and knowing with complete certainty that I was about to die, he was right.

I heard a sharp whistle and turned to look back to the line, where Vida was applauding madly. "Way to go, Becks!"

Apparently, not being killed outright was cause for celebration. And once I realized I hadn't died, I got a burst of exhilaration that forced a joyful scream out of me.

I did it twice more, but my arms rebelled at the suggestion of a fourth trip out past the breakers. It really was amazing, once the phrase "dashed upon the rocks" stopped playing in my head. I actually even managed to stand up with the last wave. At which point I realized I had no idea what to do next, and I was instantly pitched back into the waves. Still, for about ten glorious seconds, I was a surfer.

When we finally called it quits, I had my last nasty shock of the day. The changing-in-the-parking-lot aspect of surfing was another thing Vida hadn't fully disclosed. I'd always seen half-naked surfers at the beach and assumed they were exhibitionists. It had never occurred to me that they had nowhere else to go.

Vida had this whole dance routine in which she held a towel in her teeth to slip out of the top part of the suit, then deftly placed it under her arms while she shimmied the rest of the way out. I was doubtful I'd be able to carry it off so gracefully.

I unzipped the top of the wet suit and shook out my wet hair. When I looked over at Vida, she was staring at me with a funny expression.

"What?"

She shook her head. "You won't like it."

"What, I'm too fat for this outfit?"

"No, actually, you look damn good in it." Vida grinned. "In fact, you look a little like Vladima."

I glanced down at my neoprene-clad body. "Maybe with six-inch heels and some serious implants. What?"

She was still grinning. "Just be glad Josh isn't here to see you in that or there would be a whole new plotline. 'Vladima, the Surfing Vampire.'"

"Very funny."

Twenty-one

I was late for my meeting with Josh. We were "doing lunch" because Josh had said that's how CEOs and their marketing execs communicate. He'd had his people (well, Alice, the woman who came in three times a week to restock supplies and keep the office running) call my people (actually, my answering machine) to set it up. I think Josh was finding our new relationship just the slightest bit amusing.

He looked at his watch significantly as I spied him at the bar at Bizou, one of those expense-account places popular with the digerati.

I'd dashed home from Pacifica to shower and put on one of the outfits I'd bought in London. It was a sleek gray pantsuit—very hip, according to Max. "Sorry I'm late." I pointed to his drink. "Are we having a boozy power lunch today?"

"It's club soda. Do you want something to drink?"

The bartender was hovering. "Iced tea," I told him.

I was suddenly nervous and I didn't know why. Josh and I had a lot to go over—ideas about publicity, possibilities for a print media campaign, coverage in some of the "What's

Hot on the Web" columns in the magazines where I still had contacts—so why did it suddenly seem awkward?

Josh cleared his throat. "What kept you?"

"What—? Oh." I took the glass of tea from the bartender and squeezed the lemon wedge. "I was surfing."

The eyebrows went up. "You surf?"

"As of today, I'm officially a surfer chick. Although for some reason they kept calling me 'dude,' which I hadn't realized was gender unspecific— Are you all right?" Josh looked a little weird.

"I'm just surprised. I didn't know you surfed."

I grimaced. "It was more like clinging to the board and getting pounded," I admitted. "Today was my first day. Vida finally talked me into it. It was pretty amazing, really. The worst thing was the rental wet suit." I shook my head. "Never again."

"Wet suit?"

"I think I'll have to get my own if I go out again. Oh! Vida said the funniest thing. She said I looked like Vladima. You know, in the wet suit. I told her I'd need some— Josh?"

He'd choked on his club soda. "I'm fine," he said in a strangled sort of voice. "Let's get our table."

MAYBE I WAS A LITTLE RUSTY because I never used to get the jitters before a pitch, but for some reason I suddenly had butterflies.

The good news was, I needn't have worried. Josh was great. He was interested in everything and enthusiastic about a lot of it, asked the right, smart questions and focused on what was important. He was a dream boss.

And it felt so good to be useful. Like the first time you walk again after you've been in a cast.

We talked through ideas for optimizing viewer feedback on the Web site and building a Vladima virtual community, including a chat room and occasional "live" Internet appearances (whatever that might mean for a fictitious undead character). Josh seemed impressed that I had contacts in the press and could pretty much guarantee Vladima some exposure in the mainstream media, but he wanted to be cautious that we didn't alienate our current fringe fans when we went wide.

The only real hurdle I'd anticipated was persuading Josh to start releasing Vladima as a comic book again.

"You mean instead of the Web animation?"

I shook my head. "In addition to it." Before he could object to the increased workload, I made my arguments. "It gives us a whole different distribution channel. There are additional events and cross-promotional opportunities—"

"I get that," Josh said. "And I'd like to go back to doing a book." He seemed to be weighing something in his mind. "There's a comic book convention in a couple of months in Vegas that would be a perfect place to launch it."

"I know." I also knew we had only a few weeks to register if we decided to go.

"But," Josh continued, "more work means more staff, and we're maxed out already."

Which brought us to the interesting question of how he could afford the staff he already had. Including me.

"Josh," I said seriously. "We have to talk about money."

He looked wary, but I had to go on. In order to do this job properly, I needed to know where things stood financially.

"How are you keeping Vladima afloat? Because I can boost your current pitiful revenue"—I won't even mention how laughable it was—"but I need to have a target. What's your burn rate? How far are you from any sort of profitability? And how have you been covering your expenses up until now?"

He was definitely looking cautious, which confirmed one of my darker suspicions. I had a horrible theory about where the money was coming from, and I wasn't sure if I wanted to know if it was true.

Here's what I did know: Despite the initial Internet hoopla, there still wasn't a lot of profit to be made from Web sites that provided content rather than commerce.

When the Web was shiny and new and there were fortunes to be made, everyone from highbrow magazines to online game developers thought they'd make millions from people subscribing to their sites. But after the bubble burst, as far as my research could tell, the only content providers who were making any real kind of a profit were, well, pornographers.

Of course there were a few exceptions. Research sites for lawyers, doctors, and other specialized groups could charge monthly rates. And there were child-friendly sites where, for a monthly fee, parents could know their kids wouldn't be redirected to anyplace inappropriate for them.

But by far the biggest slice of the subscription-site pie was adult content. Naked people. Doing all sorts of things. And as much as I didn't want to know, I had a hideous suspicion that something like that might be going on in the mystery office over Josh's studio, and that he might (yuck) have an interest in it.

I mean, how the hell else could he sustain the financial drain of the minions? Not to mention the studio itself. And he already had all the infrastructure in place for Vladima, so it wouldn't be much of a stretch to use the same servers and equipment to host any number of lurid sites. Profitable lurid sites.

It was a question that there was no delicate way of phrasing, and Josh was waiting, so I spit it out.

"Josh, are you running a porn site?"

"Am I *what*?" He nearly knocked over his water glass.

"Josh, you can tell me if you're running adult Web sites or . . . something. I mean there's nothing illegal about it. I just figured—"

"You just figured?" He stared at me. "There are a million ways to make money in this world and you assume I'm running a porn site?"

"Josh," I shushed him. People from other tables were starting to glance our way. "Look at the facts. I don't see you working at anything other than Vladima—which we know isn't bringing in enough to cover the electricity bill, let alone the whole operation—and I know your startup tanked, so you can't be living off that, and I don't think you've got some enormous trust fund . . ." I stared at him. "Do you have a trust fund?"

He was still staring. "A trust fund or a porn site. Great choices."

"Okay then, you tell me. How have you been paying all the salaries, including mine? And why don't you want to tell me about it? How can you afford all the equipment? How have you been leasing the studio? And what the hell goes on in the office upstairs?"

He gave me a last hard look and seemed to make up his mind about something. "I don't lease the studio. I own it." He signaled the waiter for the check.

"What?"

"What, exactly, do you think you know about me?"

I was stumped. "Just what you've told me." I realized that might not be true. "And what other people have told me. I mean, I know your fiancée left you because your company went under, and . . ." Just what other personal information did I have about Josh? Not much.

He looked at me with the same expression Miss Jolly had worn when I'd washed out of the fifth-grade spelling bee in only the second round. Profound disappointment.

"My company didn't go under."

"What?"

"I admit it lost a lot of its value—"

"Right. It tanked." It had happened to a lot of people. Most of the people I knew, in fact.

He sighed. "But it netted me roughly eighteen million dollars when I sold it to UniSoft."

I blinked about a hundred times in the next split second. "You made eighteen million dollars?" I blinked some more. *"Net?"*

He gave me an look that said "duh."

"And everybody knows this but me?"

He shrugged. "I doubt many of the minions stop to think about where their paychecks are coming from. But a sharp business mind like yours—I assumed you'd done some research before you got involved with Vladima."

I shook my head. I think I was still a little shocked because I heard this muffled buzzing sound while he spoke.

"I never researched you. I didn't think . . . I mean I never thought . . ."

"You mean you never took me seriously."

I winced. But it was true. Josh—Vladima—had just been a mortifying way to make my mortgage payments while I waited for my next real job. I'd never done any research in the beginning, and when I'd started looking into things lately, I'd let my assumptions about Josh stand instead of going out and finding concrete facts. Good Lord, I'd never even Googled Josh.

I couldn't seem to get past one-word questions. "You . . . ? UniSoft . . . ? *Eighteen* . . . ?"

He took pity on me. "It's okay, Becks. I wouldn't expect anyone to assume that I'd be crazy enough to fund the whole Vladima thing out of my own pocket for all this time."

"No, well . . ."

He made a face. "That's what I meant the other day when I told you the whole thing had just snowballed. I started out drawing pictures to get over a bad breakup, and the next thing I knew I had a payroll with eight people on it."

I stared at him. "Why did she break up with you?" I knew it was a rude question, but in my own defense, I was still pretty flustered. "I thought it was because you lost all your money."

"That's how it played out in the comic book." He looked down at the tablecloth and shrugged. "The real world was more complicated. She wasn't about money. She was about power." He looked up. "She wanted to be with a CEO, and I wanted to take the money and do something fun with the rest of my life."

"Enter Vladima? Being a cartoonist is fun?" I cleared my throat. "It is kind of an expensive hobby."

He gave me a look. "It's gotten a little out of hand."

"Although," I considered, "I suppose it's not as expensive as racing yachts or attempting to circumnavigate the globe in a hot-air balloon."

"True. But I have to tell you, the thought of Vladima bringing in enough revenue to earn her keep is appealing. Right now she's costing me around six hundred thousand a year."

I resisted the impulse to say "chicken feed" and did some quick thinking. If that was the goal—just to break even—I was sure we could do it. I opened my mouth to answer him, then closed it again as the real impact of Josh's wealth hit me. And I think I got a funny expression on my face because he seemed just a little bit alarmed.

"What?"

"You're not a pornographer," I said.

"I sometimes feel like one when I see what Jeremy does to Vladima's breasts," he admitted. "But no. I'm not."

I beamed. I couldn't help it. I was ecstatic. Not only was Josh not a morally reprehensible human being, he was solvent. More than solvent. Loaded.

He interrupted my train of thought. "I'm glad to see you're so happy. I wouldn't have though a cold-hearted corporate type like yourself would care whether she was being paid from ill-gotten gains." He put some money on the table for the bill and looked over at me. "I'm a little bit relieved you do."

I refused to be distracted. "Josh, do you know what this means?"

"You now know how to introduce me at parties?"

I waved his joke away. "It means you can afford to put out the comic book as well as the Web site."

He winced. "I walked right into that, didn't I?"

"You did. When can I see the new script?" He'd said he would bring it to the meeting, so I assumed he had it with him.

He hesitated. "Let's hold off on that, okay? I think I have some rewrites."

"Rewrites?"

"Yeah." He stood. "I'm thinking about having Vladima go surfing."

"Go ahead and mock me," I told him. "I'll make that vampire rich and famous yet."

Josh gave me a crooked smile. "I have every faith in you."

I PUT ON MY PARTY CLOTHES that night with sore surfer arms and a feeling of déjà vu. Max put it into words when I answered the doorbell.

"Gosh," he greeted me, "how long has it been since we've gone someplace to celebrate Connie and Ian?"

Vida pushed her way around him and into my kitchen. "Just tell me we're having drinks before we go."

I held up a cocktail shaker. "We're so having drinks."

Connie and Ian were back from their honeymoon. It was hard to believe it had been only a few weeks since the whole English disaster. I'd managed to put Sir I Can't Even Remember His Name out of my thoughts completely, and I was just hoping I wouldn't get dragged into reliving the whole event with Connie.

"Okay, now remember," Max warned us. "We don't know anything about Ian having paid for the use of Lakewood, right?"

"Right," I agreed.

"Right." Vida nodded cheerfully. "And while we're at it, Phillip's not gay and I didn't sleep with the vicar."

"Who wasn't really a vicar," I added. "Hey, just to keep things simple, how about if we agree that nothing happened between me and the LOTM?"

"Sure." Max assumed a resigned expression. "So nobody tells the truth about their sex life and we don't discuss money. Sounds like Thanksgiving at my mother's house."

"Ah"—I handed him a drink—"but would your mother serve raspberry flirtinis?"

"Not on her best day."

THE PARTY WAS ONCE AGAIN hosted by Connie's parents. There was once again a fleet of handsome waiters circulating with champagne and various nibbleable things. Once again an ice sculpture (this time of a mermaid—I couldn't begin to guess the significance) contained an extravagant amount of caviar. Once again it all hit Vida the wrong way.

"Do you think they'll have to walk in backward?" she asked, as we all turned to the staircase following the announcement that Mr. and Mrs. Ian Hastings were about to make their grand entrance.

"It does feel a little bit like we're playing the reel in reverse," Max agreed.

"Except this time all the presents are unwrapped," I pointed out.

Connie's mother had been busy in her daughter's absence. She'd unwrapped all the gifts that had been given on two continents, made a careful list of who'd sent what so

Connie would have an easy time with the thank-you cards, and set all the glittering swag out in an ostentatious display on the long dining room table.

Vida had gasped when she'd seen it all, and Max had started whistling "Who Wants to Be a Millionaire"?

"Max!" I elbowed him. "This is not a road company production of *High Society*. Cut it out."

At least this time there were no speeches. When Connie and Ian hit the bottom step they were swallowed by the party like the rest of us.

We mingled.

"Becks," Vida said suddenly, "don't look now, but there's a guy over there who's been checking you out."

"What guy?"

She not-so-subtly jerked her head. "The one by the mermaid."

"Never go into undercover work," I told her, and looked over by the mermaid.

There was someone looking at me. I didn't think I knew him, but he had one of those faces that could have been on anyone. And now he was smiling.

I turned back to Vida. "I'm not up for flirting tonight."

"You're never up for flirting."

"Um—I was at the last party we went to, and look how well that turned out."

"How well what turned out?" Connie materialized to Vida's left. We both jumped.

"Connie! How are you? How was Venice?" Vida and I babbled.

Connie's party smile wobbled. "Let's go out to the terrace." She turned away.

Vida and I took the time to exchange one raised-eyebrow

look before we followed her, grabbing Max by the French cuff on our way to the door.

As soon as we hit fresh air, Connie burst into tears.

"It was awful," she sniffed, reaching for Max's pocket handkerchief. "It was supposed to be paradise, but it was so hot and there were so many bugs, and there was nothing to do." She looked at us wildly. "Absolutely nothing to do. No clubs, no restaurants or theaters or museums, just fourteen days of Ian and . . . nothing."

"Connie," Vida said. "You make it sound like you were on some desert island. I thought you two were going to Paris and Venice?"

"The two most romantic cities in the world," I agreed. "Wasn't that the plan?"

She blew her nose violently. "That *was* the plan. Before Ian decided to *surprise* me by changing everything and taking me to that godforsaken hellhole."

"What hellhole was that, exactly, Connie?" Max asked.

"The Four Seasons on Maldives."

Vida was the first to speak. "Maldives? As in the islands in the Indian Ocean? As in the best scuba diving on the planet?"

Connie sniffed. "We did go diving a few times."

Now it was Max's turn. "The Four Seasons? As in luxury I can't even imagine?"

Connie enlightened us. "As in a thatched-roof water bungalow on stilts and our own private lagoon."

I stared at her. "That bastard. He made you have your own private lagoon?"

"Connie." Max struggled to understand. "You're saying that Ian swept you away to the most exotically romantic honeymoon destination on the planet and you're . . . pissed?"

"He didn't tell me!" She stamped her foot, which didn't really help if she was trying not to look like a spoiled princess. "Do you know how much planning went into Paris and Venice?"

Oh, the planning. I think the three of us got it at the same time. "Connie, sweetie, did the change in plans mean you'd packed wrong?"

She turned on me. "I did not pack wrong! I packed perfectly appropriately. I even sent things by FedEx to both hotels so we wouldn't have to carry too much luggage. And I had reservations at restaurants that I'd made *months* before. And I knew exactly what we were going to do every day, and there was *so much* to do, and then . . ." Her voice trailed off. "Maldives."

I don't think I'd ever heard the name of an island paradise spoken with such complete loathing.

"There must have been a shop," Vida said hesitantly. "I mean, you must have been able to buy a swimsuit and some sunscreen, and really, what more do you . . ." The remains of the sentence were withered by Connie's glare. "I get it," Vida backpedaled. "That's not the point."

"Of course there was a *shop*," Connie said acidly. "There were several quite lovely *shops*. And there was swimming, and snorkeling, and diving, but when all was said and done in the evening, there was only . . ."

"Ian?" Max suggested.

"Ian," Connie agreed.

Something told me the honeymoon was over.

Twenty-two

Publicity. The next few weeks were all about getting Vladima's name in print. She was already an underground goddess to the poorly socialized Goth set, but I wanted to bring her out of the darkness, so to speak, and into the light of mainstream entertainment. Being careful, as Josh continually reminded me, not to kill her in the process.

"Vladima does not drink Pepsi," he said.

No problem. But in the back of my mind I wondered if she might wear an outfit from Bebe. I didn't bring that up yet.

THE FIRST STEP in the comic book project was to take the storyboards Josh had created for the past three Vladima plot lines and turn them into a graphic novel. For that job we hired a twitchy guy named Rabbit (for reasons I refused to investigate) who seemed to be born for the job.

I also had the Web master, Alex, add some simple code to the site so we'd be able to tell how many hits we got in a day, as well as track the relative popularity of different areas of the site.

I knew that if we could get Vladima's visitors to log in when they came to the site, we'd be able to get even more session information. Like where they visited first and how long they stayed with each page, and how often the same user came back for more—useful information if you want to know what's working and whether your advertising dollars (which I now had) were paying off in new viewers.

But getting people to log in was tricky. You need to give them something in return for the information they give you. We talked over a lot of ideas, but everything we could think of ended up sounding silly. Not that the idea of a crime-busting vampire sex idol wasn't silly already, but you know what I mean.

It was Jeremy, the AniSplash programmer, who came up with the idea of the Vladima screensaver. We'd just take a dozen or so of the more compelling panels and turn them into a slideshow. Jeremy told us it would be easy to create, and we could offer it as a free download from the site.

"Free?" Josh had said doubtfully. "I thought the idea was to make money somehow."

"Getting them to download something is one step closer to getting them to buy something from our online store. It takes the Vladima experience from passive—just viewing—to interactive."

"The Vladima experience?" Josh echoed.

"Online store?" Jeremy asked. "What online store?"

"That will come a little later, when the demand for Vladima T-shirts reaches critical mass."

"There's a demand for Vladima T-shirts?" Josh asked.

"There will be." If I had anything to say about it, a Vladima T-shirt would be mandatory fashion for every beginning freshman in America. Especially if I could get some member of a reasonably cool band to wear one in a video. And really, how hard could that be?

THE SECOND WEEK IN JULY, Vladima got mentioned in both *San Francisco* magazine and *Entertainment Weekly*. Josh called an all-minion meeting to mark the occasion, and when I walked into the break room, I was doused with champagne by the entire staff. That sort of thing had never happened in any of my previous jobs. I was now officially a member of Vladima's cult.

The meeting turned into a full-on party, which I enjoyed with sodden clothes and wine dripping from my hair as we discussed in all seriousness the relative merits of garlic necklaces or vampire teeth for the freebies we'd be handing out at our booth at ComixCon.

"What about wooden stakes?" Raven, the sound engineer, wanted to know. "Wouldn't they be good? And cheap to make?"

"I don't think we should hand out actual weapons," Josh told her. "There might be a vampire at another booth, and we wouldn't want our fans to go around the convention trying to slay the competition."

"There probably will be vampires at other booths," I told him. "Vladima isn't the only undead hero on the market."

Which led to a round of supportive shouts such as "She's the best!" and "Vladima rocks!" and "She could kick Vampirella's ass!"

"Hey," Donovan said suddenly, "are we going to have a live Vladima at our booth?"

All heads turned to me. Except Josh's. He suddenly found something in the microwave that needed his attention.

"I'm auditioning actresses next week," I told them all. "It's going to be tight, but we should be able to cast someone and get a costume made in time."

"That'll be some costume," Alex commented.

"Um, yeah." I looked at Jeremy, the creator of Vladima's magnificent breasts. "Well, the reality of an actress's actual body might not live up to the animated version, but we'll see what we can do."

The thought of an actress's actual body had quite an effect on the group. Four dateless guys spoke as one. "Can I come to the auditions?"

I looked over at Josh, who was blushing if I wasn't mistaken. "No you can't," I told them.

That sort of broke up the party.

Josh threw me a towel as the minions filed back to their cubicles. I looked down at myself in dismay and started dabbing around the edges.

"Um." Josh looked at a spot on the wall behind me as he spoke. "I've probably got a T-shirt or something I could lend you upstairs." He glanced at my face quickly, then looked away again. "You could, uh, get cleaned up."

"Upstairs?"

"Yeah." Now he started straightening scraps of paper on the bulletin board.

The only thing upstairs was the mystery office. "You know what's upstairs?"

"Of course I do. What do you think is up there?"

Since I'd found out Josh wasn't running a porn studio

upstairs, I hadn't really thought about it. "I don't know. A drug lab? A front for the mafia?"

He stared at me. "That's quite an imagination you've got there."

"Why? What is upstairs?"

"My apartment."

"You're . . . kidding."

"Sorry to spoil whatever little fantasies you've got going, but it's not exactly a den of iniquity."

I don't know why I was surprised. Maybe it was because I'd always figured something sinister was going on up there. And maybe it was because I'd never really thought of Josh as having an apartment.

"You're still dripping," he said.

I came back to my senses. "You're not exactly fresh as a daisy yourself, pal." He'd caught more than his share of the spraying champagne earlier.

He looked down at his soaking shirt. "So let's go dry off, and then we can go over the new storyboards."

"Deal." After all, it was just an apartment, and it was just upstairs.

So why did I suddenly feel as if I'd had a lot more than two glasses of champagne?

HERE'S MY PRIMARY IMPRESSION of Josh's loft: weird.

Not that it was weird-looking or anything. In fact, I was a little startled by how nice it was. The space was huge, and tall windows let in all the light that had been banned from the downstairs studio. Josh had sectioned areas off with bookshelves and modular units to establish clearly defined spaces for everything.

There was a living area with a sofa and massive amounts of audio and video equipment. Another space was set aside as a reading nook, with one comfortable-looking leather chair, one good lamp, and a lopsided stack of books. The open-plan kitchen had up-to-the-minute fixtures and trendy track lighting. Beyond the kitchen, behind some modular closet units on wheels, I saw the corner of a large low bed.

It was comfortable. It was surprisingly tasteful. It was immaculate. And it was weird. Weird to rinse myself off in Josh's bathroom and pat myself dry with Josh's fluffy towels. Weird to be sitting on Josh's sofa wearing Josh's U2 T-shirt, and waiting for Josh to come back from the kitchen with a cup of tea. Very weird to be in his home rather than downstairs in his office, and extremely weird that, despite the weirdness, it was nice.

He sat next to me after handing me a steaming mug. I just had time to notice how close he was when he spoke.

"There's something you should know."

I've never had a conversation start with those words and end well. I braced myself. "What?"

"I've given Vladima a partner."

"A . . . ? Oh. Um . . ." For some reason I was completely flustered. "A partner?" I wished I could stop looking into Josh's eyes. "A partner." Then I realized what he'd said. "A *partner*?"

He explained. "I think she needs someone to—I don't know—to hang out with. I mean, I've been thinking for a while that she needs a Watson, you know? A Robin to her

Batman? A partner." The way he was looking at me made it clear that it was important that I agree with him.

But I wasn't so sure. "You created another superhero?"

He shook his head. "I messed around with that for a while, but then I decided on a mortal." He reached over to the coffee table and opened a folder. "Dr. Ethan Black."

I looked at the drawing. A dark-haired guy in a lab coat wearing glasses. "He's a research scientist?"

"Among other things." Josh explained. "He used to work for the FBI crime lab, but he got fired because he kept insisting there was a female serial killer who was gruesomely murdering all the mobsters and drug lords."

Ah-ha. "He was on to Vladima?"

Josh nodded. "That's what the new storyline is—Vladima's pursuing a pedophile, and Dr. Ethan Black is pursuing her."

"Let me guess," I said. "By the end of the third issue he'll have decided that her vampire vigilantism is just what this town needs."

Josh grinned. "Something like that. Will you read it tonight?"

I took the folder. "Sure."

When I looked at him, I felt there must be something else I should say. I opened my mouth, but suddenly the weirdness came rushing back and choked me.

So I took Vladima and we got the hell out.

I DIDN'T HAVE TIME to go home and change before meeting Max for dinner at a little restaurant on Fillmore that probably had a name, but that we always just referred to as "the cheap Thai place."

"What's this?" He gestured to Josh's T-shirt. "Are we into vintage rock fashion now?"

"It's borrowed." I pecked his cheek. "It was either wear U2 or smell like a wino."

"Tough call." He put his menu aside and clasped his hands. "So what's new? Tell me everything. I want to get all the boring 'you' stuff out of the way so we can spend the rest of the evening talking about me and my brilliant new show."

He produced a stack of postcard-sized flyers for *San Francisco Follies*, the show he was backing, which would be opening in a few days at the Next Stage Theater (which was actually the auditorium of an Episcopal church on Gough Street, but who cares—it's showbiz).

"I want you to give these to everyone you know," he instructed. "And at some point you'll need to explain to me why, if you can get that damn cartoon vampire mentioned in every column in America, you can't generate a little heat for your oldest and dearest friend, but that can wait."

He gave me a dazzling smile. "You didn't answer me. What's new?"

I set the folder of Josh's storyboards on the table. "New story for the cartoon vampire, no new story for me."

Max opened the folder and started leafing through the pages. About halfway through, his eyebrows went up. "She has a love interest." He looked at me. "She has a love interest?"

I shook my head and took a break from Max to order a Thai iced tea and some red curry. "Not a love interest," I told him when the waitress had gone, "a partner."

"You don't sound very happy about it."

I made a face. "I really don't care one way or the other."

"I believe you. Thousands wouldn't, but I do."

"It's just that if she has a partner, there's bound to be a

power struggle as he tries to control her, and I— What?" Max was giving me his Dr. Freud look.

"Just because your relationships are about power doesn't mean Vladima's are."

"We're not talking about me. And anyway, my relationships are not about power."

"Uh-huh." If he'd had a beard, he'd have been stroking it.

"Oh, come on, Max, aren't all relationships about power? Connie says—and I'm not saying Connie is in any way my romantic role model—but Connie says in any relationship you're either the hammer or the nail."

That seemed to shut him up for a minute. "Well, that certainly explains a lot about her marriage," he reflected.

"And how the hell did we end up on the subject of relationships anyway? I thought we were going to have a nice quiet dinner where we'd talk about what a marketing genius I am and how you're the next Flo Ziegfeld."

"All right, all right." He held up his hands in surrender. "You win."

"Good. Are you going to eat all of those spring rolls?"

He held out the plate. "I'll only say one more word on the subject."

"Max!"

He snatched the plate away before I'd had a chance to take anything.

"Not until you listen to me."

I stared at him. "Fine." Whatever.

"I only want to say that you do have a relationship with a single, straight guy that isn't a power struggle."

"I do not." I speared a spring roll and did my best to ignore Max.

"What about Josh?"

I rolled my eyes. "Josh isn't a guy."

"I wouldn't count on that."

I gave Max a look. "He's a colleague. There's nothing personal about our relationship and there's certainly nothing sexual."

"Right. Just out of curiosity, have you seen the way he draws you?"

"He doesn't draw me. He draws Vladima."

"Uh-huh. Maybe that was true once, but after a while there got to be a definite resemblance. And in this new one—" He opened the folder and turned a page to face me. "Baby, that is you in a black leather bustier."

"It is not!" I looked at the drawing. It was Josh's original pencil sketch, unaltered by either Donovan's ink or Jeremy's animation. Vladima was rearing back to strike, standing tall over her victim, strong and fearless and gorgeous with her waving dark hair and flashing eyes. "It's so not me."

Max sighed. "All right. This is pointless. But at least we got it over with, so now we can talk about me."

"Fine."

"Good. Do you still have Shayla's number?"

"I think so. But I haven't seen her since we got back from the wedding. Why? Do I need another makeover?"

"We're talking about me, remember? I'm wondering how much she might know about the proper application of feathered eyelashes."

"Oh . . ."

So we had a lengthy conversation about everything from glitter to boas to body paint while devouring really good curry. But all the while a phrase kept repeating itself in my head.

Josh? No way. That would ruin everything.

Twenty-three

As it turned out, Shayla did know a lot about false eyelashes (feathered and otherwise) and she was happy to help Max and his partners in theatrical crime with their stage makeup on the night of the show. Not that the cast of four semiprofessional quasi–drag queens needed much help, but they appreciated her enthusiasm.

I'd been running late all day, and I met up with Connie and Ian on the sidewalk outside the theater. "Have you talked to Vida?" Connie asked in greeting.

"My cell phone battery died," I told her. "Why? What's up?"

Connie looked over my shoulder and grinned. "She's bringing a date."

A *date*? Vida? I turned and saw her talking animatedly with some guy as they waked toward us. When he got closer, I thought he looked vaguely familiar. But it wasn't until he spoke that I recognized him.

"Dude!" he said delightedly.

"Tim!" I pulled his name out of the air just in time. Tim, who was Vida's surfing-and-work buddy. Oh, well, then it probably wasn't a date. It was just Tim.

Introductions were made, and Ian was just saying something about going in when Vida's eyes widened as she focused on someone behind me. "Josh!"

Josh? She'd only met him once or twice, so she was probably—

"Hi," I heard his voice, low and close to my ear, and got a little disoriented. Like when you see someone from your hometown while you're away on vacation and the context is wrong.

I turned. Yep, it was Josh.

Vida was introducing him to Tim and then he was congratulating Connie and Ian on their wedding, and they were saying how nice it was to finally meet him, and then he turned to me.

"Hey, Becks," he said softly, "Max invited me. I hope you don't mind."

There was something about the way he was looking at me, waiting or watching for I didn't know what, that caught my reply in my throat. Vida slapped me on the back to dislodge it.

"No, hey, great. Good to see you." I nodded. "We should go in."

So I could kill Max.

ALL THE OTHER BACKERS of the *Follies*, like Max, had real careers—dentist, lawyer, investment banker, and accountant—but even if their mothers had made them go to college, their hearts still belonged to Broadway. Or at least to a fifty-seat hall behind the Trinity Episcopal church.

The production was heavy on show tunes, with the lyrics

rewritten to include witty commentary on everything from the latest ballot initiative to the mayor's sex life.

In addition to the production numbers, there were a few skits, some improv, and a horrifying attempt at audience participation that involved a woman of a certain age seated in the front row, who would probably never be able to wear her wig in public again.

But aside from that, the whole thing came off without a hitch.

A quick surreptitious look to my left revealed Josh convulsed in laughter during a number about venture capitalists during the dot-com boom, sung to the tune of "La Vie Boheme."

Ian, on the other hand, looked a little confused.

AFTER THE SHOW, the cast went off to a party at the End Up, and the rest of the investors tagged along with them, but Max said he'd rather hang out with "the little people." He met us out on the sidewalk after the show, dragging a breathless Shayla along behind him and greeting us modestly with "How fabulous was it and where are we going for drinks?"

Comments were exchanged to the effect of "Very fabulous and we haven't decided yet."

Tim suggested a place out by Ocean Beach, but we decided it was too far away. Ian suggested the Irish Bank, but Max said he couldn't handle the tedium of the financial district set after the glitter of an opening night. Then Josh made my jaw drop when he suggested Martuni's.

Connie shouted "Perfect!" at the exact moment Ian

yelled "No!"—which didn't bode well for the rest of the evening.

"I know," Vida broke the awkward pause. "The Lush Lounge."

"Brilliant," Connie said, giving Ian a we'll-talk-later-in-the-car look.

The Lush was a sort of shabby-chic retro-something place that had the added advantage of being within walking distance, so we set out.

We formed into clumps of two, with Max and Shayla in the lead, discussing every detail of the show. They were followed by Tim and Vida—arm in arm, so maybe it was a date after all—and a dangerously silent Connie and Ian. That left me and Josh to bring up the rear.

I rummaged around in my brain for something to say to him, and all I came up with was "What did you think of the show?"

He shot me a sideways grin. "I think I'm required to say it was fabulous."

"You catch on quick."

"I was kind of surprised when Max invited me."

Uh-huh. I planned to corner Max at my earliest opportunity and have a little chat with him about that. "I was kind of surprised to see you," I admitted. "When did Max invite you?"

"This afternoon. I was trying to find you at every number I could think of, and I finally reached Max. He didn't know where you were, but he asked me to come see the show."

I noticed Josh didn't come out and ask me where I'd been all day. Which was just as well, because for most of the afternoon I'd been facedown on a massage table at Spa Radiance.

Who could have predicted that the most significant thing to happen to me in England would have been my introduction to spa pampering? But I was now officially addicted. When Josh was talking to Max, I had probably been soaking my toes in a lavender-and-rose-petal-infused milk bath.

"Why were you trying to call me?" I asked him.

He grinned again. "It can wait."

Okay. So what else could we talk about? "I didn't know you liked Martuni's," I tried.

We'd just reached the Lush, and Josh held the door open, which provided him with the opportunity to give me one of those unnerving looks of his. "We'll just add that to the very long list of things you don't know about me."

Which, for some reason, made my lavender-and-rose-petal-infused toes start to tingle.

This was not good.

"TIM?"

Vida and I were in the ladies' room, and it was the first chance I'd gotten to grill her about her date—for a date it was.

She held up her hand for me to high-five her. "Tim!" *Smack*. "Isn't that the weirdest? I mean, one minute we've got our heads together debugging this wicked memory leak, and the next minute he's telling me he's had a crush on me for ages."

"Don't tell me, let me guess," Connie spoke up from the stall. "The next minute you were making out on the conference room table."

"No way," Vida protested. "We broke into the VP's office. She has a couch." She giggled.

"You like him?" I said dubiously. Then I remembered how supportive friends behave. "I mean—you like him!" With enthusiasm this time.

But I still found it hard to believe. In my experience, when a guy you've known and worked with for ages suddenly breaks down and confesses his long-term crush on you, the best strategy is a quick exit and a firm follow-up e-mail.

Not so for Vida, who was nodding vigorously. "I totally like him. I always have. But I didn't realize I was *into* him until he made a move, and then it just hit me, and I was *so* into him." She beamed.

Connie joined us at the mirror. "Sounds like she's got it bad, Becks. What do you think?"

What could I say?

"Thank God for wicked memory leaks."

BACK AT THE TABLE, Shayla was holding the attention of the men in the palm of her hand. Actually, she was holding a quarter in the palm of her hand, but since she was demonstrating her ability to flip it upward and make it land perfectly wedged between her impressive breasts, it's safe to say she had the market on male attention pretty much cornered.

"I don't understand it," Max whispered to me as I sat down. "I don't even like those things, and still I can't look away."

Josh was missing, but he returned soon after we did and

sat next to me. He took in Shayla's bar trick and shot me a grin. "I usually don't go in for matchmaking, but we just have to fix this girl up with Jeremy."

I choked on my mojito. "You're right," I told him. "She's perfect." And then it hit me. I grabbed Josh's arm. "Josh, she's perfect for Vladima!"

The exuberant makeup artist was making Tim blush furiously and Vida giggle uncontrollably by demanding that he pluck the magic quarter out from her low-cut dress. Then she looked over toward me. "What?" she asked. "What's with you two?"

"Shayla," Josh said seriously. "No pressure here, but have you ever considered wearing a long black wig?"

She grinned. "Honey, if that's what you want, you got it."

At which point Josh blushed. Which pleased me for some reason.

"Shayla," I said. "You don't know it yet, but you've just been discovered."

She laughed and fished the quarter out. "Okeydokey."

I'D TAKEN A CAB to the show because I'd known there would be drinking afterward, but I noticed Josh had only one beer, so when he offered me a lift home, I took it.

When he'd parked outside my building, he shut off the engine and walked me to the door, looking as if he wanted to say something. I ransacked my purse for my keys.

"Becks?"

He kept fighting back this smile, and since I didn't know why he was smiling, it was just the slightest bit unsettling. I thought up a brilliant reply.

"Yeah?"

"Do you want me to tell you why I was going nuts trying to find you all afternoon?"

Oh, so he wasn't going to follow Tim's example and confess to a giant crush on me. Whew. That was good news. That was probably good news. Was that good news? How much had I had to drink?

"Becks?"

"Oh. Yeah. Tell me."

He unleashed the smile. "I got a call today."

"Oh?" From his ex? Wanting to get back together? Why did that pop into my head?

"From . . . ?"

"From a guy named Alan Turnbottom."

So probably not his ex. "Alan Turnbottom?"

Josh nodded, doing that trick of his, where he looks at me so I can't look away. "He's an exec at Fox."

"Fox?" I echoed. That was nice. Wait a minute . . . "Fox as in the movie studio?"

Josh nodded, and the wattage on the smile went up a notch. "Fox."

"Fox?"

"They want to talk about making a Vladima movie."

He watched me carefully for a reaction, but as I'd completely frozen, he didn't get one. After a moment, he took the keys from my hand, unlocked the door, and pushed me gently into the lobby. Then he leaned against the open doorway. "You okay?"

I looked at him.

Josh. Real. Not a dream.

"I'm fine."

Fox. Real. Not a dream.

He reached out slowly and moved a stray strand of hair off my face. "You did it, Becks."

Then he was gone, and I was blinking under the fluorescent lights of the lobby, staring at a wall of mailboxes and telling myself I did *not* wish he'd stayed.

Twenty-four

I woke to the sound of Josh's voice, but that was only because when I rolled over to hit the snooze button, I hit PLAY on my answering machine instead.

Over the course of four messages, Josh dropped enticing hints about the possible movie deal and offered vague inducements to call him back immediately. I resolved never to let my cell phone battery die again. His last message informed me that he'd spoken to Max and he'd see me at the show. If I had come home to change after my spa day, I wouldn't have been so completely blindsided by his appearance at the theater. And I probably would have worn a better outfit.

Now why did I think that? But I didn't have time to wonder about it because the next voice on the machine sucked every other thought out of my brain. It wasn't who was calling, it was what he said.

"This is Joe Elliot for Rebecca Mansfield. Rebecca, I'm head of Marketing for WorldWired, and I've been hearing some great things about you. I'd like you to give me a call if you're interested in exploring a fairly high-level opportunity. And if you're not interested, call me anyway and I'll talk you into it."

At this, the voice chuckled and left a local number.

I sat up in bed and reached to make sure my head was still on. WorldWired. The foremost telecommunications firm on the planet. The leader in global wireless communications strategies. The hottest company on every list of hot companies in every hot magazine.

And they wanted me.

I took a minute to jump out of bed and dance around singing "They want me, they want me, they want me" until I saw my reflection in the mirror and realized that big cheese executive types who held high-level positions at WorldWired probably didn't compromise their pre-breakfast dignity by doing the twist in their pony-print jammies.

How could this have happened? Who did I know at WorldWired—or, more important, who knew me? Who could have put in a good word with that charming and obviously brilliant Joe Elliot? Someone I'd worked with in the past must have gone there recently and—

And then it hit me. I sank back onto the bed. I did know someone at WorldWired. I knew their corporate spokesman. The Olympic champion, soccer star, and closeted lover of my oldest friend. I knew Phillip Hastings.

I picked up the phone and dialed. "Max? You darling, darling man. Put the coffee on. I'll be there in thirty minutes."

VIDA OPENED MAX'S DOOR. "What's going on?"

I looked beyond her to Max in the kitchen. "I called Vida," he explained. "With the amount I had to drink last night I didn't think I could handle your level of excitement without reinforcements. Now come have some coffee and tell us what's got you so energized at this ungodly hour."

Vida looked at her watch as I came in. "Maxie, it's ten o'clock. I mean, I'm supposedly telecommuting, but don't you have patients or something?"

He tightened the belt on his bathrobe and gave her a wounded look. "Did you forget about last night already? I cancelled all my appointments today so I could stay home and read the reviews of last night's theatrical triumph."

"Oh." Vida gave me a "whoops" look. "How are they?"

He gestured to a crumpled copy of the *Noe Valley Voice* in his trash can. "I don't want to discuss it." His gaze turned back to me. "Becks, you look like hell. Did you even dry your hair this morning?"

I hadn't. I'd jumped in and out of the shower and tossed on the most convenient clothes in my closet. Then I'd rushed right over, ignoring the fact that if I didn't blow my hair dry, it inevitably curled into a wild mess.

"Who cares about my hair," I trilled, "when I have news this good?" I took the mug Max held and plopped myself down at his table, pausing only to plant a kiss on his forehead. "And when I have friends this fabulous?"

They both looked baffled. Vida asked the obvious question. "Huh?"

I told them about the call from Joe Elliot at WorldWired. They both made very gratifying squealing sounds, but neither of them looked particularly self-satisfied about it.

"Come on," I said. "Which one of you asked Phillip to say something?"

"Phillip?" Vida contracted her brows.

"Phillip. As in Phillip Hastings, the spokesman for WorldWired and your best new buddy from the wedding?"

"Wow," Vida said. "You really think he had something to do with this?"

"Who else?"

"Wow," she repeated. Then she shook her head. "But, Becks, I'm pretty sure we never talked about work stuff. I mean, I told him what I did, but I never talked about you looking for a job." She looked doubtful, as if she was searching her memory. Then she shook her head again. "No, I'm sure I didn't."

We both looked at Max, who was steaming his pores over a cup of Costa Rica's finest. "What?" He looked up. "You think I spent my valuable pillow-talk time discussing your stalled career?"

"Maxie, you're an absolute sweetheart. I don't care what anyone else says." I beamed.

"Becks." He took my mug and held both of my hands, looking a little haggard but completely honest. "There are many, many extremely good reasons to have sex with Phillip Hastings. But getting you a job is not one of them."

"I'm not suggesting you prostituted yourself on my behalf," I explained. "I just don't know why in the world Phillip would have said something about me to WorldWired when I never talked to him about work and he had no reason to do me any favors."

"Are you sure it was him?" Vida asked. "I mean, it's a big company . . ."

"I don't know anyone else there," I insisted. "It had to have been him."

"Well, maybe it was," Vida admitted. "But not because of anything Max or I said."

Then who?

"You don't suppose . . ." Vida hesitated. She looked at Max.

"Overcome with remorse for behaving like such a schmuck"—Max's eyes widened as he picked up on her thought—"the Lord of the Manor has tried to make amends?"

The both turned to me.

Absolutely not. I refused to believe Sir Vile Excrescence had done me any favors whatsoever. "No," I said firmly. "No way."

"Of course not," Vida agreed. "That's crazy. He wasn't even real friends with Phillip, remember? It was Trinny—" She snapped her jaw shut and winced. "Sorry."

"Uh-huh," I said. "I think we can be pretty sure neither of them would be very interested in doing me any favors."

We all thought it over silently for a minute.

"I suppose," concluded Vida, "there's no way of knowing until you call them back."

"Have you called them back?" Max asked.

"I didn't want to look too eager. I thought I'd give it until this afternoon."

"Becks, this sounds like it could be the job you've been lusting after for your entire working life. Do you really think you should play hard to get?"

Max answered for me. "It may take until this afternoon for her to calm down enough to set up an interview without sounding like a work-starved lunatic."

And with that, suddenly, I didn't care who had suggested me to the delightful Joe Elliot of WorldWired. Because whoever it had been, it had worked. I was getting an interview.

I felt another dance coming on, but before I could jump around the kitchen, Max asked a particularly disturbing question.

"What did Josh say about it?"

Shit . . . Josh . . . Vladima . . . Fox . . . Shit.

Vida was looking at me narrowly. "Becks, you're not just going to ditch Josh, are you?"

"Of course not." But it probably wasn't a good sign that I'd forgotten all about him and the movie deal the minute I'd heard Joe Elliot's voice. "Of course not," I repeated. "Especially now." I told them about Fox's interest in Vladima and was rewarded with the morning's second round of excited shrieks.

They had a thousand questions, and I had exactly one answer. "I don't know anything else." I told them. I checked my watch. "But Josh scheduled a meeting for noon." Which had been the very last message on my machine. "I suppose I'll hear all about it then."

I WENT to the nearest coffee joint and settled in with a latte and a lemon scone, pretending to watch the dog owners in Dolores Park while trying to figure out exactly how I was going to handle telling WorldWired that I had this commitment to a cartoon vampire. Somehow, that didn't seem as nerve-wracking as telling Josh about WorldWired.

I kept reassuring myself that everything was going to be fine. If Fox was serious about making a Vladima movie, I could stick around until the deal was finalized, right? I could get everything squared away before making the transition. I mean, WorldWired probably wouldn't expect me to start immediately. And, to be realistic, I hadn't even gotten a job offer yet. But, barring any bitter ex-employees who'd pop up at the eleventh hour to accuse me of being a bitch, I probably would.

Why did I feel like gagging when I thought about telling Josh I was dumping him? I mean, not dumping him, but dumping Vladima. Actually, not dumping anybody, just making a simple and straightforward career move. And not even doing that until I'd fulfilled my commitments.

So why did my chest get all tight when I thought about not working with Vladima and the minions anymore? I'd gotten to be rather fond of the collection of dedicated weirdoes. I'd even gotten to be fond of the immortal vamp herself. I shredded my napkin into neat, precise strips and mentally rejected any possibility that I might also be fond of Josh.

No, the only reason I felt the slightest bit conflicted about talking to WorldWired is that I'd made a professional commitment to help Josh with Vladima's marketing. And really, with a movie in the near future, my work there was done. Besides, I'd never meant it to be anything other than a way to stay busy until a real job came along. A real job such as a high-level position at WorldWired, for example.

I gulped the last of the coffee and headed for the studio.

VLADIMA'S PAD was in chaos. Josh had planned on telling the minions all at once, in a pizza meeting at noon in the break room. But a call from the Fox exec Alan Turnbottom had been answered by Alice, the part-time office manager, and she'd whispered excitedly to Donovan, and he'd said something to Jeremy, and by the time I got there the place was a madhouse.

Josh was standing on someone's desk in the field of cubicles, looking like a mad conductor whose orchestra was running amok. It was clear he had zero chance of bringing the group under control.

Suddenly, as I was swept into the bedlam, there was an unholy, earth-shattering, earsplitting scream. The anarchy ground to a halt, and everyone looked around to see what the hell had just happened.

"Sorry!" Raven's cheerful voice called out. "But it was the only way I could think of to shut you all up so we can hear what Josh is trying to say." The tiny sound engineer grinned mischievously. "And by the way, that's the new shriek for the ENTER button on the Web site." She tried to look modest.

"Thanks, Raven," Josh said. "I think it works. Now will everybody just come grab some pizza so we can talk about this like normal people?"

The meeting didn't last very long because really there wasn't much to say. Josh had accepted an "exploratory lunch meeting" with Alan Turnbottom for Monday, which meant we'd all have a long weekend before we even knew if anything was likely to happen.

But the minions didn't let that get in the way of their wild excitement or their paranoid fears. The tantalizing possibilities of fame and fortune were mixed with large doses of justifiable apprehension.

"Suppose they do something stupid, like cast Anna Nicole or something?"

Which led to a heated debate on the relative talents of

that lady and every other well-endowed actress in Hollywood. The overwhelming consensus was that only Angelina Jolie was worthy to play Vladima.

"Or suppose they want to turn it into some stupid kid's cartoon?"

Fear of the stupid seemed to be the major theme of the objections.

Josh finally called a halt to the speculation and sent everyone home for the day. It was Friday afternoon, and there was no way anything useful could be accomplished with the state they were all in.

"Listen," he said, "Becks and I are going to talk to this guy on Monday, and we're not going to let them do anything stupid, okay? Now just chill."

They chilled. Or at least they drifted off.

I, on the other hand, caved. After everyone had gone but Josh and me, when it would have been the perfect time to tell him about WorldWired, I couldn't do it. I tried to bring up the subject, but my words kept turning around and running away before I'd actually said anything.

Eventually I noticed that Josh was looking at me as if he were afraid I was about to sprout a second head. "Are you all right?"

I nodded. "Fine." I swallowed hard.

He sat on the table and faced me. "Should we talk about this?"

This? Oh, the movie. I shook my head. "Nothing to talk about until we hear what they have to say, right?"

He nodded, still looking at me. "Becks—"

Who knows what he was going to say? All I knew is that I had to get out of there. For one horrible moment

I thought I was going to tear up if I had to look him in the eye.

"Josh, I've really got to go, you know? Give me a call over the weekend if you find out anything more, okay? Bye."

I ran away, too gutless to look back.

An hour later I called Joe Elliot's office and scheduled an interview for Wednesday.

Twenty-five

Between stress about Monday's Hollywood meeting and stress about Wednesday's WorldWired interview, I was a nervous wreck all weekend.

"Come surfing with me," Vida pleaded on Saturday morning. "I swear you'll feel totally better."

But suddenly I felt I had a lot to live for, so I decided I'd pass on being shark bait this once.

"It's Andrew Lloyd Webber night at Martuni's," Max announced gleefully later that day. "Come with me! We'll see how many Sondheim numbers we can sneak in without anyone knowing the difference!" Tempting, but Martuni's meant martinis, and I thought it might be a good idea to live a pure life until Monday.

"Come over for dinner," Connie had begged on Sunday night. "The couple I invited canceled, and if you don't come it's going to be just me, coquilles Saint-Jacques, and Ian." There was a desperation in her voice that foreshadowed an evening of hard work on my part to keep the conversation moving. I mustered up as much regret as possible when I declined.

Finally, it was Monday.

. . .

JOSH PICKED ME UP a half hour before the meeting. I had dressed in an impeccable fawn pantsuit accessorized with the tiniest black leather belt imaginable and a killer pair of Christian Lacroix pumps from my London shopping spree. I had also channeled my inner Shayla and done a fairly decent job on the hair and makeup. After all, Alan Turnbottom was probably used to movie stars, so I didn't want to look like some northern California nature girl.

Josh, of course, was in black.

We headed for the Waterfront, a seafood bistro at Pier 7 on the Embarcadero. I'd been to the "casual" dining area downstairs before but never to the "elegant" dining room upstairs. Today we'd be lunching elegantly on Alan Turnbottom's expense account.

"This should be nice," I said as the valet whisked the car away. "I just wish I didn't feel like throwing up."

Josh cracked his first grin of the day. "I'm glad it's not just me."

He placed his hand on the small of my back and propelled me forward to meet our fate.

ALAN TURNBOTTOM was Hollywood. We knew him immediately by the clothes (black cashmere V-neck over pristine white T-shirt), the hair (clearly hours of artful tousling had been necessary to achieve the perfect I-don't-care-what-I-look-like look), and the phone (minuscule and silver and permanently implanted in his left ear).

He stood to greet us, still talking to whomever (George

Clooney? Russell Crowe? these thoughts did not have a soothing effect on me). He took five more calls before the entrees came, pausing before answering each to apologize (insincerely) and tell us how fantastic it was to meet us and how he loved Vladima's high concept.

Josh shot me a look as the phone rang again. "At least the view's nice," he muttered.

I had to admit, it was. A pretty summer day with a pretty blue sky and lots of pretty white sailboats to-ing and fro-ing under the Bay Bridge. But I hadn't come for the damn view.

"I'm so sorry," Mr. Hollywood said for the umpteenth time, snapping the marvel of modern communication shut again.

"That's an adorable phone," I held out my hand. "May I take a look? I'm shopping for a new one."

He handed it over cluelessly, and I promptly shut it off and plopped it into my purse. "There, that's better," I said with a bright smile. "Now we can really talk."

Turnbottom slipped right past astonished into amused. "Am I ever going to get that back?"

"I'll make you a deal," I told him. "I get to keep the phone until dessert so we can chat about how much you love Vladima"—another smile—"and in return I'll tell you whether the flourless chocolate cake or the crème brûlée will go better with your coffee."

He turned to Josh. "Does she always get what she wants?"

That enigmatic Josh smile. "Why else would we be here?"

"All right," Turnbottom agreed. "It's a deal." He raised his sparkling San Pellegrino in a toast. "May it be the first of many."

I took a deep breath. Game time.

. . .

TURNBOTTOM WAS QUITE A TALKER. He talked about the youth demographic, and the necessity of appealing to both males and females in the critical eighteen-to-twenty-four range. He talked about synergy and branding and cross-promotional opportunities. Once he began to talk, it took me about two minutes to realize he had nothing whatsoever to do with getting a movie made. He was a marketing guy. It takes one to know one.

I let him babble on, using phrases like "goth/skateboarder/X-games vibe" and "major opportunity in action figures" while I speared my seafood and tried to come up with a strategy. I had plenty of time because he was apparently doing this speech from memory and required no feedback or input from us.

It wasn't until the waiter cleared our plates that Turnbottom finally paused for the praise he clearly expected. "Well?" He flashed a smile that had probably cost more than my loft. "What do you think? Can we do business?"

I did a quick Josh check and realized he wasn't just disappointed. He was mad. He gave Turnbottom a look I wouldn't have wished on Vladima's worst enemy. "Business?" he said acidly.

Hollywood was unperturbed. "I know you're used to thinking artistically, but you have to understand that ultimately moviemaking, like . . . cartooning . . . is a business. I'm sure you have to worry about your bottom line, right?" Another million-dollar flash of teeth.

"Actually, I don't." Josh's tone could have curdled the foam on Turnbottom's cappuccino. "That's what I have Becks for."

They both turned to me. Turnbottom's smile faltered just a bit. "So, Becks," he said conspiratorially. "You haven't said very much. I was beginning to wonder if you were just a pretty face." Which he clearly didn't realize was a truly stupid thing to say.

They were still watching me.

Fuck it.

I leaned forward so I could speak quietly.

"Alan, when you get on your plane tonight and you think back on this meeting, you're going to wonder why Josh brought along the passive-aggressive bitch."

Four eyebrows went up.

"But here's the thing," I continued. "I'm not being passive-aggressive here. I am well and truly passive. Because, in all honesty, I don't give a good damn whether you ever make a movie out of Vladima." I leaned back and shrugged. "I really don't care. Because right now, we own the demographic you've just spent all afternoon describing. We're already there. And not just with some of the kids, but with the hip kids—the trendsetters."

I caught the faintest whiff of an eye roll, and suddenly I wanted to hurt this man.

"The truth is"—I leaned in again, face to face with him—"there are going to be Vladima posters on the wall of every dorm room this fall, and the only question you need to ask yourself is whether you want the Fox logo to be on the lower right-hand corner of them. When you figure that out, you call someone who can talk to us about getting a movie made. Until then, I think we're done."

I slid his phone across the table to him, rose, and walked away from the table, praying to God that Josh would give him one of his patented darkly intense genius stares and follow me.

He did.

THE TROUBLE WAS, all Josh gave me were a few of the same stares. The one while we waited for the valet to get his car was pretty fierce, and I took it as a fairly clear indicator that I was about to be fired. The one while I was buckling my seat belt (with hands that would not stop shaking) kicked the intensity up a notch. Neither of them encouraged conversation. Besides, I couldn't think of anything to say.

Josh drove wordlessly for about a block, then abruptly pulled over into a loading zone. He gave me another look, opened his mouth to say something, then shook his head and got out of the car. He crossed the wide sidewalk of the Embarcadero until he was at the water's edge, then gripped the railing with both hands and stared out at the bay.

I let my breath out slowly and told myself that if he fired me, at least I wouldn't have to tell him about World-Wired.

I got out and went to the railing. This time he didn't look at me. He just started shaking his head. Finally, I couldn't take it anymore. "Josh?"

Nothing.

"Josh, come on!"

He gripped the railing tighter.

"Look, Josh, just call Turnbottom and tell him you fired me, and that I don't speak for you or Vladima, and that I'm an unstable, alcoholic, lunatic—"

He finally faced me. "Unbelievable."

"I know, I get that way sometimes. Poor impulse control. It was when he said the 'just a pretty face' thing, and—"

"*You* are unbelievable."

Hang on, he didn't sound mad. In fact, he sounded . . . what was it?

"Becks, did you even see that guy's face? And have you ever met a bigger asshole?"

I suddenly realized he wasn't shaking his head in a what-have-you-done sort of way, he was shaking his head in an I-can't-believe-what-you-did sort of way.

"You were *amazing*!" He grabbed my shoulders, and the look he gave me then wasn't darkly intensely anything. It was dazzling and open and unbelieving, and the heat from his hands on my shoulders burned right through to my skin. Suddenly I couldn't think straight, and my stomach did a series of backflips down onto the pavement and back again.

"Becks."

He broke the spell and I broke away. I blinked and tried to pull myself together. "I'm glad you were pleased," I said, every inch the professional. "It was a calculated risk, but—"

He was shaking his head again. "Max warned me about this."

I swallowed. "About what?"

"That you'd be completely oblivious."

"Oblivious to what?"

Which is when he muttered "Jesus, Becks," pulled me close, and kissed me.

And the earth failed to move.

It was a good kiss. It definitely got a passing grade. But it was not a great kiss. Not a Hollywood kiss. It was . . .

fine. And I was hugely relieved. Josh had no effect on me. Thank God.

He pulled away and gave me a look. One of the dark intense ones. It was a lot more effective than the kiss had been.

He spoke. "Think we can do better if you're expecting it this time?"

I couldn't answer because I was trying not to burst into flames from the heat in his eyes. He nodded slowly, holding me in place with that look. Then he moved his hands to firm positions at the back of my head and the base of my spine, and he went in again.

This one was a bone-dissolving, you'd-swear-you-were-levitating-six-inches-off-the-ground, leaves-you-with-no-choice-but-to-whimper kind of a kiss.

And there was a lag time, a blissful period of unconscious, unthinking response, when I was kissing back for all I was worth, before it hit me.

This was Josh.

Twenty-six

"Oh . . . my . . . *God!*"

I'd planned on meeting Vida at Max's that night to tell them all about the movie deal, but that now paled in comparison to the events that had unfolded after it.

"What did you do?"

"How was it?"

"Did you kiss him back?"

"Right there on the sidewalk?"

I held up my arms in defense. They finally wore themselves out, except for one final "Oh . . . my . . . *God!*" from Vida.

"Okay, seriously, Becks," Max perched on the coffee table in front of me. "What did you do?"

"I . . ." I flushed with the memory. "I returned fire."

Vida squealed, which was a little annoying. "And?"

I shrugged. "And then I realized how ridiculous the whole thing was, and I ran across the street and hopped on the light rail train."

They both yelled at once.

"You *what?*"

I held up my arms again. "I ran away, all right? Why do you think I'm still dressed like this? I'm afraid to go home. I've been riding Muni all afternoon waiting for you guys to get off work." I registered their staring faces. "What?"

Max looked away. "I think we can all agree that the key word in that explanation was *afraid*."

Vida nodded. "You think Josh will be waiting for you at your place?"

I squirmed a little. "Maybe."

"And you don't want to see him?"

"Of course not!"

"Why not?" Max asked. "Because he's nuts about you and he's perfect for you? Or because you're nuts about him and you don't want to admit it?"

"I am *not* nuts about him!"

"Oh, Becks," Vida said. "You are *so* nuts about him."

I ignored her. "And why," I turned on Max, "why is it that right before the kiss, Josh said something about you having warned him that I'd be oblivious? What the hell have you been conspiring about?"

I thought he'd crumble like the killer in the last reel of a Bogart movie, but no. "I haven't been conspiring about anything. I just had one little chat with him a while ago."

"How long ago?"

"After you showed me that storyboard for Vladima and her new partner."

"Did you really?" Vida asked him.

"Why?" I wailed.

"Because it was obvious that Josh has a huge thing for you, and I wanted to know if it was some sort of twisted fixation or if he really cares about you."

"Max, why on earth—"

"Because *I* care about you, you idiot!" He was angry now and didn't want to hear what I thought about his behind-the-scenes manipulations. "And I know you're clueless about guys who fall for you, and I wanted to make sure Josh wasn't some sort of creep who was going to haul you off to some cave and put you in a black leather bustier to act out his sick fantasies!"

That shut me up, but not Vida. "Max, you're not serious! Josh?"

He sat down and ran a hand across his face. "No. Not Josh. When I talked to him, he was . . ." Max sighed and met my eyes. "He's a normal guy who's crazy about you but smart enough to see the barbed wire and 'keep out' signs you've got posted everywhere."

"I do not," I said icily, "have barbed wire."

But Vida looked doubtful. "Maybe . . ."

"Not you too?"

"Just listen, Becks." She drew her legs up onto the sofa so she could face me. "You remember the date-laziness theory?"

Across the room, Max snorted. I held my empty martini glass out to him. "I'm going to need another of these."

Vida went on. "Well, I think Connie and I may have been a little off base about that."

"You think?" Max was as heavy with the sarcasm as he was light with the vermouth.

"Quiet, Max," Vida answered him. She focused again. "I think maybe you aren't just lazy about who you go out with. I think maybe part of you only wants to go out with guys who are . . ."

"Losers?" Max handed me the replenished glass.

She turned to him. "You're not helping." Back to me. "Look, if you only go out with men who are impossibly wrong for you, then it's impossible for you to risk actually getting into a real relationship with one of them, right? And as long as there's no risk, you're comfortable. But if all of a sudden you started going out with a guy who was right for you, things might get . . . *real* or something, and that's totally scary."

I rejected the theory immediately. With proof. "No. What about the LOTM? He wasn't a loser and I wanted a real relationship with him—"

"Oh, please," Max said. "There was nothing real about him. You picked the phoniest guy in the British Isles. There was no way that was going to work out."

I looked at Vida. "He was pretty impossible, Becks," she said. "I mean, he was a liar and a cheat, in addition to the gorgeous-jet-setting-aristocratic-playboy thing." She winced. "He was just a different flavor of impossible than what you were used to."

Great. I leaned back into the cushions and closed my eyes. "So let me get this straight. I ran away from Josh not because it was a wildly inappropriate and unprofessional thing for him to have pounced on me after a business meeting. I ran away from Josh because he's . . . right for me? And I'm . . . what? Afraid of commitment?"

Vida turned to Max. "Do you think it's fear of commitment? Because I'm thinking it's more a fear-of-intimacy thing."

I stood. "That's it. I'm out of here."

"Running away again?" Max asked sweetly.

"This is bullshit psychobabble and I'm going home." I grabbed my purse and headed for the door.

"Becks—" Vida called after me.

But I was in no mood to listen to any more.

I SPENT THE NEXT DAY and a half reading a stack of books on the state of the wireless communications industry. My future was with WorldWired, not with some cartoon vampire or her sexually frustrated creator, and I had to catch up on the last year and a half of technology breakthroughs if I was going to slay them at Wednesday's interview.

I screened all my calls. The last thing I needed was to break my concentration with some stupid conversation about relationships and feelings with Josh. But he didn't call. There weren't even any suspicious hang-ups I could assume were his.

Good. Now if only I could stop jumping two feet into the air every time some damn telemarketer called, I'd be fine.

Tuesday night I took two Tylenol PMs and washed them down with two large swigs of Johnny Walker Black straight from the bottle. That had always been my secret recipe for a good night's sleep when I'd been stressed out at work. In fact, back in the boom times, it had been my bedtime ritual more often than not. With one chewable antacid chaser to prevent whiskey-induced nighttime heartburn, I was ready for bed.

Where I did *not* think about Josh.

WEDNESDAY MORNING. Interview day. I walked into the San Francisco headquarters of WorldWired Incorporated at ten-thirty on Wednesday morning looking and feeling like their latest corporate star.

Joe Elliot was boyishly cute, blond, and British. When he was introducing himself, I was struck with the random piece of trivia that the lead singer of the eighties metal group Def Leppard had been named Joe Elliot. My college roommate had had a major crush on him. For one delirious moment I wondered if the man chatting amiably and leading me to a conference room could be the former headbanger. Then I came to my senses, and said, "Oh yes, thank you. Water would be lovely."

When he stepped out to get it, I had a moment to pull my head out of VH1 Classics and back to business. I'd wasted the opportunity to get a feel for the corporate climate on the walk to the conference room, but if the room itself was any indication, WorldWired didn't scrimp on the finer things.

The lighting was soft but clear. The wood paneling was actually wood, as was the richly polished long table. The chairs were comfortable, and the control for the video-conferencing monitor looked like something Tom Cruise would fool around with in one of his spy movies.

The view of Telegraph Hill and the bay was glorious. I had to tear myself away from it to do a quick check of the corporate portraits lining the long wall opposite the window. Self-satisfied-looking white men. Big surprise.

Joe Elliot returned, followed by a lackey carrying a crystal water pitcher and two crystal glasses. God forbid bottled Evian should cheapen the ambiance.

Now where did that thought come from? What was the matter with me? And what's wrong with having plush office space? I was supposed to be presenting myself as a finely tuned corporate asset, and I was having serious problems with both my focus and my attitude. Not good.

The lackey withdrew, and Elliot relaxed into the chair opposite me. "So, Becks Mansfield. We meet at last."

How to respond, given that I'd just heard of him five days ago? "You've got a nice place here." Accompanied by an easy smile.

"We like it." He may have winked. Or I may have hallucinated it. "I can't tell you what tremendous things I've been hearing about you."

I'm the first to admit that I'm very, very good at what I do. But, seriously, it's not like I'm famous. "Really?" I took a sip from the heavy glass and was careful to replace it on its coaster. "Hearing things from whom?" Phillip Hastings, surely. But I still didn't actually know that for sure.

Elliot laughed and gestured to the line of portraits. "Only our chairman, you clever girl."

What? I searched the line of jowly capitalists again. Who the hell did I know? Nobody . . .

And then I saw him. Almost unrecognizable in a gray pinstripe. Only the slightest of twinkles linking him to the man I'd last seen hauling a sizable white swan out of Sir I-Can't-Believe-This-Is-Happening's lake.

"George?"

Elliot laughed. "Yes, *George*." He emphasized the name in a knowing way. "The old earl doesn't often leave his estate at Lakewood to interest himself in the business anymore, but he gets the whole place buzzing when he does."

I had gripped the underside of the table to keep from falling over. George wasn't a gardener. George, according to the discreet silver plaque under this portrait, was the ninth Earl of Windercestershire. And the chairman of the board of WorldWired.

Elliot was still nattering on pleasantly, so I had time to reel mentally while maintaining a politely interested expression. Of course I'd known from my research that the chairman was a semi-retired earl. But I'd never seen a picture, or if I had, I hadn't looked at it hard enough to realize it was . . . *George*? And . . . wait a minute . . . if I'd just heard correctly, George—not Sir Charles—was the Lord of Lakewood Manor. Dear God, did that make him Charles's *father*?

"So, anyway." Elliot was obliviously winding up the exchanging-pleasantries portion of the day. "Shall we get down to business?"

I gave up trying to remember exactly how many sordid details I'd given WorldWired's chairman about his son's sexual proclivities while sobbing on a swan boat, and concentrated on applying a properly confident, competent, and professional expression to my face.

"Please."

THINGS WENT AS WELL as could be expected. I spoke to five people, and I got myself into gear about halfway through the second interview. After that, Joe Elliot took me to lunch upstairs in the executive dining room. I hadn't realized there were still companies that had executive dining rooms, and the kind of clearly defined social strata they implied. But apparently at WorldWired these anachronisms were still accepted as a matter of course.

I fully redeemed myself with Elliot over lunch. He may have been wondering what the hell George had seen in me when he'd turned me over to the first interviewer, but by the time we'd finished our excellent biscotti and espresso, I recognized the gleam in his eye as that of a man who had to have me.

Professionally speaking, of course.

And I wasn't wrong. After the last of the three afternoon interviews, Joe Elliot entered the conference room with a slim leather portfolio in his hands and a let's-make-a-deal smile on his face.

We handled the preliminaries fairly quickly. He asked me what I wanted, and I knew full well he'd already figured out what he'd give me. The only trick was to not ask for less. I'd played this game before. Finally, with a resigned grin, he slid the portfolio across the table toward me.

"I don't want you to evaluate this offer now, Becks," he explained. "I want you to take it home and study it. Give me a call in the next day or so and let me know if it works for you. I think you'll find it's very generous."

I ran a fingertip lightly over the supple leather that encased my future career. "Thank you, Joe. I will."

He gave me one last conspiratorial smile. "I don't mind telling you we usually don't act this quickly. But we're all in agreement that you've got just what we've been looking for. We need a shark in this position, Becks. A no-holds-barred, take-no-prisoners winner who's bottom-line all the way and doesn't care if she puts a few backs up as long as she gets the job done. You seem to have all of that. You're a perfect . . ." He flailed at the last word, but I suspected it might have been "bitch."

"Fit," I supplied

He laughed. "See? We're finishing each other's sentences already."

It couldn't have gone better in my wildest imagination.

And my imagination can get pretty wild. So five minutes later I stepped onto the street with the expectation of a fantastic surge of energy and satisfaction.

And why not? I deserved it. This was everything I'd worked and planned for.

So why not?

Twenty-seven

Being fabulous takes it out of you. By the time I got home I was craving my fluffy pillows and feather-soft sheets the way an addict craves a fix. I didn't care that I'd promised to meet Max and Vida at Citizen Cake for a celebratory slice of Retro Tropical Shag. I just wanted sleep. And if passion-fruit-filled, coconut-covered goodness couldn't distract me from my bed, nothing could.

Except the sight of six Hartmann suitcases piled in the center of my living room.

"What the—" I had a momentary panic, then reasoned that masked marauding burglars probably didn't bring a matched set of luggage (with makeup case) to their crime scenes.

"Hello!" I yelled up at the sleeping loft, where—if I wasn't mistaken—I could hear the shower running. "Who's there?"

Josh? For one bizarre moment I imagined him coming out of my bathroom wearing a towel around his waist and saying, "How was your day, dear?"

I shook my head. That would never happen. When the sounds of the shower stopped, I shouted again. "Hey!"

"Becks?"

Not masked marauding burglars. Not Josh.

"Connie?"

She stuck her dripping head over the half-height wall that gave the sleeping loft a measure of privacy. "Becks, I'm so glad you're home!"

She headed down the spiral staircase, pulling a yellow polka-dot terry bathrobe (mine) tight around her as she descended. Talking.

"I didn't know where you were or when you'd be back, so I used the key you gave me that one time, remember? When you went to Amsterdam for that thing and you wanted me to let in the cable guy? So I still had it and I didn't know where else to go, so I used it, and I hope you don't mind, but when you weren't here I wasn't sure, and"

I would have been well within my rights to slap her. It was done all the time to hysterical people. I'd seen it in the movies.

"Connie, calm down. Of course it's all right that you're here." I looked at the suitcases, then back to her. "Why are you here?"

She stood up straight and cinched my belt tighter. "I've left Ian."

So we went to Citizen Cake after all. I needed backup.

"YOU LEFT HIM?" Vida said, for about the fifth time.

Connie nodded and swooped Max's After Midnight cake out from under his upraised fork.

"Hey," he protested.

"I just left my husband," she hissed.

She won.

We were all a little stunned. Even though we'd all had our reservations about Ian, and even though we knew perfectly well that Connie's staff had a pool going on how long the boss's marriage would last, and even though we each, in moments of frustration over the whole elaborate wedding, had been known to mutter "I give them six months," we were still stunned.

Connie chose to deal with her emotions by ranting at hyperspeed and self-medicating with high-end pastries. We all took turns nodding our heads.

"I mean, I had certain *expectations*, you know? I thought once we were married all the stupid things he did that annoyed me would just seem unimportant, you know?" She flagged down a waiter and demanded a German chocolate cookie and a lemon tart. "But all of a sudden it seemed like there was this whole long *list* of things, and it just seemed to get more and more *huge*, and then it was like *everything* annoyed me. How he holds his knife and fork in that stupid European way, and how he crosses his legs like a girl, and . . ."

Connie was right. It was a long list.

THE UPSIDE OF connie's life crisis was that it took my mind off WorldWired and the staggering figure I'd found listed in Joe Elliot's slim leather portfolio under the line item "Annual Salary." It was an offer no sane person would refuse. So there was absolutely no reason for the little doubt seedling in my belly. If I was queasy, it was due to overdosing on the cake. I didn't want to think about it, and—thanks to Connie—for a while I wouldn't have to.

At some point, someone (possibly me) suggested that we step away from the cake and adopt a more sensible approach to the crisis. Drinking.

I dragged them all back to my place and put Max in charge of the bar.

Connie had grown more introspective on the way over. She'd gotten to the point where she was questioning every decision she'd ever made.

"I mean you just *do* things, don't you? You go to college, and then you pick a job you think you'll like, and then, whether you like it or not, you stick with it because it's what you're invested in and God help you if you have to start over, right?

"And it's the same with relationships, isn't it? I mean, you just *date* someone, for God's sake, and the next thing you know you're *living* with him and you don't remember when, exactly, you decided to stick with this *particular* investment, but you're picking out a huge white dress and it's way too late to cut your losses and start again—"

Max got a word in. "Isn't that what you're doing now?"

"Sure, *now*!" she wailed.

EVENTUALLY CONNIE ran out of steam, and eventually Max and Vida helped me make up the fold-out couch for her, and eventually she drifted off and they drifted away, and eventually I was able to crawl into my own bed.

Where I couldn't fall asleep to save my life.

The thing Connie had said about making a seemingly unimportant choice and finding yourself stuck with it had gotten to me. Not in terms of men, of course. But in terms of a job, a career, a life.

I'd gotten into marketing because it had seemed like the most exciting aspect of a business. You got to travel a lot, and you got to do a lot of your stuff in the spotlight. Bold, persuasive presentations and brash, groundbreaking ideas were your stock in trade. Not like the finance geeks or strategy wonks. Marketing had seemed . . . cool.

But in all the time I'd been working my ass off and getting ahead bit by bit, I'd never really stopped to check and make sure my initial assessment of the situation had been correct. Was marketing cool? And did it make a difference whether I was marketing animation software, a butt-kicking vampire sex bomb, or corporate telecommunications solutions?

According to Connie's theory, this job offer was the inevitable result of my years of investment. And my career was the only thing I'd ever invested in. It wasn't as if I had a fallback plan. Which is exactly why I'd been walking around with that hollow feeling ever since I'd been laid off from Megaware.

But when I checked that statement for accuracy, it didn't ring true. Yes, I had been a member of the shell-shocked digerati for a good long time after the layoff. But lately . . . lately I'd been better. In fact, it could be argued that lately I'd been better (if not richer or more powerful or more influential or more corporate) than I'd been in years. Maybe ever.

I felt better. I looked better. I didn't have to regularly knock myself out to get to sleep at night, and I didn't wake up with that sickness in the pit of my stomach that I called energy. I'd spent more time with my friends, and I liked that. I'd even built up something interesting with Vladima's marketing. And I'd built up something interesting with Vladima's creator.

Josh.

It was the last coherent thought I had before sleep.

WHEN I STUMBLED DOWN to the kitchen in the morning, I found a bright, cheerful note from Connie.

> Becks,
>
> Thanks for everything! I feel so much better today! I'm going to work! I'll call a realtor about finding a new place this afternoon! I'll pick up something good for dinner tonight!
>
> Con

She came back an hour later in tears. We ordered pizza and spent the rest of the day watching every Jane Austen movie available on DVD.

FRIDAY MORNING I had a choice. I could spend another day wallowing with Connie, or I could haul my ass down to the studio and face Josh. I was scheduled for a recording session at ten, and I could take that as an opportunity to tell Josh about the WorldWired job. Or I could drink cocoa and keep Connie company through an Audrey Hepburn film festival.

Frankly, I was leaning toward denial and *Sabrina.*

Then Vida knocked on the door.

"I got the good salty bagels from Katz, and I've made reservations for massages and things at La Belle." She swept past me, deposited the bagels on the kitchen counter, and gave Connie a quick hug and appraising look. "How much time did you spend crying yesterday?"

"Hours." I answered for Connie, who was only capable of a shrug.

Vida seemed to notice me for the first time. "Why aren't you dressed? Don't you have to be at the studio in like half an hour?"

"How did you know?"

She rolled her eyes. "You only mentioned it every fifteen seconds when we were drinking the other night."

"Did I?" The way I remembered it we'd only talked about Connie's problems.

"What's the matter with you?" Vida's hands were on her hips, and she looked at me the way the school nurse had whenever I'd tried to fake the flu on chemistry-test days.

"I thought I'd stay home and help Connie out," I offered.

Vida's eyes narrowed. "Have you even talked to Josh since The Incident? Does he even know about WorldWired yet?"

Connie perked up a little. "What's The Incident? What am I missing?"

I hadn't told her about Josh and the kiss. I kind of figured my romantic problems paled in comparison with hers.

"I'll tell you all about it later," Vida said. "I took the day off so Becks wouldn't have to miss her session at the studio and you wouldn't have to be alone."

Which caused Connie to burst into tears (again) and me to realize I didn't have a choice in the matter.

I was going to see Josh.

Twenty-eight

I let myself in to the studio at 9:58 A.M. precisely to find the place deserted. No surprise—it was still a little early by minion standards. There was a light on in the break room, so I figured Josh was making tea and we'd be able to talk privately. I took a deep breath.

As I got closer to the break room, I heard the unmistakable sound of Vladima's dialogue ("Kneel before me and die, villain!"), but *not* in the unmistakable voice of Vladima's voiceover artist (me).

Had Josh already heard about WorldWired and replaced me? Or worse, had he not heard about WorldWired and replaced me anyway because of that damn kiss?

How dare he!

I marched into the kitchen prepared for battle and found Raven deep in serious conversation with my hairdresser. Not a Josh in sight.

"Okeydokey," Shayla said to Raven. "More like '*kneel* before *me* and'—Hey, Becks!" Shayla spotted me in the doorway and gave a very un-Vladima finger wave. "Raven's teaching me how to be just like you!"

"God help you."

I'd totally forgotten that Shayla was scheduled to come in to try on the Vladima costume that morning. And that I should have been there an hour ago. "Sorry I'm late."

"No worries," Shayla said brightly. "I think we've made a lot of progress." She looked tremendously pleased with herself.

"Thanks for helping out, Raven."

The tiny sound engineer, swathed in a full black skirt and black poncho sort of thing, looked more likely to be giving instruction in the proper serving temperature for eye-of-newt casserole than doling out acting tips. She waved away my appreciation.

"This one's not bad. She'll need to work on lowering her voice a bit if she's going to sound anything like the real Vladima—" Raven looked momentarily flustered. "I mean you—oh, you know what I mean."

"I've got CDs of all your recordings," Shayla said. "I'm going to listen to them constantly until I've got it right."

Odd. Of course I had realized that someone else was going to dress as Vladima—which hadn't for one instant been something I'd ever wanted to do. And I was happy we'd picked Shayla for the part. She had the classic comic book babe figure and could work wonders with wigs and makeup to get the rest of the look right. Plus, with her personality she'd probably be able to spend hours in the ComixCon booth talking to fans without wanting to slap anyone.

Still . . . I'd placed the orders for Vladima's costume and Vladima's boots, and everything else a real-life Vladima would require, but it had never really hit me that someone else was going to be Vladima's voice at the convention.

I mean, Vladima's body was one thing, but Vladima's voice . . . it felt odd. Really odd.

Which was the perfect description for the look Raven was giving me. "Are you all right, Becks?" Her bright little eyes didn't miss a thing.

"Fine."

"Great, then why don't you find the costume for Shayla? We can get started recording while she tries it on."

I must have misheard her. "Get started recording? Is Josh around?"

Raven smiled in a way that made me think I'd just confirmed something for her. "Josh couldn't make it this morning. He asked me to take your session."

"You?" I realized how rude that had sounded but couldn't think of how to make up for it.

"I do all the voiceover recordings except yours, you know." She was looking up at me like a curious black bird, and I suddenly realized why she went by the name Raven.

"You do?"

"Of course," she said briskly. "I have no idea why Josh has been doing you all this time."

Shayla stifled a giggle. I probably flushed.

"Let me get that costume."

I couldn't get out of there fast enough.

"OKAY, BECKS, TAKE IT FROM 'What can I do for you, Doctor Black?'"

Here's something else that was odd—Raven's voice coming through my headphones as I sat alone in the recording booth. I'd never realized how much the sound of Josh's voice had soothed me when we'd worked. How it had relaxed me. How it had made me—

"Becks!" Raven's sharp cry made me jump. "Can you hear me?"

I looked over at her, perched in Josh's room at Josh's soundboard, and gave her a thumbs-up.

Where the hell was Josh?

IT WASN'T UNTIL AN HOUR LATER, when Raven was finished with me, that I was able to answer that question.

I'd emerged from the recording booth to the unmistakable sounds of minions in full-riot mode. Apparently Shayla was a hit. A quick trip down the hall to the cubeyard confirmed her status as the reigning sexual fantasy object of Vladima's largely dateless staff.

"Becks!" She spotted me and came bounding over, with alarming results to her . . . do you still call it décolletage when the neckline plunges all the way down to the navel?

"Shayla, you look . . ." Words failed me. She'd poured herself into the costume and zipped herself into the thigh-high patent leather platform boots. The black wig was long and luxurious, and the pale makeup with scarlet lips and deeply shadowed eyes was . . . "perfect."

She broke character completely by squealing in delight, which had a profound effect on Jeremy, who stood back and regarded her silently with worshipful adoration.

"Josh says I completely freaked him out," Shayla told me, clapping her hands with glee.

"Josh?"

"He's in his office." When she swiveled at the waist and pointed behind her, I thought Jeremy might go into spasms.

"Thanks." I went around the corner and saw Raven in Josh's office. What a quick little bird she was. As I got closer, I noticed that the door was closed. The door was never closed. Josh was looking at something on his monitor, then looking at Raven, then back to the monitor. It took a minute for him to notice me on the other side of the glass.

Our eyes met and I froze. There was a flash of . . . something . . . in his look, then heat, pain, anger. It was over in an instant, leaving me feeling like someone had run a wooden stake through my heart.

He broke away and turned his attention back to Raven. He seemed to be concentrating very hard on whatever the hell she was saying.

I stood there, being ignored, until I could draw a breath again. Then I grabbed my bag, cut quickly through the crowd of minions, and half-stumbled out the door to the street. I pulled out my cell phone and dialed.

I got his voice mail, thank God.

"Hi, Joe, it's Becks Mansfield. I'd like to accept the offer. I'll see you at WorldWired in two weeks."

I MADE TWO STOPS on the way home. Cheesecake and Katharine Hepburn movies. I figured between Connie's separation and whatever the hell had gotten into me, we'd make a weekend of it.

I unlocked my door calling Connie's name. She'd left me a note.

Becks,

I feel so much better after having spent the day with Vida. She really helped put things in perspective.

I finally got up the guts to call my folks and tell them the fortune they spent on the wedding might have just as well been tossed into the bay. We're going out to dinner and I might spend the night at their place, so don't wait up for me.

Thanks for everything. Oh, and the detoxifying aromatherapy treatment at the spa really seemed to work—you should try it!

Con

I looked around the empty loft and realized that if I was going to wallow, I was going to wallow alone.

I couldn't face it. Instead I picked up the phone, figuring if Vida could turn Connie around, surely she could talk some sense into me.

I was even willing to try aromatherapy.

Twenty-nine

Vida arrived with strawberry sauce for the cheesecake and an armload of yoga videos.

"Your mind-body connection is all out of whack," she informed me. "Neither is listening to the other." She'd been getting all Zen ever since she'd started dating Tim. "No wonder you're a wreck."

"I'm not a wreck!"

She pointed an accusing finger at the pile of DVDs I'd just rented. "*Summertime*? *The Rainmaker*? You've got a spinster film fest and a billion calories on your table and you don't think you're in a little trouble here?"

She called Max. Her end of the conversation went something like "Yes, I know it's Friday night and you have three parties, but I also know you wouldn't be caught dead at any of them before eleven, so get your ass over here. Becks needs us."

I winced. I hate to be needy. I don't like being weak and I don't like being dependent. Hell, I don't even like being taken to the airport.

But the truth was, for reasons I couldn't begin to figure out on my own, I felt needy. All I really wanted was to put on my fuzzy slippers and have people say nice things to me. Things like "There, there" or "Everything will be fine."

Because—and this is where I didn't understand myself at all—everything *was* fine. I'd just landed my goddamn dream job, and once Josh got over that goddamn kiss and we got back to a normal, professional relationship, everything would be goddamn perfect.

Vida disagreed.

"I can't believe you still haven't talked to Josh. What are you so afraid of?"

"I'm not afraid!"

"Right. You're just running away every time you see him for the exercise."

"I'm not—" Well, perhaps the way I'd left the studio that morning could have been construed as flight. "I'm angry with him. There's a difference."

She gave me severely raised eyebrows, so I elaborated.

"He should have had the decency to call and apologize for his behavior the other day." Even I realized I sounded like a prim version of Marion the Librarian, but I went on.

"Or he could have kept our recording date—appointment—this morning, or at the very least acknowledged my existence when I stood outside his *closed* door!"

Vida wasn't buying it. "Did you ever stop to think you might have hurt him? That he wasn't just being rude? That maybe he's trying to protect himself from you now that he's finally made a move and you've totally rejected him?"

I remembered the look on his face through the glass wall and felt that stake go through my heart again.

"Listen, Becks," Vida adopted a less accusatory tone, "I know it's terrifying to start something new. Especially with someone you're already friends with. There's just so much more at risk if things don't work out, you know? I mean, when Tim and I got together, I was totally stressed about what could happen if we broke up and still had to work together."

I nodded, glad to hear I wasn't the only one to worry about the consequences of inappropriate romances.

"But the thing is," she went on, "one day I started thinking about what could happen if we *don't* break up."

"What could happen?" I asked.

"We could live happily ever after." She smiled one of those Renaissance Madonna smiles. Radiant.

And extremely irritating. But before I could respond, the doorbell rang.

Max, thank God. And in full take-charge mode.

"All right," he announced, flinging off his jacket and checking his watch. "I've never met a romantic problem I couldn't solve in under thirty minutes, so mix me a cocktail and tell me what's going on."

"I don't have a romantic problem," I explained. "I don't know what my problem is. I've just accepted the kind of job I've been lusting after for my entire adult life, and instead of going out to celebrate I feel like complete shit. And through no fault of my own"—I stressed this point—"I haven't even been able to discuss the situation with my current employer."

"Uh-huh." Max reached for the cocktail shaker, as I hadn't leaped into service quickly enough. "And when does this feeling of complete shit date from? Perhaps around the time you ran away from the fevered embrace of your current employer? Who I think we can all agree is the only man you've met in years who might possibly be right for you?"

"She hasn't called him," Vida informed on me. "She hasn't even told him about WorldWired, and when she saw him today, she ran away again."

"Will you two please give it a rest? This isn't about Josh!"

As I yelled at my best friends, I caught a glimpse of myself in the little mirror over the bar cart. I had strawberry sauce on my chin. My hands were shaking so badly I risked losing the remnants of my drink. My mascara had settled in murky pools under my eyes. I looked like a crazy woman. I looked like hell. Worse, I looked like Vladima in the middle of a feeding frenzy.

Seeing myself in the mirror, I finally saw what everyone else already had. And the last of my denial came crashing down.

Oh, fuck. This was about Josh.

I'VE HEARD that the first step in any twelve-step program is admitting you have a problem. I'm inclined to go along with that. Because once I admitted I was in a mess over Josh, I lost it. Big time. I had thought it was serious when I'd cried over Sir Meaningless Interlude in England, but this—this was in a whole different league.

The bright side of my complete breakdown was that Vida and Max finally broke out the "There, there's" in full force.

It was horrible. Every hideous sentence beginning with "what if" that a woman has ever asked about a man came pouring out of me. What if he . . . What if I . . . What if we . . . What if he *doesn't*?

Vida and Max had some answers, but not all. It kept coming back to the same thing—did I care enough about

Josh to risk all those horrible what if's on the off chance that, against a lifetime of history and staggering odds, everything might turn out all right?

By the time Max left at eleven, I had at least summoned the strength to wash my face.

By the time Tim picked Vida up at midnight I could contemplate the thought of going to bed without drinking the rest of the vodka.

And by the morning, I told myself, everything would be fine.

All I really needed was a plan.

AS IT TURNED OUT, I slept through the morning. A clear course of action had failed to come to me magically in a dream, dammit, so I tried to think of one while I manically cleaned my loft all afternoon.

One part of my brain echoed Vida's last words to me—"Just call him." But that would only take me so far. Because once I called him, in all likelihood I'd have to say something to him.

After I'd scrubbed everything I owned, I decided to scrub myself and I ran a hot bath. Baths were good. Some of my best plans had their origins in the bath. And incredibly, possibly due to the citrus aromatherapy that Vida had provided for mental energy, a plan did come to me.

It was so obvious. I needed to write a script.

I threw on my coziest sweats, all fluffy from the dryer, and sat down at the dining room table with a glass of Zinfandel and a legal pad.

I could do this. I'd written hundreds of persuasive talks in the past. If I could script Q & A sessions that persuaded

CEOs to write multimillion-dollar contracts, I could script a dialogue between Josh and me that would get the result I wanted.

Oh fuck. What was the result I wanted?

But before I could start banging my head on the newly polished table, the doorbell rang. Saved.

"Max?" I called. "Vida?" I opened the door.

Josh.

Thirty

I stared at him blankly for I don't know how long. Long enough for him to take the initiative.

"Think I could come in?"

"Oh!" I stepped back as if the doorknob had given me an electrical shock.

"Look"—he got as far as the hall closet and closed the door behind him—"I was going to call—"

"I was too."

He gave me a quick glance. "You were?"

I nodded. "I was just"—I stopped myself from telling him I was just drafting out the optimal dialogue—"going to call in a few minutes."

He shrugged. "Right."

"I was! There are a couple of things I need to talk to you about—"

"Such as?"

I backed down. "Well, you might as well come in if you're going to come in."

We made it the three steps to the kitchen. The living room, with its single sofa and floor pillows, was too cozy to even contemplate.

"I didn't think you'd want to talk to me." Josh said, not looking at me.

"Why ever not?" *Why ever not?* Now I was channeling Bette Davis. Not good.

Josh risked a cautious glance. "When a woman runs away from me, I tend to think the worst."

I bit back my automatic reply denying that I'd run away. He'd been there. He knew. Instead I offered an explanation. "Oh. That. Yeah. Well . . . sorry."

"So am I. Sorry." He looked it. "About, you know, everything."

"Yeah. Well. Whatever."

Is it obvious why I'd wanted a goddamn script for this conversation?

"Anyway . . ." We both said it at the same time, and finally there was a hairline crack in the ice.

"Look, Josh." I decided to wing it, starting with full disclosure about the WorldWired job. Maybe he'd be so mad about that news that he'd storm off and I wouldn't have to deal with the rest of it. "There's something I have to tell you."

"Yeah." He nodded. "There's something I have to tell you too. About Vladima."

"Oh." I felt the giddiness of the reprieved convict. "Great. You go first." If we could just keep it professional for a few minutes, I might get over the feeling that I was dancing on knives.

He cleared his throat. "I got a call that day after we . . . met with Alan Turnbottom."

Good save. I imagined he'd been about to say "after we made out like sex fiends on the Embarcadero."

"A call?" My voice came out a little huskier than I would have liked.

He nodded. "From Turnbottom's boss. Chloe Stevens. Apologizing for sending Mister Slick to see us when she should have handled it herself."

"Damn right she should have. Who is she?"

"The head of some division. Whichever division it is that buys properties to make movies."

"So she still wants to buy Vladima?"

"Well, in fact . . ." He examined the intricate pattern of slashes on my cutting board. "She already has."

She . . . what?

"You sold the movie rights?"

"Lock, stock, and coffin."

"Without me?"

"Oh," Josh looked a little alarmed. "Well, yeah."

Great. Only the biggest negotiation he'd probably ever handled, and he hadn't even picked up the phone to call his resident expert in such matters. This is how one kiss can ruin everything.

"Becks, it was a good deal. I'm sure I could have used your advice, but it was pretty cut and dried. And I'm not a total idiot, you know. Just because I've been hanging out in the graveyard for the past few years doesn't mean I've forgotten how to run a company."

I did forget, occasionally, about Josh's life before Vladima.

"I'm happy for you," I managed. "I'm sure you made a great deal." And it was too late now, anyway, if he hadn't.

"You can look it over, if you want. I've got a copy back at the studio."

"Fine, if you'd like me to." I sounded less than enthusiastic.

He tilted his head and sort of stooped over to make me meet his eyes. "Becks, this is a good thing."

Oh, shit. Why did he have to get so close when I was still trying to process everything? It made me want to just say "okeydokey" so we could get around to the kissing part.

No it didn't, I mentally corrected myself. Out loud, I snapped at him. "Josh, I can't believe you made such a huge commitment without consulting me."

He didn't flinch. In fact, the steadiness of his gaze was a little unnerving. "I would have. If I thought you might return a call."

Of course I wouldn't have returned a call. But he couldn't have been sure about that. "If you had called about this, about business—" Didn't the man ever blink? I felt as if I were being pulled toward him, and if I didn't do something about it immediately, I'd never be able to recover.

I switched gears. "What about everything else?"

"Good question." He straightened and moved a little closer. "What about everything else?"

I was finding it hard to keep hold of my thoughts. "Are you planning to keep doing the Web site? And the comic book?" I made the mistake of looking into his eyes again, and my voice came out about an octave higher than usual. "What about the ComixCon convention? Do you still want to go? Do you still want Shayla as Vladima? Do you still want me—"

"Oh," he said, his voice softening. "I want you."

There was a buzzing sound in my ears. I shook my head to try to clear it. "In what capacity?"

"As Vladima's voice," he said. "And handling her marketing."

I closed my eyes, but I could still see him. "Great. Perfect." I let out a deep breath and looked at him again. "Good."

"And in whatever other capacity you want."

I opened my mouth, but no sound came out.

"Becks." Josh touched my arm lightly, sending a little heat wave from my elbow to my shoulder. "You know, just because someone wants you doesn't mean you have to say yes. You're free to just . . . walk away."

I'd dated a lot of men in my life that I should have just walked away from. Was this still about Vladima? Or was Josh telling me I should walk away from him?

"And," he continued, his voice going all warm and liquid, "I'm very aware that just because you want something doesn't mean you're going to get it."

I nodded, the image of the LOTM springing to mind. I tossed it away and floated a little toward Josh.

"But," he was so close now that I was staring at his shirt buttons. I could feel his breath on my forehead as he spoke. If I looked up . . . I didn't dare look up.

"But, sometimes, if you're unbelievably lucky"—he brushed my hair away from my face—"the one you want wants you."

Everything went a little soft around the edges and the buzzing in my head got louder. I took a slow breath and looked up.

"Fuck Vladima," I told him. "I want you."

Thirty-one

Whenever I'd imagined sex with Josh (okay, yes, I admit it. I'd imagined sex with Josh ever since that kiss), I'd thought it would be the sort of wild, frenzied thing I'd had in England with what's-his-name.

It wasn't.

I can't even begin to . . . I mean *slow* isn't really sufficient, and *languid* is too poetic for . . . maybe some mixture of *intense* and *aching* and *deliberate* and *right* could give a general idea, but honestly, it was just so . . . *Josh*.

AFTERWARD, when we were all tangled up in each other and gasping for air, I had a hard time thinking anything other than WOW.

That lasted about a minute and a half. Then faint alarm bells began to ring. Alarm about the inevitability of post-sex embarrassment. Alarm about what this meant to him. Hell, alarm about what this meant to me.

So when I said out loud the four words that any rational woman knows she should never say out loud, especially after the most incredible sex she's ever experienced, the only possible explanation is that I hadn't eaten anything all day and I'd had wine on an empty stomach. And I was still buzzing from the most incredible sex I'd ever experienced.

So yes, I said it.

"What are you thinking?"

He caught my hand as it went automatically flying to my mouth to stuff the words back in.

Hideously, he seemed to take the question seriously. "I'm thinking about that first kiss the other day and how terrible it was."

Great.

"But the second kiss . . ." A smile hovered on his lips. He seemed to lose his focus for a moment and shook his head to get it back. "And I'm thinking, suppose the same thing were to happen in bed?"

This was getting interesting. "You mean . . ."

He nibbled a little on my knuckles. "If the second time is that much better than the first . . ." He gave me the wickedest grin I'd ever seen. "I'm a dead man."

I blinked. Josh had made a joke. *Josh!* He had taken the moment with more potential for excruciating embarrassment than any other, and he had . . . lightened up.

Which made me do something I've never, in all my post-sex experience, ever done before.

I relaxed.

And I felt the beginnings of a wicked grin of my own. "I vote we test that theory immediately."

Which was the last sensible thing either of us said for several hours.

. . .

I WAS HUMMING to myself in the shower when I felt, more than heard, the door slam. Had he gone out for a supply of flaky croissants and the Sunday papers? I dried off to this cheerful fantasy.

There was no note on the riotously disheveled bed. I pulled my best robe around myself and padded down the stairs. No note anywhere there either. But the message light was flashing on my answering machine. Had he recorded a memo for me?

I pushed the button and listened with growing dread.

"Becks! It's Joe Elliot! I'm so pleased you've decided to join WorldWired! The only thing is, instead of starting in the San Francisco office in two weeks, I want to talk you into coming to New York for a meeting a week from Tuesday. Now, I know you said you had some silly little commitment, but I think you'll be able to get out of it, won't you? So give my girl a call and she'll organize all the details. See you soon!"

Click. Buzz. As the little red light stopped flashing, I did the only thing possible. I screamed.

"NO!"

"ARE YOU SURE he heard the message?" I'd reached Vida on her cell phone. She and Tim were on a wine-tasting weekend in Sonoma. They were always doing things like that these days.

"Of course he heard the message! Why else would he have slammed out of here with no explanation?" I'd sunk down onto the kitchen floor with the phone in my hands and my back against the cabinets.

"But, Becks, you can totally explain it to him—"

"I can't explain anything if he isn't talking to me!"

"Okay." She went into logical mode. "I'm assuming you've tried to call his cell."

"Of course I have! It's turned off!"

"Okay, take a deep breath. What exactly did the World-Wired guy say?"

"Just that I'd need to start the job earlier and had to get rid of 'some silly little commitment' so I could fly off to New York."

"'Silly little commitment.' That's bad."

"I *know*!"

"Okay, breathe . . . breathe . . . how long has he been gone and how far could he have gotten? Do you think he's home? And is it better to let him cool off a little or to go over right away—"

I stopped listening to her, because I could have sworn I heard a key in the lock. I popped my head up over the kitchen counter.

"Josh!"

"He's *there*?" Vida shrieked over the phone.

"Gotta go." I hung up on her.

"Hey," Josh said, "I didn't think you'd be up yet. I hope you don't mind, but I took your key."

"Where . . ." My voice didn't seem to be working correctly. I tried again. "Where were you?"

He held up a white bag. "Two double lattes, assorted croissants and Danish—because I don't know what your favorite is—and the Sunday paper."

I must have been staring or something because he looked at me kind of funny. "What's wrong?"

I wrapped my arms around him and held on.

Nothing was wrong.

. . .

"YOU STILL HAVEN'T TOLD HIM?" Vida stared at me, her fork halfway to her mouth. I'd met her and Connie for dinner the next night to bring them up to speed on . . . well . . . my love life.

"Of course I told him. Not until later in the afternoon, but I told him." After a shameless interlude on my living room floor. Thank God for throw pillows.

"What did he say?" Connie demanded. "Was he furious?"

"Not furious," I said.

"But what did he say?" Vida insisted.

I shrugged. "He said, 'Congratulations.'"

He'd actually said a lot more, like how he'd known I'd eventually land on my feet, and how brilliant he'd always thought I was, and how happy he was for me. It was rather nice, having my own personal cheering section who also happened to be a major sex god.

"Anyway." I couldn't take their beaming faces anymore. I needed to change the subject. "Connie, do you think you'll be staying with your parents for a while?"

She turned to Vida. "That's a polite way of asking me to get my stuff out of her loft so she can turn it into her official palace of sin."

"Don't be ridiculous. I wouldn't begin to know how to decorate a palace of sin. But, um . . ."

"I'll get my stuff tonight," Connie assured me. "And stay at my folks' place until I find a flat somewhere."

"You really don't think you and Ian might work things out?" Vida asked.

Connie grimaced briefly. "Let's put it this way. I'm willing to make you a good deal on a slightly used wedding dress."

Vida's eyes widened. "I think I'll pass."

Connie turned to me. "Shall I hold onto it for you?"

Sometimes I have no idea if she's serious. "Just let me get through the first week of this thing, all right?"

THE FIRST WEEK of this thing was bliss. It was like all those jazz-in-the-background, walking-through-the-park, laughing-at-the-same-things movie montages that let you know two people are meant to be together.

We were kept from being completely nauseating by the fact that we were both so busy. He had to finish the monthly animation for the Web site—the last before the introduction of Dr. Ethan Black—and I had to get everything ready for Vladima's appearance at ComixCon. I told Josh I'd keep handling the Defender of the Night's marketing despite the new job. I like to see things through. Besides, I kind of felt like I owed it to Vladima.

I was also gearing up for WorldWired. I had ten days to organize my life around a demanding job again. I called Connie's cleaning lady and arranged for her to come twice a month, reasoning that I'd never have the time to keep my loft as tidy as I'd grown to like it. I called a drycleaner and arranged for weekly pickups and deliveries, knowing that business suits were far less forgiving of casual laundering than the comfortable clothes I'd been wearing lately. I called Shayla and asked for a suitably executive new haircut.

With all that going on, Josh and I spent every minute we could together. We strolled around Clement Street, browsing for books and picking up vast amounts of takeout dim sum to be eaten in bed. We went to Martuni's for Gershwin night and sang along to sappy songs. We met people for dinners where we ignored them and rushed to get home. We rented a lot of movies we never watched.

The night before I was scheduled to fly off to New York to meet Joe Elliot, I finished the recording for Vladima's last episode as a solo act. After I'd snarled my last sarcastic line ("I love eating in Chinatown . . . everyone's so spicy"), Josh came into the booth, took my headphones off, and kissed me the way no vampire should be kissed. Then he took me upstairs, where we never got around to opening a bottle of Dom Pérignon.

Everything was going to be perfect from now on.

Thirty-two

I hadn't done nearly enough to prepare for WorldWired. It wasn't until I was out of the cab, through the gauntlet of security, and seated in business class on my way to New York that I began to think of all the things I should have already taken care of.

I should have read everything that had been written about the company, its competitors, and its target market for the past six months. I should have memorized the entire management staff and organizational structure so when people casually referred to "Mark" or "Bill," I'd know who they were talking about. I should have analyzed every ad they'd put out for the past two years—particularly since the meeting I was flying to New York for was with an ad agency to discuss a television campaign.

I should have made a to-do list.

There was nothing I could do now but break out my new laptop (which had arrived on my doorstep three days ago, courtesy of Joe Elliot's "girl," who turned out to be a very nice woman named Chris).

When I opened the computer, there was a small piece of paper on the keyboard. I got a little melty because I knew it had to be a note from Josh.

It wasn't.

It was from Vida. She must have slipped it in the night before when she, Connie, and Max had come over with pizza and wine for a sort of impromptu good luck party.

Becks,

Remember that life, like surfing, is all about balance.

V

Tim was definitely having a Zen influence on her. Six weeks ago she would have just said, "Becks, don't get crazy on us." And she would have said it to my face.

I tucked the note away in a pocket of the computer case and gathered my thoughts.

The one thing I had done since getting the job was send a note to George—Sir George—thanking him for recommending me to WorldWired. I'd written it on a sheet of thick creamy stationery embossed with—what else—a swan.

I started my to-do list with "Send thanks to George." Then I checked it off. It made me feel better to have one sign of accomplishment among all the tasks I had yet to complete.

I worked at the list until the flight attendant came around with breakfast. By then it was three pages long.

I was already completely behind.

THAT NIGHT, after checking into the very hip Manhattan hotel the company had arranged, meeting Joe Elliot and a few of the guys for dinner, and coming back to my room to raid the mini-bar for chocolate and Scotch, I fired up the laptop again.

I knew I could find a lot of background material on

WorldWired's ad agency online, so I figured I'd spend most of the night doing research, prepping for the meeting with them the next day. I can never sleep the first night in a strange hotel room, so why not put the long dark night to good use?

I clicked open my Web browser, and it sent me directly to Vladima's lair. Josh had been with me when the computer was delivered, and clearly he had done some fiddling with the default settings.

Josh.

I realized with alarm that I hadn't been thinking about him all day. If he was my boyfriend, wasn't I supposed to think about him all day?

Hang on, maybe I had been thinking about him all day. I just hadn't registered it. Now that I set my mind to it, I remembered seeing a young gothed-out couple in the airport and guessing they were Vladima fans. Then, as the couple had started making out in the security line, I'd wondered whether Josh had plans for Vladima and Dr. Ethan Black to get carnal any time soon. Then my mind had wandered to the practical implications of vampire teeth during sex. That just led to thinking about sex, which had made me wonder whether Josh was still warm in bed as I passed through the metal detectors. So I had been thinking of him.

I'd left him sleeping at my place. He'd come over late, about the time the pizza party was breaking up. He'd wanted to take me to the airport in the morning, but I told him I wouldn't let him. So he'd washed the dishes while I'd packed—which somehow made me feel as if we were playing house, but in a good way. Then we'd gone to bed and—just for one instant—I'd wondered why in the world I was leaving him in the morning.

Now I glanced at the clock and realized he'd probably still be at the studio. I opened my e-mail, ignored the messages from WorldWired strangers introducing themselves, and sent Josh a note. It said:

I miss you, I miss you. Really.

I hit SEND feeling like the biggest geek in high school. But there was no retrieving it.

I switched back to the browser and left Vladima to go to WorldWired's home page. Thirty seconds later I got a message notification. He'd written back.

I miss you more.

I shut down the computer and called him.

"THEY'RE KIND OF FREAKS."

It was an hour later and Josh had just asked me about my new colleagues. Actually, he'd asked me that as soon as he'd answered the phone, but I refused to answer until he gave me a play-by-play of everything that had happened in Vladima's world that day. The plans for ComixCon were heating up, and I didn't want anything to go wrong while I was gone.

But eventually we'd gotten back to WorldWired.

"Becks, you know people who think drinking blood is socially acceptable, and you're telling me the marketing staff of your Fortune 500 company are freaks?"

"Okay, maybe not freaks. But they're *such* corporate citizens. Every sentence seemed to start with 'We at WorldWired . . .'" I sniffed. "And who do I know that drinks blood?"

"I'm afraid to tell you. But I wouldn't worry about the WorldWired guys. Maybe they were just indoctrinating you. They'll probably ease up on that stuff after you've been there a while."

"I hope so." I made a face. "And maybe it was just this crowd. They were all that prep school, frat boy, captain-of-the-football-team, aggressively clean-cut and competitive-as-hell type."

"Were there any women?"

"No." We'd gone to a fantastically expensive place for dinner. It was all wood paneling and dim lighting and pictures of dead animals on the walls, and they specialized in wild game—buffalo and venison and things I didn't even want to speculate about. "No women except for Bambi—and I ate her for dinner." Or at least her cousin.

"Bambi was a boy."

"Really?"

"Trust me, I'm a cartoonist." I knew exactly the grin that would flash across his face as he said this.

"So it was just me and the manly men, and I had the feeling that after I went back to the hotel they were probably going to go out and do some manly things."

"Like get lap dances?"

"Something of the sort. Why? Is that what you do when you go out of town?"

"I don't go out of town," he pointed out. "I just sit here at home and pine away for you."

"Are you pining?" The thought of that was completely delightful.

"Can't you hear me?"

"It might help if you inserted a heartfelt sigh here and there in the conversation."

"I'll work on it. So what's the plan for tomorrow?"

"A breakfast meeting with the same crowd, then we go to Madison Avenue to meet with the advertising firm about the new campaign."

"You've got a breakfast meeting? Isn't it two in the morning there?"

I looked at the clock. "Uh-huh."

"Shouldn't you be sleeping?"

I rolled over on to my back. "That's not going to happen."

"Oh, I get it. 'We at WorldWired' don't sleep."

"You're so very amusing. No, I just don't sleep in hotel rooms."

There was a significant pause. "Ever?"

"Not on the first night someplace. After that I can usually manage, with the help of some Tylenol PM." And some Scotch, but he didn't need to know all my secrets right away.

"But that doesn't work on the first night?"

"No." I reached for an exorbitantly priced bag of M&Ms.

"It only starts to kick in about an hour before I have to get up, and that just makes me groggy all the next day."

"You're serious about this." Josh sounded disbelieving. "How do you make it through the day?"

"That's why they invented caffeine." I told him. "And look who's talking. I think this is the sleep-deprived calling the kettle exhausted."

"Yeah, but I only have to stumble downstairs to a nice dark office whenever I drag myself out of bed. I don't have to impress a room full of hotshot New York ad types."

I stopped in mid-M&M toss, and they went spilling all over the bed instead of anywhere near my opened mouth. "Did you really have to say that? I'm trying not to think about the hotshot New York ad types."

"Don't tell me you're intimidated? Aren't you a hotshot San Francisco marketing genius?"

"Well"—demurely— "yes."

"Okay, genius, I want you to do something for me."

"What?" I reached for a pen.

"First, set your alarm."

"Totally unnecessary."

"Humor me."

I humored him.

"Okay, now, what are you wearing?"

"Josh! Are we going to have phone sex? That's so cool!"

I finally earned the heartfelt sigh I wanted. But I'm willing to bet it was accompanied by an eye roll. "Just tell me."

"A French maid's uniform."

"Seriously."

"Seriously? One of the sample Vladima T-shirts."

There was a pause. "Okay, that actually does more for

me than the maid thing. But never mind. What's on the bed?"

"The laptop." And scattered bits of colored chocolate, but I didn't really want to tell him that.

"Turn it off and put it on the desk."

"Hang on." I put the phone down and did as he asked. I stopped for a minute to look at myself in my V-wear—a black oversized T-shirt with Vladima in full leather gear emblazoned across it. Yep, I could see why Josh would like it.

"Okay, I'm back. Now what?"

"Now get under the covers."

I complied.

"And get comfortable. Turn on your side the way you do when you're ready to stop talking to me and go to sleep."

"But I'm not ready to stop talking to you. And I'm not ready to go to sleep." I eyed the computer with a twinge of guilt.

"I thought you were humoring me."

I grumbled, but I turned.

"Now what?"

"Now just listen to me. I'm going to read something to you."

"Josh—have you started a new script?"

Another sigh. "This is you not talking now, all right?"

"All right. This is me not talking."

He started to read. It wasn't a new Vladima script. In fact, it was just about as far to the other side of the literature spectrum as you can get.

It was *Little Women*.

I recognized it after about two sentences. "I used to love that book!"

"I know," he said. "You told me once. I just got you a first edition for your birthday, so be quiet and listen, and you can say 'Thank you' in four months."

"Josh!" How long ago had I even mentioned *Little Women* to him? How could he have remembered that? Did he think we'd still be together in four months?

He didn't answer me; he just read. And I listened. And it felt so nice to be lying in bed listening to that voice of his swirling around in my head. His voice and the story I knew almost by heart.

And the next thing I knew, it was morning.

I'll be damned.

Thirty-three

>he read you to sleep?

It was four days later and I was on my way home. Actually, I was at JFK sending instant messages to Vida from the laptop.

<every night this week

>!!!!!!!!!

<I know!!!

>why haven't you called?

<work

>how is stupid work?

<stupid

I sent it before I even thought about it. I don't think I'd ever said anything bad about a job since I'd gotten my first college internship. Except for the Vladima thing, of course, before I'd developed an appreciation for the undead.

Now Vida pounced on it.

>then QUIT!

<ha ha

>seriously!

<gotta go—they just called my flight

They hadn't really. I just didn't think I could discuss my

extremely mixed feelings about my new position in the United boarding area over a wireless connection. A connection that was probably, now that I thought of it, provided by WorldWired.

Ugh.

It had all started out manageably enough. The ad agency—KMD—was one of the biggest in the world, and the people we'd met with had been sharp, bright professionals who had actually come up with a campaign that seemed pretty good to me. The team assigned to us consisted of two men and two women who took turns explaining the various facets of the proposed media onslaught.

We of WorldWired met afterward in the back room of another dimly lit restaurant, this one specializing in fish and decorated with lush oil paintings of glistening trout and salmon. Not my kind of joint.

I assumed at some point I'd get a glimpse of the WWHQ, as they referred to the company's reportedly palatial headquarters in midtown, but apparently post-pitch reviews were traditionally held, accompanied by vast quantities of expense-account liquor, "off-campus."

The meeting had included more people than just those I'd met through Joe Elliot the night before. It had even included a few other women.

"Be careful," said one. Thalia, I think, although we hadn't been introduced. "*They* can drink themselves into a stupor and boast about it the next morning, but if one of *us* gets a little tipsy . . ." She eyed my martini, then gave me a look filled with dark portent about the swift and vicious nature of office gossip.

I paced myself.

At some point amid the predictable posturing among the

guys I'd met the first night, I must have tuned out the conversation. It was probably when one of the guys—Chip? Skip? Kip?—was droning on about targeted market areas. As if he was original or insightful or something.

I was thinking about whether the addition of Dr. Ethan Black would be likely to increase the female Vladima fan base, when I sensed someone looking at me. Everyone, in fact, was looking at me because Joe Elliot had apparently just asked me a question.

Were they still talking about targeted markets? I tried to keep my face neutral while my brain did a series of U-turns. In an attempt to avoid Joe's stare, I looked up at the wall behind him. Then I said the first word that popped into my head.

"Fish."

A quick check of my new boss's expression showed he clearly expected something more of me. Can I help it if I was distracted by the portrait of a large-mouthed bass hanging over his head?

"Fish?" I heard someone echo.

I nodded, cleared my voice, and said as assertively as I could: "Fish where the fishing is good."

I looked Joe Elliot in the eye. "It's something my Grandpop used to say, but it sums up my thinking on targeted markets pretty well." A complete lie, but one I was willing to commit to.

Joe blinked rapidly, and I held my breath. Then he smiled. "I suppose you'd say we should use the right bait for the right fish as well, wouldn't you?"

Saved. For the rest of the evening the fishing metaphors flew, and I did my best to keep my mind on the conversation.

This was not a good start.

. . .

"THIS IS THE WORST BAND I've ever heard in my life."

I had to agree with Josh's assessment. We'd met Max, Connie, Vida, and Tim at the Hotel Utah on Saturday night to hear a group called Bag O'Cats—a name that did not bode well. The band was fronted by one of Tim's best friends, which was the only possible reason for subjecting ourselves to a truly awful performance involving guitar, bass, drum, and bagpipe (seriously).

Immediately following the first set, Josh said something about desperately needing me to look over a clause in the contract for the movie with Fox, and we fled the joint.

We went to his place, where—much to my surprise—he handed me the Fox contract along with a glass of Pinot.

"I thought you were just making an excuse to get us out of there."

"I was, but I also want your take on this section." He pointed to a page he'd flagged. "I've gone over it twenty times and I still can't tell whether it means we need Fox to approve of our plans for Vladima at ComixCon."

"What?" I put the wine down and searched through the section.

"It just has me worried because it's so vague about exactly what kinds of things they do or don't get to say something about," Josh elaborated while I read.

I glanced up at him. "It's vague, but it's lawyer-vague."

"Meaning?"

"Meaning they intentionally left it vague so other lawyers could interpret it in their favor if we do anything that they weren't foresighted enough to tell us not to do in the first place." I read over the section again in silence. When I looked over at Josh, he was rubbing his eyes.

He saw me watching him and stopped. "What do you think we should do?"

"You really want my opinion?" I asked.

"Of course I want your opinion. You're my resident genius, remember?"

I thought about it, about a dozen what-if scenarios playing out simultaneously in my mind. "I think we need to bring them in."

Josh looked a little deflated. "Really?"

I nodded, a plan taking shape. "But not to ask their permission. We'll say that we're doing this major event and launching the printed comic book—"

"They're happy about the book," Josh interrupted. "I just never brought up the convention because . . . well, it never came up."

"It's fine," I told him. "We'll call Chloe, and tell her what we're doing, and that we're expecting to make a huge splash at the convention, and then we'll make her an offer she can't refuse."

"Which is?"

"She gets the perfect venue to announce the Vladima movie."

Josh looked doubtful. "Will she want to announce it? So soon?"

I picked up my glass and raised it in a toast. "She will when I get through with her."

I took a moment to enjoy the look on Josh's face, then stretched and picked up the contract again.

"Don't do any more reading tonight." Josh got up and stood behind me so he could rub my shoulders. "You're exhausted. You didn't get much sleep last night, and you really didn't need to spend all day coaching Shayla on her Vladima performance."

His hands felt fabulous. Just the right amount of pressure in just the right places. "First," I told him, "I particularly enjoyed the way I didn't get much sleep last night—even though I still say it wasn't necessary for you to pick me up at the airport."

"I'll pick you up if I want to pick you up," he said reasonably. "Eventually you'll get used to it. Then we can work on me taking you to the airport."

"And second," I continued as if he hadn't spoken, "I enjoyed the day with Shayla. She's fun to hang out with and she's going to make a perfect booth vixen at the show."

"I can't argue with that."

"Good. Oh, that feels good." I leaned back a little. "Nobody at WorldWired ever gives me a backrub."

"That's a relief," Josh said. "Because I wouldn't want to have to kill anyone." His fingers slowed. "How are things going, anyway?"

So I told him a fish story.

"HOW'S YOUR OFFICE? Do you have a fabulous view of the bay?"

It was Monday, and I was on the phone with Vida. "I don't know," I told her. "I'm in Dallas."

"Dallas?"

"I spent the weekend at Josh's, and when I got home this morning at six to get ready for work, there was a message on my answering machine telling me I was booked on the eight-fifteen flight to Dallas. It was just a good thing I hadn't unpacked yet from last week."

"What the heck are you supposed to be doing in Dallas?"

"Going to a series of seminars on the future of telecom. I'm on a break from one of them now."

"Yuck. How long do you have to be there?" Vida sounded appalled. She didn't approve of cities that were more than a half-hour's drive from the beach.

"All week—but it's not that bad. At least I'm alone out here, so I can cheat on WorldWired a little and spend time on the phone with the guys at Fox."

"What's going on with Fox?"

"An elaborate series of manipulations. You'd lose all respect for me if I told you."

She didn't answer.

"Vee? I'm kidding."

"I know. I'm just starting to get worried about you."

"I'm fine," I said automatically.

"Did you ever get my note?"

Note? "What—" Then I remembered. "Oh, the surfer thing."

"The balance thing," she said. "You've only had this job two weeks and your life is totally out of balance already."

"It is not," I told her. "It's just full. And rich. It's full and rich. And diverse." I had a suspicion I wasn't convincing her, so I stopped.

"Do me a favor," she said. "Every now and then, just to humor me, stop what you're doing and breathe, okay?"

"Breathe?" I was pretty sure I did that fairly regularly.

I heard her take a slow breath, then release it. "A count of five breathing in, and a count of five breathing out."

I assumed this was an instruction. "Five and five. Got it."

"Oh, Becks."

We said good-bye and I went back into the seminar, where I sat in front of my laptop and completely tuned out the speaker. Was Vida right? Was I getting too wrapped up in the new job? Ever since my last layoff, all I'd wanted was to get too wrapped up in a new job. But that had been before I'd taken on Vladima. And before I'd . . . before . . . well . . .

Before Josh.

If Vida was right, I needed some sort of tool to help me keep things in balance. I feigned attention in the general direction of the speaker and opened a new file on the computer. I titled it "My Balance Sheet" and began naming the columns. *WorldWired*, *General to-do*, *Vladima*, and *Friends*. Then I wrestled with myself about the fifth column. *Boyfriend*. No. Backspace. *Relationship*. No. Backspace. Finally, I admitted the truth and simply typed *Josh*.

Then I started filling it in. The WorldWired list was fairly straightforward. Show up at meetings this week in Dallas, show up in the office next week and see what they'd throw at me. That, and the items from last week's uncompleted to-do list of research. Oh, and figure out what exactly I was supposed to be doing in this job.

The general list would be boring things like paying bills on time and not forgetting to go to the dentist. That could wait.

The Vladima list was potentially endless. Finalize all the ComixCon plans—that could be broken into several dozen sub-tasks. Successfully negotiate with Fox—there were probably another fifteen phone calls for that one. Then there were discussions with the printer and distributor for the comic book, and calls to about a hundred comic shops across the country to make sure they'd stock the thing when we released it.

Yep, the V list was horrific. In fact, I realized I would be wasting valuable time just by filling in the remaining empty columns of the balance sheet.

I looked up suddenly when the people around me burst into applause at something the speaker had just announced. Damn. I had no idea what he'd said, and to be honest I just couldn't find it in myself to care about the future of telecom when I had a jillion-item to-do list for Vladima.

She is one demanding vampire.

Thirty-four

Joe Elliot was sending me on the road. Maybe it was because, as he explained in an e-mail, I needed to visit the various far-flung branches of the WorldWired empire in order to understand the company better, or maybe it was because my new boss just wanted to get me out from underfoot. In any case, I was racking up the frequent flyer miles.

"HOW'S ATLANTA?" Josh asked.

"Peachy."

"What are you supposed to be doing there?"

I was supposed to be learning everything there was to know about the Southeastern wireless market from the hot-shot VP who owned the territory. But someone had neglected to tell Joe Elliot that said VP had just resigned. Or had Joe intended to send me on a wild goose chase? Either way, I got to the Atlanta office just in time to tag along on a lavish farewell lunch and wave bye-bye to the departing genius. I had a feeling the group would be in chaos within two weeks without him, so I made a couple of halfhearted recommendations, but it wasn't worth spending my valuable phone time with Josh discussing it.

"Never mind," I said. "What's happening with Fox?"

We'd spent the weekend between Dallas and Atlanta strategizing. Well, mostly strategizing, with only a few interludes of massive sweaty sex getting in the way of our business plans. On Monday, I'd made a series of phone calls to Chloe from various airports, but Josh had had to fly to LA for the important face-to-face meeting with our executive champion on his own.

I thought I had her convinced, and that Josh would just have to tidy up the details, because I thought I'd come up with a fairly brilliant idea. I'd told her there was going to be a monumental e-mail campaign, beginning at the grassroots level with Vladima's most fanatical followers and growing until it reached every corner of comic fandom. By the time ComixCon came around, every attendee would have at least seen the e-mail petition, even if he hadn't in fact signed it and passed it on to twelve unsuspecting friends.

And what would the petition call for? What would it demand as an inalienable right?

Why, a movie featuring Vladima, of course.

Which would give Chloe the opportunity of swooping in for the grand finale event of ComixCon and announcing Fox's intention to make the movie in direct response to the power of the geeky people.

It was a bold spin on the concept of viral marketing, and I was pretty proud of it. I'd be even more proud if it worked.

"Did she go for it?" I held my breath.

"Not only that," Josh told me. "But I think she wants to offer you a job."

When it rains, it pours. "I don't think I could handle another."

"I can't believe you can handle what you've already got," he said.

"Don't be silly. I'm fine. Now tell me every word she said."

I could feel Josh's grin. "Becks, she thinks it's a brilliant publicity stunt and she's totally on board. Just tell me you're coming home so we can celebrate."

"I'm coming home," I told him.

"Good, because—"

"On Friday."

"Friday? You have to stay in Atlanta all week?"

"No, but apparently my life won't be complete without stopping in Baton Rouge and Chicago." At least, that's where I thought I was going. I'd have to check the itinerary lurking in my e-mail inbox again to be sure.

Josh gave me one of those heartfelt sighs. "Okay, Friday. But this weekend you're all mine."

"Deal." The only thing I'd have to do for WorldWired over the weekend was make sure I stopped off at home to pick up my passport. Because the following week I was scheduled for Frankfurt.

"WHAT ARE YOU DOING in Germany?"

Connie's voice sounded tinny and far away. That, and annoyed.

"I'm working. How did you get this phone number?" I wasn't even sure of the hotel's name, let alone its internationally complicated phone number.

"From Josh. Did you know about Phillip?"

"Phillip?" Connie had woken me from a fairly sound stupor and I was a little fuzzy. Perhaps that had something to do with the Oktoberfest party my hosts had taken me to the evening before. It's possible they'd spent the day giving me oodles of precious information about the European markets, but I'd never remember it. Because when the meeting ended they'd encouraged me to destroy most of my brain cells in an overcrowded beer hall. I glanced at the clock. Three in the morning. I'd only been in bed an hour.

"Phillip Hastings!" Connie said sharply. "Did Vida tell you?"

Alarm bells went off in my head. And they didn't mix well with whatever I'd been drinking out of those gigantic mugs. "Tell me what?" I must have blocked out entire days of the English wedding disaster because now I couldn't remember if Connie knew about Phillip and Max or not.

"That he's coming!"

"Oh." I sank back into my pillow. "Is that all?"

"Is that all?" Connie's words dropped like ice chips. "You knew my brother-in-law was coming for a visit and you didn't tell me?"

"Actually, I didn't know," Not the exact date, anyway. "What's the big deal? He's a nice guy."

"He's my *brother-in-law*!" Connie wailed. "He's going to expect to stay with us!"

Oh, I got it. "You mean he doesn't know you left Ian."

"Finally! Now do you see why I'm upset?"

Actually, no. But I didn't dare say so. "Don't you think Ian might have mentioned the separation to him?"

"Of course not. Ian thinks this is just postwedding jitters."

*Post*wedding jitters? Ian clearly had an advanced degree in denial. "Okay, then he'll tell Phillip that. No problem."

Connie latched on to the thought. "Do you think so? Because I'd hate for Phillip to think—or for his family to think—that after that huge wedding and everything and after they went to so much trouble with all the parties and everything—"

"Listen, Connie," I really needed to learn the German word for "aspirin." "If you're so worried, why don't you just move back in with Ian while Phillip visits? He can't be staying long, and it's not as if there isn't a precedent for shams where you and Ian are concerned. I mean, after that whole phony English estate wedding—right down to the fake vicar, for God's sake, and—"

And then I realized what I was saying. And who I was saying it to.

"What?"

I really needed to learn the German words for "Oh, shit."

>>SHE'S NOT *speaking to me*

I read Vida's message with no surprise.

<<*why? I'm the idiot who told her*

>>*we're all guilty—we knew*

It was the first time Vida and I had connected since I'd unleashed Connie's fury. I still hadn't spoken to Max, although I had gotten one terse e-mail in response to the panicked message I'd left on his machine.

From: maxie@doctormax.com

To: bMansfield@worldwired.net

Subject: Fuck!

She's on a rampage. If you're a smart woman, you'll stay in Europe.

—M

Now I could at least gather a few more details from Vida. <<*how did this get to be our fault?* I keyed.

>>*she's mainly mad at Ian*
>>*but since she already wasn't speaking to him*
>>*we're caught in the crossfire*

<<*what can we do?*

>>*Max says she'll get over it*

<<*ha!*

>>*when are you coming home?*

<<*on my way—see you this weekend*
<<*should we talk to her?*

>>*if we can*
>>*but don't count on it*

I didn't.

. . .

SATURDAY WAS SCHEDULED for the studio. Josh would be putting the finishing touches on the new Vladima Webisode, which would have its premier at ComixCon, and I needed to finish organizing the distribution for the first flood of Vladima comic books. Which would have been doable if I hadn't slept through the entire day.

"Did you drug me or something?"

It was six o'clock in the evening before I staggered down to the studio from Josh's loft upstairs. The place was dark, except for the dim glow of a computer screen in Josh's office. There wasn't a minion in sight.

He didn't answer, so I tried again. "Is Jeremy around? We were supposed to go over the Web promos. Have we got any stats on the e-mail circulation? Why did you let me sleep so long?"

"You've been lying to me." Josh didn't look up from his work.

"That's what I do. I'm in marketing." I sank into a chair. "Is there any coffee?"

"Becks." Something in his tone got my attention. "What the hell do you think you're doing?"

"What?" I sat up with a sick feeling. Had I missed a deadline? What had I forgotten about that was now going to mean a ruined ComixCon debut? Or had Connie come by looking for blood?

Josh stood up suddenly, seemed about to say something, then just muttered and left the room.

Okay, not good. I followed him to the break room, where he started making coffee, still muttering and still not looking at me.

"I get it, Josh, I messed up. Just tell me what it is and I can fix it. Don't be angry."

He slammed a prerelease V-mug on the counter with a crash. "Jesus Christ, Becks, I'm not angry with you!"

I blinked.

"Okay, maybe I am angry with you." He blew out a breath and ran his hands through his hair. "What the hell is going on with you?"

"What do you mean?"

"I mean, you told me you were getting plenty of sleep on the road, which was clearly a lie, and then you spent the whole night last night thrashing around and talking in your sleep."

"I talked?"

He nodded grimly, and I had the horrible feeling he was about to tell me what I'd said. What could I have said?

"You're fired," he told me.

"I'm *what*?"

He shook his head. "That's what you kept saying—'You're fired' and 'Now boarding,' and a bunch of other gibberish I couldn't understand. What the hell is going on? What are you doing all day that's giving you nightmares?"

I swallowed. "I'm just doing my job."

His expression hardened. "Well, I don't like what it's doing to you."

I felt cold suddenly, and sounded it when I answered him. "Well, forgive me if I disturbed your sleep last night."

He moved toward me, his voice harsh. "This isn't about my sleep. This is about your sleep—or lack of it. And about the way your hands have been shaking for the past week. And about how you don't seem to want anything other than caffeine and alcohol these days. When was the last time you had a decent meal?"

"Stop attacking me!"

"I'm not attacking you, I'm worried about you! Can't you tell the difference?"

"Well, who asked you to worry about me? I'm fine! I'm a big girl and I can take care of myself. And if I'm so hard to be around these days, I'll just get out of here."

I spun around for the door and would have made a seriously dramatic exit if I hadn't gotten dizzy and stumbled.

Josh caught me by the elbows. "For Christ's sake, Becks, you're a wreck. I know you want to think you can do everything, but you can't keep living out of suitcases and doing God knows what for WorldWired, and then expect to come back here and have the energy to run everything like you've been off relaxing at a spa."

He forced me into a chair and I waited for the room to stop spinning. "Josh, I may be tired these days, but I haven't been dropping the ball. We're completely on schedule for ComixCon, and—"

"Fuck ComixCon! This isn't about ComixCon!" He brought his fist down on the table.

I jumped up. "Stop yelling at me!"

"I'm not yelling!" he yelled.

We glared at each other for a moment, then he took a deep breath. "Christ, Becks, I'm just trying to tell you I'm worried about you. If you want to keep doing whatever you're doing for WorldWired, that's your choice. But if it means you can't help out with Vladima anymore, just say so. I'd rather deal with that than deal with you killing yourself."

Suddenly he was the one who looked exhausted.

"Josh, don't worry. I'm fine. Everything's fine. I—"

He grabbed my hand. "Will you please stop saying that?

Would you please stop telling me you're fine and everything's fine, and it will all be *fine*!"

"Josh, I'm sorry." I didn't know what else to say. "I just didn't want you to think you had to . . ."

"To what? To worry about you? To try to make things easier for you? To help you?"

I looked at him, and what I saw made me want to kick myself. "I'm sorry," I said again, and not just as a reflex this time.

"I know." He shook his head. "I love you, Becks, but you're a damn difficult woman to take care of."

I nodded. "I don't like being taken care of."

"No shit." He looked at me.

"Hang on a minute." Something just caught up with me. "Can we rewind a few lines? Did you just say you love me?"

He met my eyes. "God help me."

The room started to spin again. Or maybe it wasn't the room. Maybe it was the whole world. So I took the only sensible action I could. I grabbed the man who stood in front of me and held on as if my life depended on it.

Maybe it did.

Thirty-five

"Did you say it back?" Vida had let me get through almost an entire phone call filled with excuses about why I hadn't seen her over the weekend and halfway through my whole you-won't-believe-what-Josh-said story before she demanded an answer.

"Well . . ."

She groaned. "Tell me you said it back."

"I—" The truth was, I didn't quite remember. "It's all kind of a blur."

"Becks!"

"Well, he did catch me a little off guard," I snapped. "I mean, one minute he's yelling at me and the next—"

"Stop! If you tell me you didn't totally fall into his arms right there on the spot, I'm never speaking to you again."

"Vee—"

"And I was already never speaking to you again because of the Connie thing."

"Have you talked to her? What's happening?" Connie hadn't returned any of my calls on Sunday. I hadn't had a word from her since I'd let it slip about Ian's subterfuge at the wedding—which I completely blamed on Oktoberfest and the evil Germans who'd dragged me to it.

"Don't change the subject. How did you leave things with Josh?"

She was my best friend, but I balked at telling her the details. About how we'd just clung to each other silently in the studio for a while. About how he'd carried me—*carried* me—up to his loft. About everything he'd said, and the very, very good things he'd done afterward.

"Becks!"

"We left things, um . . . nicely."

"Oh my God. You're impossible. Did you at least—"

"He took me to the airport this morning."

That stopped her. At least for a few seconds. "You let him?"

"Not only that," I told her. "I liked it."

"Becks! This is *huge*!"

I HAD LIKED IT. And it was huge.

I never let people take me to the airport. I hate it. I hate that they're doing me a favor. I hate that I have to make conversation with them all the long way there, and keep telling them what airline I'm on because they *always* forget and have to circle the departures level *forever* after they've missed the right turnout. And I have to be cheerful about that, even though it means I won't have time to stop at Starbucks before getting on the plane because this person is taking time out of their life to get me to the damn airport.

I'd much rather just pay an anonymous cabbie who does this for a living, doesn't care if I want to spend the time in the taxi thinking about everything that I have to do once I get wherever I'm going, and who knows when to turn to get me to the right drop-off zone.

But Josh had woken me up early that morning, taken me to my place, and made coffee while I threw things out of last week's suitcase and into this week's. And then we hadn't even discussed it. He'd taken me and it hadn't felt like a gigantic *thing*, and the conversation hadn't been forced, and he'd known better than me what flight I was on, because he'd printed my itinerary out from my e-mail while I'd been in the shower.

It had been . . . nice.

"WHERE THE HELL ARE YOU?"

It was Tuesday and I was talking to Max. "Boston."

"Why?"

"Because I work for a living."

Actually, I hadn't done any work in the two days I'd been there. The Boston office was in an uproar because a power outage on Monday morning had thrown everyone's schedules into chaos. I'd spent the day dealing with hysterical graphic artists who were completely stressed out over their deadlines because of the precious time they'd lost the day before, and I still hadn't seen their new and allegedly brilliant technodemo.

Max wasn't impressed. "Have you even seen your own office yet?"

"No, but I've seen my paycheck," I told him.

"Money isn't everything."

"You haven't seen this paycheck."

I heard him take a deep breath. "Anyway, that's not why I called." He paused. "Vida told me something interesting about you."

"I'll just bet she did." I knew I couldn't tell Vida something as gigantic as Josh saying he loved me and expect her to keep it to herself.

"So . . ." Max said. "You're happy?"

"I think so."

"Try to commit to it," he urged.

"Max," I asked. "Would you tell me if you thought I was just being date-lazy? I mean, Josh is the one who's kind of pursued me, and I'd hate to think I was just into him because . . . are you still there?"

"I'm still here. And if I knew where Connie was, I'd slap her silly for ever putting that stupid date-laziness theory in your head."

"So you don't think that's it? With Josh?"

"Becks, from the bottom of my jaded and cynical heart, I don't think that's it."

Which was an enormous relief. I mean, I may be delusional on occasion, but if my friends share the delusion . . . maybe it isn't a delusion after all. I decided to change the subject while things were still going so well.

"So nobody's heard from Connie yet?"

"I had to promise her assistant I'd give her free Botox before she'd tell me that Connie was still alive and coming into the office. She just isn't returning my calls. Or Vida's."

"Or mine," I told him. "I wonder what the hell she's thinking."

"I'VE DECIDED TO TAKE IAN BACK."

No "Hello." No "Sorry I've been making you all worry about me." No greeting whatsoever. Just a phone call at two in the morning and an announcement.

"Connie! Are you okay? What's going on?"

She sighed with impatience. "I've decided," she said slowly, "to take Ian back."

"That's . . . great." I struggled to sit up. Josh had talked me into an elaborately comfortable position involving four pillows when I'd called him earlier, and it was a little hard to extricate myself while dealing with what apparently was not a nervous breakdown from Connie.

"You sound great," I told her.

"I've decided to interpret the entire wedding episode as an endearing attempt to please me. When you think about it, it was actually quite sweet of him to go to all that bother."

Well, yes, in a pathological kind of way.

"And now that I've adjusted my perspective," she went on, "there's no reason why we can't make a fresh start."

"Uh-huh," I agreed in what I hoped might pass as a supportive-friend tone. "Of course. Connie, where are you?"

"Home."

"I mean . . ."

"Home as in my home with Ian. Although you wouldn't recognize the place. Honestly, a few weeks on his own and he's living like a bachelor again. Would you believe I found a pizza box in the living room? And it wasn't even *empty*."

"Is Ian there now?" Because she probably wasn't going to win him back with comments like that. But where else would he be at midnight?

"He's in China."

"China?"

She sniffed. "On business."

I got a very bad feeling. "Connie." I wasn't quite sure

how to phrase the question. "Does Ian know you've taken him back?"

"Um," she answered in a very small voice. "Not exactly."

"YOU'VE GOT TO BE KIDDING."

Vida had said it that morning, Max had said it that afternoon, and now Josh said it as I steeped in the hotel bath after yet another day of not seeing the fabulous high-tech marketing blitz that was behind schedule at WorldWired's Boston office.

"She's planning on just being there when he gets home."

"When will that be?"

"She doesn't even know for sure."

"Wow."

"Uh huh."

"Listen, it's not that I'm not interested in Connie, but we need to discuss the crucifix delivery."

Things with Josh hadn't really changed much. Except, of course, that I now had a constant, rhythmic sort of pulsing refrain of *he loves me, he loves me* as the accompaniment to everything I did. But in terms of work, I hadn't taken him up on his offer to drop Vladima and he hadn't forced the issue. I didn't want to drop Vladima. I liked the work, and so far I didn't see a problem in balancing it against my as-yet-to-be-defined WorldWired duties. Despite whatever I might mutter in my sleep.

So, with ComixCon only a week and a half away, and Vladima's needs reaching the critical stage, I found myself saying those three little words that every woman dreams of someday saying to the man in her life.

"What crucifix delivery?"

. . .

"JUST PROMISE YOU'LL BE HOME this weekend, okay?" Vida caught me as I took a cab from Boston to someplace in Cambridge for something to do with communications research. "Remember? Phillip is coming to visit Max and we're all going out Saturday night."

"Does Phillip know about the whole Connie and Ian thing?"

"I don't know, but I'll find out this afternoon. I'm going to give him a surfing lesson. You didn't promise yet."

"Don't worry," I said. "I'll be there. I have to be home this weekend—I have tons of things to take care of."

"Don't tell me that! You have to go out with us tomorrow night!"

"Seriously, Vida, I don't know if I can. I've gotten way behind, and—"

"Josh already said you would."

"What?"

"I talked to Josh this morning, and he said you guys would make it. His exact words were 'We'll be there.'"

Then it must be official. We were a "we." We were a "we" with a serious amount of work to do on behalf of a certain undead someone, but we were a "we." And for once, that thought didn't give me hives.

"Becks?" Vida prompted me.

"I guess we'll be there."

"I WANT YOU IN a black leather frock coat."

Josh waited a beat before responding. "I thought we decided on work before phone sex."

"This is work. I want you in a black leather frock coat at the convention. In the booth. Walking around."

"You're kidding."

"And leather pants."

"Becks." There was something like the slightest hint of warning in his voice. "I am not the artist formerly known as Prince. I'm a cartoonist."

"You're a rock star cartoonist and I want you to dress like one."

I was getting more resistance from everyone on the ComixCon dress code than on anything else. I'd brought in a sample cloak for the minions over the weekend and you'd have thought I was asking them to eat stale spiders. But even I had to admit that it had made everyone who tried it on look like a hobbit. So we compromised on a uniform of black jeans and black T-shirts with "Vladima's Minion" written on them in a lurid red scrawl. Dripping, of course. But Josh needed to make more of a sartorial statement.

"I'll concede the leather pants," he said. "But they'll be damn hot on the show floor."

"That's true." Conventions were always a crowded, noisy, sweaty mess for those who worked them. I reconsidered the leather coat. "How about a black silk shirt?"

"Fine."

"With French cuffs."

"Whatever."

"And ruby cuff links."

Again a pause before his reply. "I'm not sure the wardrobe budget will stretch to rubies."

I rolled my eyes. "Garnets, then. Something that looks like a single drop of blood."

"Becks, are you getting just a tiny bit too into this?"

"From a man who—I'm willing to bet—right now has votive candles burning under his *Nosfuratu* poster, that's rich."

"Jeremy lit the candles."

"Nevertheless."

He was going to look good if it killed me.

"WHERE THE HELL ARE YOU?"

"I'm in an airport, Max, where are you?"

"The beach." He made it sound like the valley of the doomed. "I'm freezing my ass off while Vida and Phillip do unnatural things in the water."

"Like surf?"

"So they say, although it looks to me like it's just an excuse to swim away from everything safe so they can talk among themselves."

"Why didn't you go out with them?"

"Someone had to stay on shore and guard the Bloody Marys."

"You brought cocktails to go surfing?"

"I thought, you know . . . blood in the water . . . sharks and blood . . . I don't know. I can't think straight around Phillip."

I let that line pass without comment.

"Let's change the subject. I hear enough about blood from the minions. What's new on the Connie front?"

"She's still at the house."

"And Ian?"

"Shanghai, I'm told."

"Has she at least talked to him?"

"You can ask her yourself tomorrow night."

The phone line started breaking up as I got closer to the security check-in. "Where are we going tomorrow?"

"Martuni's. Connie says she's going to wear white and sing 'Don't Cry for Me, Argentina.'"

I lost the connection. I could only hope he'd been kidding.

Thirty-six

"I've never seen two women more in need of big sloppy martinis and sing-along show tunes in my life."

Josh stood in the doorway looking underfed, sleep-deprived, and in need of a haircut. In short, perfect.

Shayla spoke up. "I've been telling her to get out of here for an hour, but she can't make up her mind about the teeth."

We were in the studio's break room, and we'd been trying out variations on the theme of pointy teeth for, I had to admit, quite some time.

"I think I'm leaning toward just the canine extenders," I told him. "What do you think?"

"I think if she's wearing the Vladima costume, nobody's going to be looking at her teeth." He looked at Shayla. "No offense."

"Don't be silly. That's the nicest thing you've ever said to me," she beamed.

"Okay, then we'll go with these." I handed Shayla the two teeth. "Now—"

"Now nothing," she interrupted. "Now I have a hot date

with a colorist from Vidal Sassoon, and you have some big sloppy martinis waiting for you somewhere. Let's get out of here."

I looked at Josh. "Vladima speaks."

"I love this." Shayla clapped her hands and did her best to look imperious. "Leave!"

It would have been perfect if she hadn't giggled.

THE PIANO BAR BACK ROOM at Martuni's on a Saturday night. Huge drinks, wall-to-wall people singing their hearts out, and the only request that's off-limits is "Piano Man."

There were some good singers that night, and the piano player seemed to have a working knowledge of everything from *The Sound of Music* to *Hedwig and the Angry Inch*.

Connie did attempt "Don't Cry, etc." but enough people joined in so that she didn't make a complete fool of herself. Phillip got into the spirit of the thing with a fairly rousing rendition of "I Get a Kick Out of You," sung in Max's general direction, which confirmed my suspicion that he was all right.

He was also clueless about the state of his brother's marriage, but that was fine by Connie.

"He's using Ian's absence as an excuse to stay with Max," she hollered in my ear. "So everyone's happy."

Everyone was happy, including me. I was being crushed on all sides by my friends, and I knew I'd pay tomorrow for the amount of Bombay Sapphire I was drinking, but I didn't care.

"Okay! Okay!" Vida attempted to get all our attention

when a new piano player took the keys with an Elton John medley. "Okay, listen!"

We did our best.

"The comic convention is in Vegas next weekend, right?" She still had to shout to be heard, but at least "Your Song" wasn't terribly intrusive.

"Right," Josh yelled, nodding.

"Tim and I are going!"

Tim gave us all a huge grin and double thumbs-up.

"Great!" I shouted. "I'll get you both passes."

"No!" Vida yelled. "We're not going to the show! We're going to Vegas!"

We must have looked confused because Vida started laughing. Then Tim put his arms around her and shouted an explanation. "We're getting married!"

Connie shrieked. Max did a spit-take with his martini. I don't even know how I reacted.

"We're eloping!" Vida yelled. "And you're all invited!"

Which is right when the piano player launched into "Can You Feel the Love Tonight?" I hate that song—it's so sappy—but even I wasn't capable of bitching about the background music in the midst of a massive group hug, followed swiftly by a period of jumping up and down and squealing, a few tears, calls for more drinks, and lots more hugging.

Even I had to admit it. I could feel the love.

ON MONDAY MORNING I could only feel the stress. I was in LA on yet another WorldWired trip. Over the weekend I'd thought about calling in sick and canceling, something I'd never done in my entire professional life. I actually got as far as picking up the phone, but when it came down to it, I just couldn't say the words. It's hard to break a lifetime of conditioning.

Josh and I had worked feverishly all day Sunday, and he'd taken me to the airport in the morning with a huge list of things I needed to do before Thursday, when I was scheduled to meet him in Vegas. Thursday was setup day, with the show officially starting Friday morning.

I'd had a vague uneasy feeling that, in light of Vida and Tim's news, Josh might try to steer the conversation toward relationships or commitments or something, but he'd made only one comment, in the cab on the way home from Martuni's.

"I guess some people move faster than others."

I'd looked into those great big dark damn eyes of his and my throat closed up. "I guess."

And that had been it. Thank heavens.

"VIDA, I CAN'T BELIEVE you didn't tell me!" I'd been dumped in a random office after a perfunctory tour of the extremely cool and retro WorldWired Los Angeles building, and I was taking the opportunity to berate my best friend.

"When have I seen you? Saturday was the first time in weeks I'd had more than a five-minute phone call or an e-mail from you."

She had a point. "Still—"

"Still nothing. Be happy for me."

"I *am* happy for you! Which doesn't mean you couldn't have mentioned it in one of our five-minute phone calls."

"It only happened on Friday," she said. "After we got back from surfing with Phillip and Max."

"He just came out and asked you? Did you at least get to change out of your wet suit?"

"It was over a totally nice dinner at a totally nice restaurant, and we were wearing totally nice clothes. And he didn't ask me—I asked him."

"Vida!"

"What? It all worked out. He said yes." She paused. "In fact, he said 'absolutely.'"

"But why? I mean—"

"I know what you mean." She took a breath. "I think it was because of Phillip. You know how in England I went completely nuts over him? I didn't even see who he really was because I was too busy projecting all this *stuff* on him about who I thought he was."

"I remember." I remembered doing the same thing myself with a certain minor member of the nobility whose face I couldn't really recall at the moment.

"So when I saw him again on Friday, it all kind of came back to me. How crazy I'd been. And then I looked at Tim over the dinner table, and I don't know what came over me. I just knew I was *seeing* Tim, you know?"

I thought of Josh's face over the dinner table and I knew. Okay, our dinner table was usually covered in my spreadsheets, his sketches, and a few miscellaneous knickknacks from the netherworld, but I still knew.

"Yeah." My voice cracked.

"So I just said it. And Friday night in Vegas we're going to do it—no muss, no fuss—so we can start spending the rest of our lives together without wasting any more time."

I cleared my throat. "Is Connie giving you grief on the 'no muss, no fuss' part?"

"What do you think?"

"I think she's probably having a selection of bridal gowns delivered to your office today."

Vida laughed. "She *is*. With a traveling seamstress, no less, so when I pick one, I can get it altered on the spot."

"Does that make her your maid of honor?" I can't believe I felt a twinge of jealousy at the thought.

"God, no. No bridesmaids—I promise."

"Bless you."

"Shit. I have to go. There's a guy pushing a trolley full of wedding cakes down the hall, and he's headed my way. See you Friday!"

Friday. It seemed months away. Until I looked at my to-do list.

JOE ELLIOT TURNED UP on Thursday.

I was scheduled to be in the office until around noon, when I'd head for LAX and catch a short flight to Vegas, meeting up with Josh and the minions. It wasn't really the WorldWired Way to take a day and a half off when you'd been an employee something short of six weeks, but I'd e-mailed Joe Elliot about it and he hadn't seemed to mind.

Then I got a note.

> Becks,
> Joe is in town and needs to speak with you urgently. He can clear fifteen minutes tomorrow at ten. Meet him in the boardroom.
>
> Chris

Shit. Chris was Joe Elliot's assistant. The one he habitually referred to as "my girl." It was weird that, after all this time, my boss suddenly needed to see me "urgently." And it was also weird that the note was just waiting for me on my desk Thursday morning, when I would normally have expected an e-mail or a voice mail.

The timing, on the other hand, wasn't at all weird. It was just completely disastrous.

"DON'T WORRY ABOUT IT," Josh said.

"Don't worry about it? You guys are going to be setting up all afternoon." I checked my watch, grateful Los Angeles and Las Vegas were at least in the same time zone. "If you're still waiting for a cab at the airport you're already behind schedule."

"We can handle it," he insisted. "You already had everything shipped to the convention hall, right? The plans are all in place, you've triple-checked everything; you've given everyone—including me—more explicit orders than Eisenhower gave the troops on D-day. We'll be fine."

Part of me knew he was right, and part of me hated him for not needing me more.

"Besides, we can get you on your cell if anything comes up, right?"

"I can fly there this afternoon and just come back here on an early flight tomorrow. It'll only be an hour each way." I'd been checking a travel Web site while we talked.

"Don't be crazy. You'd wind up exhausted by the time the show started, and that's when we'll really need you."

"It's nice to know you'll need me at all." That came out a little more sullen than I would have liked.

"Becks, just relax. You organized this thing down to microscopic details. The booth isn't complicated, and Jeremy knows how to hook up the video displays better than you do. We'll be fine for the setup."

Relax. He wanted me to relax. And I thought he knew me.

"But if you're not here on Friday, the entire world will come to an end," he said.

Maybe he did know me. "Really?"

"Absolutely. The oceans will boil and it will rain toads and we'll all completely fall apart."

"That's nice."

"So just do whatever you have to do for WorldWired, and we'll see you as soon as you can make it tomorrow, okay?"

"I still don't like it."

"Neither do I, but we'll deal with it. We'll be fine," he insisted. "Here's the cab. I'll call you later."

I hung up. "We'll be fine," he'd said. How annoying. No wonder he didn't believe me when I told him the same thing.

BY LATE AFTERNOON I was jumping out of my skin. I knew Joe Elliot was in the building, and I didn't see why I couldn't just grab fifteen minutes with him and catch the next plane to Vegas instead of waiting around for a day.

Waiting and wondering. What the hell did he need to talk to me about? And why now, after weeks and weeks of avoiding me, was something suddenly urgent? And what could be so important that he had to talk face-to-face instead of sending me an e-mail or calling me?

Only one answer satisfied all the questions. He was going to fire me.

But why? I hadn't done anything to deserve being fired. Hell, I hadn't done anything at all.

Maybe that was the problem. Maybe all of this traveling around had been intended to give me a chance to spot an opportunity for success and seize it—or at least to send him thoughtful analyses of what I'd seen and heard everywhere.

I thought about it. I thought about how I might have handled all the travel and all the meetings if I'd been the old Becks—the one with her head in the game. I probably would have done all my research before New York and been able to come up with some brilliantly insightful feedback for the ad firm. I probably would have drunk down every word the technogeeks had spoken at the conference in Dallas, and I'd now be the WorldWired's greatest expert on future trends in the industry.

As I obsessed about everything I hadn't done, I started to feel a little feverish. My hands started sweating when I realized that the resignation of the VP in Atlanta could have been a huge opportunity to show Joe Elliot that I could pull people together in times of corporate change. The power outage in Boston could have been a providential chance to take the team back to the basics of working with pens and paper on ideas rather than on computerized visual trickery.

My hands started to shake when I realized that Frankfurt could have been an opening for me to really get a handle on the European markets, instead of tuning out what everyone was talking about until they'd said the magic word—*beer.*

I hadn't been giving WorldWired the attention I should. If I was being honest with myself, I'd known that all along. And although I'd never consciously realized it, I knew now that I'd been assuming, in the back of my mind, that eventually something would change and I'd get into gear and . . . focus.

But the truth was, I was focused. I just wasn't focused on WorldWired. My entire intellectual capacity seemed to be filled with the detritus of a cartoon graveyard and its undead mistress. Vladima was what I thought about, schemed about, dreamed about. Making her successful had become my obsession. On planes when I could have been preparing for meetings, I was writing press releases. And after meetings, when I should have been preparing insightful reports with brilliant recommendations, I'd been monitoring the progress of the Vladima movie e-mail campaign.

My head was in the game, all right. But the game was Vladima. And that had to be bad for WorldWired's investment in me. From their perspective, I was not doing a good job.

I was not doing a good job.

With that realization, I ran to the nearest restroom and threw up.

I'D BLOWN IT. I'd blown the opportunity of a lifetime, which had been handed to me on a silver platter by an eccentric earl with a fondness for swans. I'd been given the chance I'd been craving for years and I'd thrown it away in favor of a cartoon creature of the night.

I don't know how long I hid out in the restroom, mentally kicking myself while alternately splashing my face with water and holding cold compresses over my eyes. But by the time I came out, the office was largely deserted and I'd made up my mind.

Joe Elliot was going to fire me. Fine. I'd brought this on myself. In his position, I'd probably do the same thing. And now that I knew, I might as well get it over with. At least, once it was over, I'd be able to catch a late flight to the convention.

I squared my shoulders and went looking for my executioner.

Thirty-seven

I heard him before I saw him.

His voice, proper and British and unmistakable, was floating down the hallway of the twenty-seventh floor. The executive floor. I'd seen it on Monday's tour of the offices, all frosted glass and low-slung furniture in poolside colors, but I hadn't been invited up since.

It had seemed the likely place for Joe to be hanging out, and when I heard him I congratulated myself on finding him so efficiently. Then, after talking myself out of the impulse to run away, I followed his voice. As I got closer to a half-opened door, I started to make out what he was saying.

"—more talent than I'd have given her credit for."

Her who? Her me?

"No, she's really not as attractive as I would have expected."

Probably me. Was he on the phone? I couldn't hear anyone responding to him.

"Although, I have to say, in New York I really did see some flashes of brilliance."

Damn right he had. Well, flashes of desperation, anyway.

"No, no, of course I understand. Yes, the situation is untenable."

Untenable? What situation?

"Certainly. A man of the earl's age. It's not uncommon, of course—no, you're quite right."

The earl? George?

"No, I completely understand your position."

Joe seemed to be trying to reassure the other person. Who the hell was the other person?

"Yes, of course. Tomorrow. Certainly. As soon as it happens. Yes, of course, Sir Charles."

Sir Charles?

I heard the plastic clatter of the phone being hung up.

I stood frozen in the hallway. It wasn't until I saw Joe's shadow moving against the frosted glass that I fled. I ran back down the hall, sprinted past the elevator doors, and dove for the stairwell. I made it down fourteen flights before I had to stop, gasping for air and hanging on to the railing.

I'd left my purse in my temporary office. I'd have to go back and get it, and the laptop, and make my way to the hotel. I told myself this while I tried to get my breath under control. Purse, laptop, hotel.

These are the things I concentrated on. I did not think about the slimy knight who'd been talking about me. I did not think about Joe Elliot, the knight's—what? Henchman? I did not think about what plans they'd been putting in place for me tomorrow.

Purse, laptop, hotel.

Once I took care of those, I'd be able to form a plan.

. . .

"HAVE YOU TOLD JOSH?" Max asked.

"No. I've talked to him at least seven times tonight, but I just couldn't ask him to deal with my problems on top of everything else he's doing."

"Becks, he'd want to know. He'd want to deal with your problems. And what's more, he might have some good advice. He knows a hell of a lot more about office politics than I do."

"But, Max, this isn't just office politics. Not if Sir Charles is behind it. And I never told Josh about the whole idiotic Lord of the Manor thing and what a lunatic I was in England—and I don't want to now. So without knowing what a bastardly bastard I'm up against, how could Josh help?"

"Why do you suppose Sir Chuck has it in for you? I mean, it all seems a little . . . over the top, don't you think?"

"The only thing I can think of is that he doesn't like the fact that George got me the job in the first place. He seemed to hate his father for some reason, so I'm wondering if this is a lot more about getting back at him than it is about hurting me."

"Well, whatever his twisted reasoning may be, I know exactly what you should do."

Thank heaven for friends. "What?"

"March right in there tomorrow morning and quit. Better yet, send your boss an e-mail and get on a plane to Vegas tonight."

"Max! Be serious!"

"I *am* serious. What the hell do you need with that job anyway? Leave them in your dust and get out of Dodge."

"Max, I can't." Of course it had occurred to me to cut and run. But I just couldn't do it.

"It's pointless, Becks. You should have quit weeks ago. And may I point out that if you had, instead of losing sleep and getting wrinkles talking to me all night, you'd have spent the evening doing Lord-knows-what kind of debauched bachelorette things with Vida, and then gone to bed with a man who loves you!"

"I *know*!"

"Then *quit*!"

"*No!* Max, if Joe Elliot fires me for incompetence, I can deal with it. Hell, I probably deserve it. But I can't just bail without knowing what the hell is going on."

Nothing Max said, sensible as it was, changed my mind. Even as I hung up I knew. I knew that, whatever this game was, I had to play it to the end. Whatever Joe Elliot threw at me in the morning, I could take it. I would take it.

But it would help if I could summon my inner Vladima.

"YOU WANT ME TO GO *where*?"

Joe Elliot looked at me with something that might have been excitement in his eyes. "China. Guangzhou. We're thinking of opening a branch there."

"China?"

"China." He seemed a little flustered. More flustered, in fact, than I would have expected. Of course, I'd expected to be fired—not offered a huge promotion and a transfer halfway around the world.

"Look, Becks, there are some things at play here . . . I don't really feel at liberty to discuss . . . but there are things that . . ."

Definitely flustered. But why?

"Joe, what's really going on? Why China? Why all this urgency all of a sudden?" And what in the hell did the LOTM have to do with it all?

He poured himself a glass of water and seemed to collect himself. "All I can say, all I *will* say, is that there are certain pressures being brought to bear. Certain pressures that make it impossible for me to keep you on in your current position. But I'd like to offer you this not inconsiderable opportunity—"

Pressures. That clicked it all into place.

"Sir Charles wants you to send me to China." I said it flatly, cutting Joe off in midsentence.

He blanched. His mouth moved. Then sound came out. In a whisper.

"Sir Charles?"

"I know he's behind this. I know he wants you to get rid of me. What I don't know is why." I pinned him with a look, causing him to squirm in a way that would have made a certain vampire role model proud.

Joe cleared his throat violently. "What do you know about Sir Charles?"

"I heard you on the phone last night." I said it coldly, in something like Vladima's voice.

Joe blinked. He stared at me, then nodded. "So you know."

"I don't know a damn thing! I don't know why he cares what you do with me, and I don't know why you give a damn what he thinks! So why don't you just drop the act and tell me why the hell you're following his orders and sending me to *China*."

By that point I might have been yelling. It felt good. Not

as good as slapping him, or—and this is Vladima talking—snapping his neck like a twig, but good.

He sat down suddenly and shook his head. "Becks, he doesn't want me to send you to China. He wants me to fire you."

Now it was my turn to blanch. "What? *Why?*" Because I slept with him in a fit of English wedding–induced lust?

He shrugged. "He's embarrassed. He thinks people will talk about how his father got you the job. That they might think you and the earl . . ."

My jaw dropped. "That's ridiculous!" Good God. Sir Charles didn't want me fired because I'd slept with *him*. He wanted me fired because he assumed I'd slept with *George*. Yuck! I mean, nothing against George, but—Yuck!

Joe shrugged again. It seemed to be his management style. "It's what he thinks, and he hasn't given me a moment's peace since he found out about you."

"Why the hell do you care what he thinks?"

"Becks." He gave me a pleading look. "He's going to inherit it all one day."

Of course. The words just hung in the air for a while.

Finally, Joe took a deep breath. "But if there's a God in heaven I'll be retired and living in the South of France before that happens." He stood up. "In the meantime, I don't want to fire you. I think you've been doing brilliantly, and . . ."

Brilliantly? I'd been doing brilliantly? How was that possible? I hadn't gotten obsessive or controlling or even remotely bitchy on the job. I hadn't cared enough to. Was Joe telling me that the secret to professional success was to stop paying attention? I blanked out what he was saying for a moment until I heard the fatal word.

"*But* I'm sick and tired of being bullied about it, and Sir Charles insists you're some sort of a stain on the family honor. So—"

I braced myself.

"I'm going to give you a whopping salary increase and a chance to carve out a significant segment of the Asian markets. All you have to do is stay off his radar for a while until you become so completely indispensable to WorldWired that the board of directors would have his balls for firing you. Can you live with that?"

He looked at me expectantly. Could I live with that? It was the professional chance of a lifetime. Or the chance of a professional lifetime. It was huge, and more than I'd ever dreamed of being offered. More than that, it was a chance of justifying Joe's faith in me—and George's. And a way of spitting in Sir Charles's eye while making a staggering salary doing it.

"Becks, what do you say?" Joe asked.

Good-bye, Vladima would have told him. Then she would have hunted down Sir Unbelievable Bastard and made an afternoon snack out of him.

My response was more pragmatic. "When do I leave?"

IMMEDIATELY. If I was to make it look as if Joe had really gotten rid of me, it had to happen immediately. I was taken from the company office tower by the company limo to the private company jet. My bags were already packed for the trip to Vegas. I even still had my passport on me, as I hadn't cleaned out my purse since Frankfurt. It all happened . . . immediately.

. . .

THIS IS JOSH. *Leave me a message at the beep.*

But I couldn't. It was ten-thirty the morning of show day. The doors had opened half an hour ago, and by now Josh would be in the middle of the kind of frenzy only half-crazed fanatics with misplaced blood lust could create. I couldn't just leave him a message. I couldn't just tell him I was abandoning him.

Even if I was.

HI, IT'S VIDA. *If I'm not answering, I'm probably surfing. Leave me a message and I'll call you back.*

I hung up. What could I say? That I was going to miss her wedding because of my job? I didn't want her to wake up to a message from her supposed best friend telling her that "something came up." I couldn't do it.

I GOT OUT OF THE LIMO and looked at the stairs leading up to the private jet. This couldn't happen so fast. I had to have time to explain. I had to tell Josh about Sir Charles . . . and the chance of a lifetime. I had to tell Vida about . . . what? What could I tell Vida to make her understand?

"Let's go, miss." A uniformed man spoke from the top of the stairs. "We're only cleared for takeoff for the next ten minutes."

I saw my suitcase being tossed into the back of the plane. My stomach lurched.

I went up the stairs.

"Are you afraid to fly, miss?" The uniform gave me an assessing look. "You seem kind of pale."

"She'll be fine." A middle-aged woman in a smart suit and sensible heels took the laptop off my shoulder. "She just needs to get comfortable, right?" She gave me a smile that crinkled the skin around her eyes and made me want to tell her my life story.

"Just sit right here." She led me by the hand to an enormous leather swivel chair. "And as soon as we're in the air, I'll bring you a lovely cup of tea."

Suddenly, I wanted a lovely cup of tea from this nice woman more than I'd ever wanted anything in the world. I looked around the cabin. Just six comfortable chairs and a door at the back. I was the only passenger. I sat down.

Then, I think, I went into shock.

IT MUST HAVE BEEN SHOCK. I know I was numb. What seemed like ages later I watched my hand reach out for a cold teacup, but I didn't feel anything when I saw it make contact.

Odd, that.

I couldn't hear anything but a sort of *whooshing* sound. Then I noticed that the kindly flight attendant was saying something. I could see her lips moving. But I had to concentrate very hard before her words came through.

" . . . lunch? It's almost twelve, Los Angeles time." She tilted her head to one side while she waited for me to process the request.

Food. I hadn't eaten anything since noon the day before,

and I'd lost that rather dramatically in the eighteenth-floor restroom of WorldWired LA.

I shook my head, and in doing so I came to my senses. I blinked and shook my head again. It was almost twelve in Los Angeles which meant it was almost twelve in Vegas. I was on a private plane. I was going to China. And I hadn't told Josh or Vida.

Suddenly the ridiculous thought popped into my head that I might run into Ian in China and we could commiserate about those we'd left behind.

I shook my head again, hard. *I hadn't told Josh or Vida.* They'd be looking for me any time now. Vida would expect me to call her from the cab after I'd landed. Josh would expect me to show up at the booth any minute.

I grabbed for my purse and pulled out my cell phone.

"I'm afraid not," the nice lady plucked it out of my hand. "The use of cellular phones is prohibited."

I gave her my most serious don't-even-think-of-fucking-with-me look. "This is an emergency."

She pocketed the phone with a smile. "Federal regulations."

My mouth went dry. "Do you have the other kind of phone? Like on real planes? Where you pay with a credit card?"

She shook her head. "We used to, but—"

I tuned her out. I couldn't call Josh or Vida.

"What time will it be when we land?"

"We'll be in Hong Kong—we're making a stop in Hong Kong—at approximately ten-thirty Saturday night Hong Kong time."

"What?"

The woman was unflappable. "It's the time change. On a plane this size, it's about a twenty-hour flight, so—"

"So it will be what—six-thirty in the morning Saturday in LA time? In Vegas time?"

She dimpled. "Yes, you're very quick—"

She said something else, but I wasn't listening. It would be six-thirty Saturday morning before I could talk to anyone. By which time they'd be worried sick.

No, they wouldn't, I realized. Because Max would get there this afternoon. And he'd tell them that Joe Elliot had been plotting something with Sir Charles. And they'd call WorldWired to see what had happened. And they'd find out.

And they'd hate me.

While I sat there waiting for my head to explode with the hideousness of what I'd done, the door at the rear of the cabin opened. And an extremely rumpled man stepped out.

"My word! What a surprise! If it isn't my old friend and conspirator!"

George. Sir George, or Earl George, or whatever the hell I was supposed to call him. Looking like he'd just woken up from a nap.

"Well, isn't this a treat? My dear girl, whatever are you doing here?"

I gave him the only possible answer. "Making the biggest mistake of my life."

Thirty-eight

We stared at each other for a moment, while the flight attendant stared at both of us. George finally broke the silence.

"My dear, I seem to have the knack of stumbling across you at rather pivotal moments in your life."

I nodded. "Yes, you do."

"Would you like to talk about it?" He took a seat in the chair opposite me.

"Yes, I would."

I BABBLED. I BABBLED while the nice lady produced hot tea and cookies. I babbled while George had a cup. I babbled right up to the part where I told him Joe Elliot was taking orders from Sir Charles, and what the bastard knight had assumed about why George had gotten me the job.

George interrupted me by slapping the arm of his chair. "It's just what that scoundrel son of mine would do. Thinks I'm a doddering old fool, so he assumes everyone else must think so too. Damn rotten of him to think that you and I—that we . . ." He slowed down at that point and shook his head again. "Oh, um . . . well. Mustn't worry about it." He patted my hand. "I'm just very glad I had some shopping to do in Hong Kong or I mightn't have run into you."

Then the absurdity of the whole situation hit me, and I must have gotten some sort of look on my face.

"My dear? Are you all right?"

"It's just so stupid," I told him. "I mean, even if we were—who cares? I mean, in my other job, with Vladima, I've been sleeping with my boss for over a month—and it never even dawned on me until right now that I was sleeping with my boss. We were just—and everybody knows, all the minions, and they couldn't care less. Except maybe some of them are happy for us—"

I realized I was babbling again.

"Do you mean to tell me you're still involved with that sexpot vampire creature?" George looked delighted. "Why, my grandsons have been absolutely inundating me with e-mail petitions to have a movie made about her."

I made a sound that was half laugh and half gasp. "At least something's working out the way I planned."

The old earl gave me a slightly puzzled smile. "But my dear, if you have this other job, and if you have this chap that you're . . . ah . . . well." He avoided my eyes. "I have to wonder what in heaven's name you're doing on a jet bound for Guangzhou by way of Hong Kong?"

The horrible hideousness of what I'd done sucked all the air out of my lungs. "I've ruined everything," I said. "I just saw the job, and the money, and the chance to do what I'd always thought I wanted." I shook my head. "But I don't want it."

I looked at him. "And I didn't want Sir Charles to get his

way, but now I've handed over everything that matters. I didn't want to let down Joe Elliot or the company, and now I've let down Josh. I've let down Vida. I've let this stupid job destroy my entire life."

And as I said it, I knew it was true. The job I'd wanted to *be* my life was nothing more than a distraction. I had a life. And it was with Josh, and my friends, and even—damn her—Vladima.

"George, I have to stop this! I have to make it right!" I grabbed his hand. "I can't go to China!"

"Well, I must say, I feel somewhat to blame for everything, as I'm the one who recommended you for the job in the first place. But never mind." He rubbed his hands together.

Never mind? Hadn't he been listening? Why did he look so happy all of a sudden?

"Do you know, I have to thank you in advance," he said. "Because you've given me an opportunity I've been waiting for my whole life. Or at least since I first saw *Casablanca* more years ago than I care to remember."

What the hell was he talking about?

"So thank you, my dear, because—with apologies to Mr. Bogart—I can tell you that if you stay on this plane, you'll regret it. Maybe not today, and maybe not tomorrow, but soon, and for the rest of your life."

At this, the flight attendant burst into applause.

"Thank you, my dear." He blushed, as he glanced in her direction, then turned to me.

Every muscle in my body longed to wrestle him to the ground and shout *"I know!"* Instead, I took a deep breath. "That's great, but—"

He cut me off with a wave of his hand, turning to the flight attendant. "My dear, could you please tell the pilot to request a new flight plan? I think we're going to Las Vegas."

BY THE TIME I MADE it to the convention hall, the show was closing for the day. I had to fight my way upstream against a tide of pimply power geeks and sweaty costumed superheroes to make it to the door. Then I flashed my pass at the guard, and I was in.

The show floor was enormous, and it seemed bigger somehow for being mostly empty of fans. The booths looked worn and ragged. Posters were torn, drinks had been spilled, and half-eaten hot dogs and pizza slices littered the place. Racks of comics had been picked over. I knew it would be hours before most of the exhibitors were finished for the day, and by the time they left, the booths would be restocked, reswept, and ready for another onslaught.

The only problem I had now was finding the one damn booth I cared about.

Gigantic banners hanging from the ceiling indicated the major show areas on the floor. I quickly disregarded Japanese animae, children's cartoons, and the adult section. I was looking for Web-based titles, and as I jogged past a giant black sign advertising the X-Men, I saw it.

And I stopped. It was time to slow down and catch my breath. Time to approach with caution. Time to get the lay of the land and see which way the wind was blowing. Basically, it was time to stall.

The booth was about five down and to my right, on a corner, just as I'd arranged. I couldn't help but be a little proud at the empty T-shirt shelves and bare magazine racks. We'd been a hit.

The gang was all there, everyone wearing the regulation black jeans and "Vladima's Minion" T-shirts. Everyone except Shayla, that is. She was sleek and busty in her black leather costume, showing even more cleavage than her cartoon counterpart.

The place was clearing out quickly now, and suddenly the throbbing dance music from the PA system, which I hadn't even noticed until then, was cut off. A loud announcement was played to the effect that only exhibitors should now be on the floor.

I heard Shayla's voice over the general noise. "Thank God! Can I take off these boots now? They're killing me!"

I moved a few booths closer. Jeremy was tugging at Shayla's fetish footwear and looking damn happy to do it. She pulled the black wig off and shook out her blond ponytail. I didn't imagine Jeremy could take much more.

The PA system started up the music again, but now it was the kind you hear in your dentist's waiting room. I suppose the schmaltz was meant to drive the ultra-cool comic people out as quickly as possible.

I took a position at the booth diagonal to Vladima's. I didn't think I exactly blended in with the life-sized cardboard cutout figures of the Goth Girls, but their attendants seemed to be on a break, so I was able to watch the minions unobserved. There was Donovan, packing up the laptop that had been playing Vladima's greatest hits on the giant screen above the booth. There were Rabbit and Alex, pulling more boxes of T-shirts from underneath the table to be sold to Vladima's increasing number of fans tomorrow. Raven seemed to be everywhere, clipboard in hand, checking off the to-do list I'd prepared for her a hundred years ago.

And there was Josh. He was deep in conversation with an obviously star-struck dweeb. The fact that the dweeb in question was clearly in awe of Josh and not Shayla pegged him as a wanna-be comic book author, not a mere fan. In fact, he was just pulling a tattered volume out of his back pocket, offering it with shy pride to the man I was afraid to face.

Josh. He was wearing the leather pants and black silk shirt I'd picked out, and I even saw a glimmer of some deep red jewel on his cuffs. He looked exactly like the rock star of the dark world that I'd wanted him to be.

He also looked beyond tired. I couldn't imagine what I'd put him through, on top of the punishing demands of the conference itself. But he nodded and accepted the offered book, taking the dweeb seriously. He probably made the kid feel as if all his dreams could come true.

Josh was a good man.

That thought provoked a strong urge to melt into a puddle right there at the Goth Girls' cardboard feet. But I steeled myself. This was not the time for sentimentality. This was the time for a clear head and a command of language. I had a lot of explaining to do.

I'd been mentally drafting my speech all the way here, and now—at about the fifth version—I thought I had it down rather nicely. The last thing I needed was to look into Josh's eyes and go all mushy.

Suddenly I realized I'd been spotted. Shayla was beaming at me, frozen in a posture of surprised delight. Jeremy noticed something was up and followed her gaze. Then he was grinning at me too. The next thing I knew, all the minions had stopped what they were doing and were just gaping at me. It was like a *tableau vivante* of the undead. A *tableau mortante*.

Josh was the last to notice anything, and then it was only because the dweeb had shaken his hand and left. Josh looked around at his staff with a "What the hell?" expression.

Shayla nodded toward me, the look on her face encouraging. Josh turned.

And just like the first time I'd ever seen him, as our eyes met across the chaos of a show floor, everything else seemed to slide into a slow-motion blur. Josh was the only fixed point in my world.

At first he just stared. Then he looked away, and when he turned back, he was angry.

Suddenly I couldn't remember a word of my speech.

"Get the fuck out of here."

It was a keeper of the Goth Girls who gave me the order. I jumped.

"Yoki, get security. We've got another weirdo." Three Japanese teenagers in neon miniskirts and extreme ponytails were looking at me with varying degrees of hostility.

"Um . . ."

"It's okay," Josh's voice called.

I winced.

"She's with us," he said.

I opened my eyes and looked at him.

He cleared his throat and bowed his head, as if he couldn't stand to see me. Then, "She's with me."

And when he looked at me again, every coherent thought I'd ever had left me. I felt myself pulled toward him as he moved across the aisle. I dimly heard Shayla saying "All right" and someone, maybe Jeremy, whistling.

We just stared at each other, then "Becks," "Josh," both at the same moment.

He ran both hands through the mess of his hair, letting out a breath. "You're here."

"I'm here."

He nodded and looked at me again, and I had the strangest floating sensation.

"Your flight to China got canceled?" His voice was rough, whether from a day of shouting over the noise or from anger, I didn't know.

I took a breath, remembering everything I had to tell him—why I'd gone, how I'd realized what an idiot I was, how I wanted him to forgive me.

What I said was "We turned the plane around."

His eyebrows went up.

"I'm sorry I missed the show," I said. "I'm sorry I didn't call." I wanted to touch him, to make a connection, but I didn't seem able to move my arms. "I sorry—" I met his eyes. "I'm sorry."

"Why—" He cleared his throat. "Why did you come back?"

Which was the perfect opening for Phase Two of my explanation. How I realized the Vladima thing was rewarding work that I was actually good at. How I realized Vladima and the minions needed me far more than WorldWired ever would.

"Because I love you."

The look that passed between us could have kept all the lights in Vegas burning for a week. I took one step toward him.

Then the PA system started blaring a new song and everything went to hell.

"Oh, Josh," I groaned. "Not this. Not 'Can you Feel the Love Tonight?'"

"Jesus Christ, Becks." Josh pulled me into his arms. "Will it kill you to have one goddamn genuinely romantic moment?"

"Josh." I wanted his mouth on mine more than I've ever wanted anything in my life. "I refuse to have this be our song. Maybe it's okay for Vida and Tim—"

"You don't get to have a say in it." He moved his head toward me in a way that made my stomach wrap itself around my spine.

"Josh," I said firmly, "this will not be our song."

The look he gave me scorched everything around us. "Oh yes it fucking will."

Then . . . oh yes.

Oh yes it fucking was.

Thirty-nine

"You guys . . ."

I did my best to ignore the annoying voice that was attempting to intrude on the best moment of my life.

"Hey! You guys!"

But she wasn't making it easy.

"You *guys*!" It was Shayla, and now she was poking us. "We have thirty-five minutes to get to Vida's wedding!"

Josh broke away from me, panting, as I noticed with satisfaction. "We'll never make it."

I grabbed both of their hands and headed for the door. "Come on," I told them. "I have an earl in a limo waiting outside."

"ISN'T THIS EXCITING!" George greeted us as we piled into his car. "Where are we going?"

"The Bellagio," Shayla said. "Connie took over the arrangements," she explained. "And she's going to beat you senseless if you show up looking like that."

"I don't imagine she'll be any too thrilled with you, either."

Shayla still sported Vladima's leather catsuit and about a pound of vampire vixen makeup.

"Ah, but I came prepared." She opened the enormous black bag she'd been carrying and started pulling out bottles and brushes, handing them at random to Josh, a delighted George, and the friendly flight attendant, whose name was Penny and who had accepted an invitation to a Vegas wedding with evident enthusiasm.

Shayla slathered cold cream on herself while shouting out directions for me. I applied moist towelettes, moisturizer, foundation, and blush without benefit of a mirror. Then Penny did something to my eyes and lips as we crept down the strip toward the hotel.

"Do you have anything to change into?" Shayla asked me as she pulled some sort of flimsy blue thing out of her bottomless bag. She pulled it over her shoulders, then lowered it strategically while she simultaneously wiggled out of the tight leather gear. George and Josh politely averted their eyes, but Penny and I stared in fascinated amazement at her flawless technique.

At the next stoplight I hopped out and ransacked my bag in the limo's trunk until I found the dress and shoes I'd planned to wear to the wedding. And the white dress shirt I'd packed for Josh, in the (accurate) belief that he'd forget to bring one.

Back in the car, I said "Vida's going to kill me" while attempting the Shayla wriggle with less than spectacular results.

"No she won't," Josh said, stripping off his shirt. The sight of which made me wonder whether we should go to the wedding after all, or just jump out of the car and find the nearest room with a bed in it.

"You're right," I tried to focus on the zipper of the thing I needed to get into. "She won't want to get her dress all messed up. She'll ask Connie to kill me."

"Neither of them are going to kill you," Josh said, buttoning rapidly. "Because neither of them know where you've been."

I froze. Shayla zipped me up while I stared at Josh.

"They've been calling all day," he said. "And I kept telling them you were busy."

"Josh . . ." I didn't know what to say.

"Oh, well done, young man." George clapped him on the shoulder. "Well done."

Josh looked over at me, still staring at him. "After Max told me about what you'd overheard, I called Joe Elliot. His assistant told me everything. But I couldn't"—he cleared his throat. "I couldn't believe you wouldn't be back."

I looked into his eyes, and for one horrible moment I allowed myself to imagine a world in which I'd made it to China. I blinked and shook my head. It was too awful. "Josh—"

"Ah," George interrupted me before I could start blubbering outright. "It looks like we're here."

We pulled up to the massive hotel with ten minutes to spare, and we didn't look half bad. Shayla was a blond bombshell, George and Penny were perfectly presentable, I was as chic as I could manage under the circumstances, and Josh . . . Josh was the sexiest man in this world or the next.

"DUDES! YOU MADE IT!" Tim, apparently not in the least bit nervous, gave us an enormous grin as we burst through the door to the tastefully appointed and mostly deserted East Chapel of the Bellagio.

"Thank God," Max said. "If you hadn't—"

"Where's Vida?" I demanded breathlessly.

He gestured down a hallway. I ran, calling over my shoulder, "Josh, introduce George and Penny to everyone!"

I skidded to a stop at a door marked "Bridal Party." It didn't really need the label because I could hear Vida shouting at Connie quite clearly from the hall.

"I don't care when the reservation is for, Connie! I don't care if we have to go get married somewhere else! I don't care if I have to get married by a goddamn midget dressed as Elvis! I will not get married without Becks here!"

I gulped. I tried very hard not to get completely choked up. I opened the door.

"Hey, is that the sound of a bride having a breakdown?"

"Becks!" Connie turned on me, hands on hips and nostrils flared. "Where the hell have you been? Do you know what I've gone through to put this thing—"

"Shhhh." I waved at her to shut up and turned my attention to the bride.

"Vida. You're beautiful."

The dress was simple and elegant and perfect for her. And the look on her face made me redefine *radiant*.

"Becks. I knew you'd make it."

"I'LL SAY THIS FOR YOU, Becks, you know how to keep things interesting." Max plopped down next to me with a bottle of champagne in one hand and two glasses in the other. The ceremony was over, Vida was married, and we'd all adjourned to one of the hotel's many bars for dancing, drinks, and general post-wedding revelries.

"Thank you, Max." I took a glass of bubbly. I'd been jitterbugging with the bride, and it was thirsty work.

"Where's your man?"

I grinned and pointed to the dance floor, where Josh was currently cutting something of a swath with Penny, the flight attendant.

"He's got some moves," Max said appraisingly.

"He's spoken for."

"Don't worry. I'm completely harmless." He sighed elaborately and sipped his drink.

"Oh, that's convincing. What's the matter? Postwedding letdown?"

He shrugged. "It's stupid of me, and I know it's stupid of me, but I wish Phillip were here."

Phillip. Yikes. "Have you heard from him since . . . God, was that only last weekend?"

"It was, and I haven't." He shook his head. "And I probably won't."

I slid around in the booth until I could lean my head on his shoulder. "I'm sorry, Maxie."

He put his arm around me. "It doesn't matter. I don't need a man." He gave me another melodramatic sigh. "I'm just going to get two cats, name one Sky Masterson and the other Nathan Detroit, and reconcile myself to being a big fat bitter old queen." He sniffed.

"Don't be silly," I told him. "You're not fat."

He pushed me away and pinned me with a very evil look. "For that remark, you bitch, you're going to have to dance with me."

. . .

"ISN'T IT WONDERFUL?" Connie was standing at the bar watching Vida and Tim engage in some sort of free-flowing movement that would have been more at home at a Grateful Dead concert than on the dance floor of the Bellagio, but she'd had enough champagne not to judge. "Aren't they wonderful?"

"Wonderful," I agreed. It was getting late and I felt as if I'd been up for at least three days. Two of them in uncomfortable shoes.

"I wish everyone could be married," she sighed.

I choked on my drink.

"Are you all right?" She turned to me.

"The bubbles went up my nose."

She smiled, and I swear I felt an arctic chill move up my spine. "So, Becks, about you and—"

"How's Ian?"

It was a cheap shot, I know, but my self-preservation instinct had kicked in, and it doesn't play fair.

"He's fine. He got back on Wednesday."

So I wouldn't have run into him on the Silk Road, after all. "Are you two . . ."

"Talking." She nodded and looked out at the dancers again. "Aren't they beautiful?"

I thought things over. If Ian could see her like this, all her sharp edges blurred by French wine, they'd probably do more than talk. "Connie?"

"Hmm?"

"Where are you staying?"

"Here. Why?"

I took her glass from her. "Because you should go to your room."

She gave me a puzzled, tipsy grin. "Why?"

"Because now might be a very good time to call your husband."

"Call Ian?"

"Call Ian. You know. On the phone . . ." I raised my eyebrows suggestively. "Ask him how he's doing. Maybe ask him what he's wearing . . ."

She opened her mouth to speak, then stopped. "Becks!" Then the grin came back, this time not at all puzzled. "Will you say good night to Vida for me?"

"I promise."

She pecked me on the cheek. "The man won't know what hit him."

"I have every faith in you."

I watched her navigate her way to the door.

"What's she up to now?" Josh came up from behind, putting his arm around my waist and observing Connie's departure.

"Phone sex with Ian."

He winced. "There are so many things you shouldn't tell me."

"You have no idea."

He moved me out to the dance floor, where we swayed sleepily to a lovely rendition of "Bewitched, Bothered, and Bewildered."

"Josh, can we have this be our song?"

His mouth twitched. "Nope. We're stuck with Elton for the rest of our lives."

I leaned my head on his chest and closed my eyes. "Bastard."

We moved around the dance floor. "Josh?"

"Mmm?"

"Did you really believe I'd come back?"

He didn't break his rhythm for an instant. But it took him a while to answer. "I had to."

It was good that I was leaning on him because that way I didn't have to look him in the eye. "I'm so glad I did."

He lifted my chin with his fingertips until I was looking up at him. "I know."

I reached up to touch his face, tracing the little lines at the corners of his mouth. I knew myself too well to promise him I'd never do anything stupid and pigheaded again. But there was one promise I could make.

"I'll always come back."

He pulled me in close to him again, still moving to the music. "I know."

As we swayed silently for a while, I began mentally going over everything we'd have to do for the rest of the ComixCon weekend. I knew I didn't need to worry about WorldWired anymore because George had promised, with much delight, to deliver my resignation to Joe Elliot personally in the morning. Then he and a clearly besotted Penny had headed off to the airport again.

That left only a million and one Vladima tasks to take care of. I needed to follow up on how her press coverage was going, how the e-mail campaign was progressing, whether we'd have critical mass for the big Sunday night party when Chloe, the Fox exec, was going to announce the movie.

"Josh?"

"Still here."

"Did you hear anything from Chloe today?"

He groaned. "We're not going to talk about work now, are we?"

"I just want to know if she's still coming on Sunday."

"She's coming. Now can you please relax?"

"Of course."

I snuggled into that spot by his shoulder and we danced for a while.

"Josh?"

He tipped my head back and kissed me. "What?"

"Do you think Chloe was serious about offering me a job at Fox?"

Acknowledgments

First and always, thanks to my parents, Dolores and Keith Dumas.

Great big bouquets of thanks to the people who braved the early drafts. Denise Lee, who tells me the truth while distracting me with shiny objects; Erick Vera, who is usually right, dammit; Carole Dumas, who gets the award for best long-distance comments; and Rosanna Francescato, who's edits are happily accompanied by martinis.

Many thanks to Ann Parker, Janet Finesilver, Carole Price, Rena Leith, Michael Cooper, Clair Johnson, Gordon Yano, and Colleen Casey for sticking with the book in the every-other-Thursday critique group—even though I know I disappointed you by not murdering anybody.

Huge thanks to the fabulous Amy Rennert, for letting me be able to say "my agent, Amy," and the amazing Marjorie Braman, who might be the world's most delightful editor.

Thanks to everyone who's had to put up with my endless blathering about the book over the past year or so. The list is long, but includes Christine Dorffi, Karen Mcintyre, John Dumas, Richard Dumas, Mary Dumas, Josie Wernecke, Eric Laine, Peter Conrad, and Camille Minichino.

And finally, would it be weird to thank the people who put me on a layoff list a few years ago? Maybe not, because that's what it took for me to finally figure out the balance thing.